STEEL ROOTS

BY

S.J. ROBERTS

Dedicated to my parents, Beth and Peter.

Your patience and help made this possible.

Thanks go out to my brilliant editor, Steven Moore - Condor Publishing

Natasha, an immense help throughout.

My dog, Bodhi, for not always trying to rest your chin on my keyboard.

Copyright © 2024 S.J. Roberts
All rights reserved

"Power corrupts, and absolute power corrupts absolutely." - Lord Acton

CHAPTER ONE

Life spiralled into death from the top down.

Brady Drummond's lungs had spent twenty-four years trying to extrapolate any of the good left in the oxygen particles in Ranley City. The air was stagnant, yet moving. It was an ever-present and invisible contradiction. Air was a misnomer. Every particle had been filtered so many times, they each carried the memories of everyone with it. Genetically imprinted vapour may have been a more accurate description of what was keeping him alive.

He spent most of his life in the mid-levels of his tower block. In the top twentieth percentile of citizens for quality of life. Half way up, but a long way above the lifestyle median and he still felt as though his status in life had a stranglehold on him. How anyone who lived below him managed, he couldn't fathom.

Without the respiratory particulate filter implants that most of the citizens had, he should have been affected by the depleted air by this point. For anyone outside of the Fighting League without the enhancements, they would have been emphysemic long ago. His access to pure oxygen tents kept his lungs in a semi-permanent holding pattern, circling the drain.

He was one shuttle wait away from his next pre-fight treatment and it felt about time. His chest was heavy with nerves, as though his diaphragm was caught in a spider's web, but he had adrenaline too. Lots of adrenaline. He hadn't felt that pre-fight buzz for a long time.

This would be his forty-third bout in the Natural Class League and the first time he would face one of the Central Tower champions. Hitting his forty-third fight at the age of twenty-four practically made him a veteran of the circuit already. His win to loss ratio was none too shabby either. Victory today would be number thirty, a nice round figure. He'd like that. It wasn't going to happen, but he would like it nonetheless.

He had his childhood carer, Elena Martin, to thank for his involvement in the Natural Class Fighting League. His Grandmother, as she insisted on being called, had been a staunch advocator for living life free of intrusive bio-tech enhancements, and had fought in the early days of the league herself. Without the tech to keep up with the rest of the citizens of Ranley, Brady had little choice but to follow in her footsteps to make ends meet.

Brady looked down at his knuckles, thankful the damage he was about to receive would at least be somewhat hidden by his dark skin tone. He tensed his hand, gripping tight, and watched his triceps pop and ease beyond his quarter-length jacket sleeve. His eyes moved down to his knuckles, gnarled and enlarged from hours of bag training in preparation for what lay ahead.

The transit lounge was clean and well lit. Holographic advertising drones danced around the immense building, intrusively seeking out passengers. They peddled the latest in bio-tech implants and enhancements and sundry tech and consumables. They made sense to him, unlike the ones pushing virtual reality immersion holiday software to a market that could never leave the city. *Why waste all that effort advertising something that sells itself?*

It was a virtual reality break, or nothing. By the time the company had put together the advertisement for their new vacation experience, everyone had already upgraded.

Brady considered himself one of the lucky ones. His fighting career had afforded him access to the city rooftops. There, he had witnessed sunlight and seen the stars, whilst millions had lived and died without such pleasure. Despite his privilege, he still craved the scripted experiences of holidaying in a virtual world.

The transit lounge was divided into two sections. One internal, one external. As Brady took a seat in the external section, he noticed it was marginally busier than usual. For a moment, he convinced himself the waiting passengers may have been there to travel with him in support. He was, after all, their tower's champion. External passes were so hard to come by, nobody would waste the opportunity to leave their tower on something so trivial.

Crowds were always one hundred percent partisan wherever he went. Worse yet, he had heard rumours of just how hostile the Central Block fights could be.

Brady had worked his way inwards from his early days on the outer circuit. Fights had become progressively harder and crowds progressively more hostile. The closer to the Central Block he got, the larger the crowd and the larger the purse. He couldn't shake the feeling that his promotion from the middle circuit to the Central Block had come a little too easily.

The leap in standard of living was astounding as well. The city was like a cut section of a tree. Outer rings were thickened and dying, but with each movement closer to the centre, the more life there was. He had never been to the central towers, but from all he had seen and heard, life grew there and decayed as it pushed concentrically outwards.

He knew the odds were stacked heavily against him. The elite fighters of the Central Block circuit were leap years ahead of anything else he had faced. Worse yet, every fighter he knew had subtly hinted at a high level of corruption and match fixing.

The fact that gambling went hand in hand with the Fighting League was not news to Brady. On the outskirts, it was always fairly above board. People bet what little credit they had with small-time brokers. If they had no credits, which was often the case, they would use their cybernetics as collateral. Either way, it was honest and straight up. The closer to Ranley City's Central

Tower the fights got, the higher the stakes became. With high stakes came corporate involvement.

Brady was headed towards the rooftop stadium in Central Tower East's premier entertainment district. The thirty floors below were home to Ranley's most affable private citizens, including his opponent, Nikolai Sciano. Still, knowing he was en route to a loss wasn't the reason for his adrenal alertness. It was something else. A tension. Imminent.

MediTech's security presence was no higher than usual. They had not put a security premium on anything coming in to Brady's tower since the last high-tech business that operated there moved centrally. Nobody of any value visited, so it got the basic treatment. A team of two seriously armed guards patrolled the platform, so heavily adorned with cybernetics it made them the ultimate in no-holds-barred trouble dispersion. They had carte blanche to act in any manner they deemed necessary to keep the status quo. Though it was rare for them to face a test of their authority.

Even the minimal security force had control, so Brady could not fathom why the atmosphere was rife with tension. He had scanned the platform back and forth for the last ten minutes, scrutinising all the waiting passengers. Nothing out of the ordinary aside from the slight increase in volume. A handful of families inexplicably excited to visit a carbon copy of the block in which they had lived their entire lives, the usual splatter of business people waiting to visit another branch. The rest were made up of indeterminate agendas and the ever present service people who spend their lives flitting between blocks as and when required.

If nothing else, the consideration of his surroundings had managed to pass the time before his shuttle arrived. He watched it glide into the docking bay quickly and quietly. It was efficient and clean. Most people would live and die in their tower, never gaining access to the external shuttle system, so wear and tear from passengers was kept to a minimum, and it showed. Brady often wondered why they were still running that many services when they remained mostly empty, but not much that happened at MediTech's discretion was logical.

Elena had often told him that many years before he was born, transit was not only permissible, but actively encouraged. Though in his lifetime it seemed the profit margin of transit passes didn't meet the security costs required to make everything run smoothly. It was more financially viable to keep everyone in place and cut patrol costs by funnelling resources into transit lounge security.

The shuttle engaged with the platform, opening for turnover. Passengers disembarking numbered around the same as those waiting to embark. Rarely was there an imbalance. The scurry of interchange was always confusing for the day trippers; those with a history of exchanging went through the motions on auto-pilot. Retina scan at the doors of the shuttle, body scan at one of the applicable pillars on the platform.

Brady waited this time. It seemed he was the only one who felt the tension. Perhaps it was just in his head, but he couldn't shake the feeling something wasn't quite right.

MediTech's guards closely monitored the body scans, knowing that's where any trouble might be. Sure, someone could get on the shuttle without scanning their retinas, but as long as they did, the shuttle would never set off. The body scanners, however, were circumventable. Most of the waiting passengers had entered the shuttle. Only Brady, a few latecomer business travellers and a mother with her young daughter remained.

He'd get on last regardless of the atmosphere. Brady never understood the rush to get into the shuttles. Each had a thousand seats, yet he had never seen so much as half capacity in his time using them. Probably the same reason almost everyone else had been deathly silent for fear of bringing attention to themselves, regardless of the fact they had legitimate transit authority. For them, it was the fear of the unknown. He was one of only two people in the lounge who felt relaxed enough to have even taken a seat in the waiting area.

The MediTech security guards continued to deal with the passengers scanning themselves, ready to leave the platform for the tower block elevators. A couple of queries here and there, nothing serious. One or two call-ups to Ranley City Central to confirm transit passes, but no more than usual. And then, just as he stood up to start the boarding procedure, he saw it.

A blur at first, then a blip in the corner of his eye before it disappeared. That's all it was, a scrambled blur of confused light particles making a break for the shuttle. If he hadn't have been looking in the right place, at the precise moment it glitched, he never would have seen it. But, Brady knew instantly what it was —the effects of a crude prism field disruptor. The question was whether the guards had seen it too.

He referred to them as chancers. People without transit authority so desperate to get between tower blocks, they would take this risk. Brady had no idea what the success rate was, but he would have placed good credit on it being absurdly low.

There was a sliver of a window for the chancer to make it. It would take a perfectly timed sprint, and a seamless leap and clamber up the side of the shuttle to take a position on top. Then, if they were one of the few who managed to make it that far, they'd need a hell of a tight grip on the panel gaps of the shuttle as it hurtled, suspended in the air at upwards of four hundred miles per hour to get to their destination. And if they did manage all that, they would have to beat an equal one in a million shot at bypassing the guards at their destination as well. One thing was abundantly clear to Brady: it must be one serious circumstance to even consider such a gamble.

Brady rooted for the chancer, not because he cared for their plight, but because witnessing a successful break would make for a far more interesting story than all the ones he had seen fail.

He watched eagerly, snapping his eyes between the guards and the distortion. It was getting really close. Far closer than he had seen anyone get before. A few more feet needed. One clean jump might well do it. Nothing from the guards. *Go!* he thought. The chancer took their leap; they timed it perfectly. The thud as they hit the side of the shuttle. It was too loud. *Game over.*

As the flickering light particles scrambled to the top of the shuttle, one guard swiftly jerked around; but they would have heard the thud even without their auricular implants. A flip of the safety latch on his MT-720 assault rifle sent enough charge through the magazine to liven the first cluster of rounds with an electrical crackle. His retinal targeting system automatically switched to thermal imaging and picked out the optimal targeting points for him. The chancer managed to get to the roof right before the muzzle flash.

The MT-720s fired silently, utilizing MediTech's recently developed miniaturised ionic propulsion system. Too often, the field reports from operations that suffered loss of life cited enemy technology staying in line with MediTech's own. More often than not, from cases where their technology had fallen into enemy hands. They were in a constant push to stay one step ahead of anyone else and silent firing technology allowed sniper activity to remain undetected by most auditory sensors.

Four shots peppered strategically around the chancer's light blur, each landing with a flesh and bone clattering thud; however, one missed. The guard would have to deliver a lengthy field report for that later, even though he already knew it was a targeting calibration error.

Red mist escaped the scrambled prism, closely followed by the lifeless body.

The prism field disruptor fell behind the shuttle, a small hand-held trigger device, no longer functioning without the pressure of the corpse's finger. His bloodied, partially charred body fell backwards onto the platform in front of the shuttle, startling the passengers waiting to embark. The guard sprinted towards it, barrel steadily held in place locked on his target. Not needing to be, but ready nonetheless. Momentarily prioritising the tech over the life he had taken, the guard aimed a single shot, shattering the prism field disrupter where it lay.

The guard grabbed the corpse by the ankle and dragged it back towards the security pillars. A trail of blood smeared across the cold masonry floor in a messy reminder of the swiftness of justice.

The ordeal was over, the passengers safe to continue their days. The mother and her young daughter, a cherubic blonde eight-year-old with a smile that could turn the devil, were next to board. Taking her hand, she led her daughter towards the shuttle, crossing paths with the guard. They stepped over the body just like it always been inanimate, with not so much as a curious glance. In just a few years of life, Brady suspected the little girl had seen so many indiscriminate public executions that she was already desensitised.

Brady watched as the guard opened a large hatch on the security pillar and bundled the body in like a bag of refuse. For years, the mystery of the carcass chutes had played heavily on his mind. From the rumours during his early years of education at the academy that the bodies fell to a rendering plant and turned into the meat that was sold under the guise of being synthetic, all the way to being burned in sub-level furnaces to run the tower heating systems.

Even though he had left the academy and had a taste of reality, he hadn't ceased to believe either were possibilities. That would explain the noxious odours that perpetually lingered on the lower levels of every tower he'd ever been to. Rather, his curiosity regarding the corpse's final resting place had been superseded by a more grown up intrigue about why it was that the death of any citizen incurred such a steep credit charge. Especially when the corpses were handled with such nonchalance, regardless of the cause of death.

The armour didn't bend quite as much as the guard would have liked, so he struggled to stuff the torso down the chute and shut it, employing a callous technique more suited to trying to get a few too many items into a suitcase than disposal of a human body. His partner cut off the mother and daughter as they headed towards the shuttle, her imposing demeanour stopping them dead in their tracks.

'Scan for transit authority,' the guard ordered as she thrust a fingerprint scanner at them. If they struggled to understand her voice, muffled by the encapsulating helmet, the sharp stabbing motion of the scanner provided ample subtitle.

The mother and daughter pressed their index fingers onto the scan plate of the guard's pad with unquestioning compliance. Print, chip and DNA scans matched for both mother and daughter, not that there could be any doubt. Brady could feel the mother's anxiety as she waited. He was certain she had never so much as paid off a credit balance late, let alone commit transit fraud; yet, the nervous energy emanating from her was apparent, even from across the room.

As quickly as the burst of activity had broken the calm, it died down. Spectators who watched with bated breath had already forgotten about the fracas and moved on with their lives. Brady was the only person who could not. For some reason, it resonated with him, whereas any other day it wouldn't have registered. He wondered if it was as simple as the fact he knew he was about to walk into a viper's nest; or just the result of the tension in the buildup.

Either way, he felt a fire beginning to burn a hole in his

stomach. He knew he shouldn't let it flare up, but the anger kept growing as his rationality tried to douse it with water. The two emotions continued to swell and suppress, the anger taking two steps forward, one step back until it managed to spill out. It was subtle.

Brady stared at the male guard, and an almost unnoticeable snort of derision escaped his nostrils. For a brief moment, he thought he had gotten away with it. He had momentarily let the fact that the MTSG were heavily adorned in the latest cybernetic enhancements slip his mind. They could hear a pin drop on a cushion three blocks away, and he knew it.

'Is there a problem, citizen?' the male security guard snarled, fresh from disposing of the corpse.

'Talking to me or the dead guy?' Brady kept his head down as he spoke.

'I suggest you drop that attitude!'

Brady was buzzing. He knew nothing good ever came of challenging MediTech, but he couldn't help himself. 'Drop it like you just dropped a human being into oblivion?'

'I'm warning you.' The guard's response was calm, as though they wanted him to disregard their orders.

'Why? You didn't warn him.' Brady stood sharply. It was instinctual to put himself in a position to defend himself.

Brady realised he had taken it too far. He knew full well he should have cut his losses, but he was already too far down the rabbit hole, driven by compulsion. He had always been in opposition to MediTech's totalitarianism, but until that moment, he, like everyone else, had managed to keep a lid on it. But the broth was boiling over and the heat was still on.

'Last chance to shut that smart mouth!' instructed the guard, aiming his rifle in Brady's direction.

'Your boss wouldn't like that.' Brady grinned with a cocksure arrogance. 'He's probably got a lot riding on me.'

The guard laughed. 'Trust me kid, nobody is betting *on* you.'

Brady squared up to him, shoulders as wide as they would go. 'I gotta get there in once piece though.'

'Kid,' the female guard said from behind, startling him, 'you just gotta get there.'

She struck the back of Brady's head with enough force to send him to his knees and no more. It was perfectly weighted. If she had wanted to knock him out, even kill him with a blow, she had the strength.

The male guard jabbed Brady in the chest with the point of the rifle. 'Get on the shuttle!'

CHAPTER TWO

Brady sat in his corner, battered, bruised and alone. The packed crowd inside Central Tower's multi-purpose stadium neared two hundred thousand, all seated and looking down on a fully caged fighting pit. He hadn't fought in front of so many people before.

In the opposite corner, surrounded by his team of trainers, nutritionists and a plethora of indeterminable entourage members, Nikolai waited to dish out another round of annihilation. Brady could make out the sadistic grin of his opponent. A small gesture, but one that had an immense impact on Brady's resignation.

He hunched over with his head in his hands, both covered in blood mixed with saliva as it drained through them, down to the canvas. Each drip was like a metronome repeating that he was out of his depth.

He grimaced, ribcage radiating pain as he attempted to take in enough air to give him a half shot at making it through the next round. No help from the heavily partisan crowd, all booming their support for Nikolai in a deafening cacophony. Were Brady to have had any confidence left after the opening round, they would have sucked it out. He popped in his mouth guard as the bell rang.

Nikolai's 6'4" frame carried his bulk well. His body was far from crafted to perfection, but it held raw power. In contrast, giving up four inches in height, Brady's lean muscular figure was more a vision of agility and explosiveness. As the combatants approached each other, it was clear that Nikolai had the upper hand. He casually sauntered towards Brady, who readied his footwork. He was cautiously waiting for the next big hit to come.

Right on cue, Brady noticed the wind-up. Nikolai's right hand sliced through the air with far more speed than he expected from such a behemoth. Brady felt the air pressure before he felt the fist itself, and the following impact sent signals to every synapse in his body as they desperately tried to tell each individual cell to recoil and protect itself.

By comparison, the impact of the canvass was a blessing in disguise. Maybe if he lay there and didn't move, he could make it out alive. Maybe he'd get to see the South Pacific islands again, stand under that beautiful waterfall and feel the fresh water he hadn't tasted in… Actually, he never had. He'd never been out of the city. *Where is that place?* he wondered. Except it wasn't him. It didn't feel like his body. He was shorter, older, stronger, faster. His synapses were firing much faster. He knew things he knew he didn't know. He had one foot in another body, he just didn't know how or whose.

'What am I doing?' He pressed his fists into the canvas to try to separate himself from it. 'Get up!' He struggled with his own weight, wobbling at the elbows like the two-hundredth push-up in a set.

Nikolai smirked. It wasn't the first time he'd knocked an opponent into someone else. Probably wouldn't be the last.

Brady gingerly picked himself up, hoping Nikolai would let him stand at least. His mind defeated before his body, Brady knew he'd have to snap himself out of this slump just to survive this fight. He sucked fortitude out of thin air. *Just move quicker than him!* he told himself.

With his footwork and body movement, Brady was as agile as anyone he'd fought in his brief career. If he stepped up his game, he couldn't be hit, and that was his only hope. All he could do was to try to stay out of Nikolai's way until the bell. To his surprise, he matched him step for step.

'How do you move that fast for such a fat man?' Brady could barely speak with lungs of fire. He wished he hadn't.

Nikolai didn't like it. He stood off. Left an opening, obviously by design. He was offering a challenge that Brady accepted.

Brady knew he shouldn't, but his body moved ahead of his mind every bit as quickly as his mouth did. His bravado was just that one step quicker than his intellect.

Brady deftly shifted his weight onto his back foot to launch a full speed attack in an attempt to capitalise on his opponent's dropped guard. Nikolai's wry grin told him he'd made the wrong move. He wanted to back off. Every inch of matter in his brain slammed on the brakes, but his ego had cut the brake line.

He launched a fly kick, right foot aiming true at Nikolai's chin. For one glorious millisecond Brady thought he had him, but his confidence didn't last.

Nikolai's head and body seemed to skip to one side as though it defied the laws of physics, a minute movement to avoid the strike, more like the movement of a hummingbird than a man. As Brady hit the air, Nikolai caught him, bringing him crashing to the deck with such force the audience in the top rows could have felt it.

The crowd hushed in unison with the final blow, knowing that bar a miracle, the fight was over. Nikolai had made a career finishing his opponents with a rear naked choke hold once he had them tired and on the canvas. Brady was victim two hundred and something. The crowd knew the fight was done and their collective gasp almost felt strong enough to take all the oxygen out of the arena. Nikolai didn't need to breathe and he would make sure Brady couldn't.

**

Brady had lost consciousness, but the imagery of his dream was as vivid as real life, maybe more so.

Who was that guy? he thought, as he watched him through the binoculars.

He knew him. He'd seen that man before. Watched as he laughed in the face of suffering. No idea who it was, just knew it was the face of everything he stood against. The man was waiting for someone, calm and collected.

Shouldn't be so chilled, he thought of the man who was utterly oblivious to the fact he was under strict surveillance.

It wasn't just surveillance. He knew there were four guns currently trained on the meeting site. Besides, the man was clearly not a regular visitor to Santiago's street cafés, nor Cuba itself. The sheer amount of sweat dripping from his brow was evidence the climate was new to him. Anyone else may have mistaken that sweat for nerves, but he had a well-trained eye and could see the man was perfectly comfortable with everything aside from the unrelenting heat.

The target remained calm as a party of three armed militia joined him. The surrounding crowd was on edge and the atmosphere between civilians and the militia was obvious, even through the binoculars. His earpiece crackled.

'Mr James,' one militia member said, greeting him cordially as the other two nodded politely before all three parties took their seats.

Mr James sat back, relaxed in his chair. 'Where are we with the operation?'

'Everything's set to go ahead on Mr Braunschild's say so, Mr James,' another militia member stated.

'We have the plant ready to get raw footage at the scene once everything is in motion,' the first militia member added.

'He's a risk.' Mr James calmly sipped through the curly straw in his cocktail. 'Make sure he is among the casualties.'

'That is not possible,' the third member nervously clarified. 'He will be too far from the impact zone.'

'Then move him closer.' Mr James slid his drink away, as the sweetness had become too much. 'We need total destabilization, we can leave no loose ends hanging.'

'Then what are we if not loose ends?' the first militia member queried.

'It doesn't bode well for you to ask questions.' Mr James removed a slim cigar from his gilded case. 'The uniform is because you follow orders. If you made them, you would be wearing a suit and tie.' He slipped the cigar between his teeth. 'Frankly, our organisation has no problem with your government being dragged into this, but we would suggest you keep your ship in order to avoid what would be a very costly revelation.' Mr James pulled a gun lighter from inside his jacket and pressed the trigger, the flame dancing across the tightly coiled tobacco leaves. As he set the lighter down, he eyed every one of his table guests.

***

Brady woke up backstage on a cold table. No head support, just the steel on the back of his head. It was a slow stir rather than an abrupt coming to. Although his sight was glazed over, he could just make out the fight officials in the room. *Where was this Mr. James and the Cuban militia?* he wondered. *Better yet, what is Cuba?*

He began to lose sight of the dream, as he did so often. Their clarity had scared him as a child, but he had grown so used to them, they barely registered beyond the initial confusion of waking up.

As it faded, he wondered if he had seen that one before. They often repeated but began to blur into one a long time ago. He had a vague recollection of hearing about Cuba in history class back when he cared about learning, long before his grandmother had set him straight about how the education system they entrenched him within had been designed solely to push the agenda of, and glorify the establishment. Something about the race for control of South America, a conflict with China, though the details had faded in his memory.

Brady shook off the dream and got himself back in the room. He knew the procedure like the back of his hand; hop into the body scanner so the league's technicians could confirm he was carrying no bio-tech modifications. The Natural Class league had found its share of people trying to cheat the system with hastily installed tech between the pre-fight scan and the bell ringing. Brady had beaten a fair few of them himself.

Brady shrugged off his helper as they led him to the body scanner and stepped into the machine, remaining motionless whilst the technicians performed the scan. Two techs manned the operation desk, both carefully studying their monitors. Brady's scan image appeared normal at first, but the primary technician's brow furrowed as she studied what she saw. A small red blurry patch in Brady's brain scan, just on the periphery of his cerebellum. She got the attention of his secondary technician.

'Take a look at this,' she said and pointed to the close-up of Brady's brain scan on her monitor. The secondary technician looked equally bemused. He leaned in.

As Brady watched them, with furrowed brow, confused at the delay to his normal quick release, the technician gestured to the controls. 'Expand it.' As his counterpart obliged, he saw the magnified image was no clearer. 'I'm not sure that's anything. Blood clot probably, he got hit pretty hard.'

'I'm reporting, regardless.'

'It's not worth the paperwork.' He fiddled with his personal comms ear cuff, sending out a signal without anyone knowing. 'It's a clot, just forget it.'

Brady noticed the female technician study her counterpart carefully. 'Is it worth your job, though?'

Brady moved out of the scanner and headed for the exit just as

Nikolai entered to applause, handshakes and high fives. Nikolai went straight for the scanner and took his position. Neither technician paid any attention to the numerous bio-tech infractions on his results. If Brady didn't already know the fight had been rigged due to the complete imbalance between Nikolai's size and speed, the lackadaisical approach to Nikolai's mandatory scan confirmed it.

The crowd impatiently chattered among themselves as Brady stood in the centre of the ring, nervously fidgeting as Nikolai confidently strode inside. On seeing him emerge from backstage, the crowd's disconnected chatter focused into unified chants for their home-town hero.

The two men feigned respect for each other with the standard combatants' embrace before the public address system and the large screens floating above the ring fired up. The contrast in their post-fight state was clear.

The P.A system boomed: 'Ladies and gentlemen!

The winner of today's contest, by way of knockout in the third round, and still undefeated,' it continued, being met by an instantaneous roar of applause, 'your 2302 Central Tower west champion. And the reigning champion of Ranley City. Nikolai Sciano!' yelled the announcer, to rapturous applause and the live shot of Nikolai on the giants screens.

The announcer's tone shifted solemnly as he continued. 'Information has just been brought to our attention.'

'The challenger, Brady Drummond, has been flagged for illegal enhancements.' The news elicited a booing from the crowd. Brady looked around, utterly dumbfounded by the announcement.

He threw his arms up in protest. 'What?'

'As a result, all bets for tonight's fight have been voided.' The boos erupted into a direct, sustained attack on Brady as he looked around frantically for some kind of sense to be made.

'We remind you that all bets are undertaken at your own risk and no refunds will be given,' concluded the announcer, causing the crowd to raise their discontent with Brady tenfold.

Bottles began raining towards the ring, smashing on the cage and showering it with glass shards. Brady quickly covered his face as he turned to run for the exit, noticing Nikolai had left the arena already.

He was alone, more alone in that moment than he had ever felt. Adrenaline pumped through his body as he watched the arena guard shut and lock the cage door. From the moment the fight had been booked, he'd had a sense of unease. He was trapped. In the ring, the arena, the tower block and his mind. All he could do was stand and take it.

***

The transit shuttle hummed quietly on the tracks. Transport moved slower than usual. Brady had no idea why, but the last thing he needed was a slow journey home.

The carriages were predominantly empty. A handful of well-tailored citizens casually waited for their exit in the first-class lounge. Brady sat alone in the rear carriage, battered and bruised from his ordeal with Nikolai and the subsequent barrage of bottle shards courtesy of the disgruntled fans.

Brady tended his wounds with the first aid kit that travelled with him for every fight. He had never needed to replenish it, but the sheer amount of damage inflicted on him had almost depleted it. He was well versed in patching up, a skill he learned in childhood, tending to his adoptive carer Elena's wounds.

Elena had moulded Brady in her own image. She had carved a long career fighting in the Natural Class leagues and used her earnings to take in orphaned children under her care. He had been the only one of her adopted children she had trained in martial arts and, long after her death, he felt that bond.

As he finished bandaging his left bicep, the shuttle carriages echoed with an almighty bang and the otherwise smooth ride trembled. Startled, Brady looked around for the cause, panicked because in all his years using the shuttles, he had never witnessed anything untoward before.

From his position, Brady couldn't see through to the other carriages. *'Did they hear that?'* he wondered. His heartbeat surged such that he could feel the ebb and flow of the blood through the veins in his neck. There didn't seem to be any follow up from the noise; the shuttle continued along smoothly once more.

No noise from the other carriages. Brady wondered if he imagined it. He could feel the definite effects of a concussion, and he worried that it had caused some form of delusion. Somewhere between the edges of reality and paranoia, he fell into a daze.

He remained within himself as the gangway doors slid open. It took him a while to acknowledge there was movement, but as he dragged himself out of his head, he saw a middle-aged woman approaching from the adjacent carriage. A look of panic on her face put him at ease. Unless she was an incredibly vivid manifestation of a concussive paranoid delusion, he wasn't crazy. Something had happened.

'Did you hear that?' she asked, her voice shaky, yet Brady felt it was a little of an overreaction.

'Yeah, I heard it.' Brady stood slowly to greet her.

'What was it?'

'Uh...' He wanted to ask why she thought he would be party to information she wasn't, but decided that would come across stand-offish and clearly the woman meant no ill intent. 'I'm not sure.'

'You think something's wrong with the shuttle?' He could tell from the look on her face she was seeking reassurance.

Brady shrugged. 'I guess it could be.'

'Are we going to be okay?'

Brady could sense her breathing becoming erratic, and knew she needed comforting words, but he didn't feel obliged to lie. 'I don't know, probably.' He saw the fear in her widened eyes. 'I mean, everything seems okay now.'

'Sorry, I'm a just bit scared.' Her hands trembled. 'I've never been on one of these before.'

Brady had developed a callous shell to fellow passengers over the years. For them, it was always the same thing. Heads down, get where they were going, no nonsense. Until he heard the wavering in her voice, he had forgotten what it was like the first time he'd taken a shuttle.

'Hey, don't worry.' Brady stopped looking around elsewhere and focused on her. 'It's probably nothing, happens all the time.'

'Oh okay. Thank you. I'm just going to—' She stopped herself mid-sentence as she pointed at a vacant seat. Brady nodded, smiling gently as she took the seat.

Brady grabbed his medkit and took a seat a couple down from her to finish his repairs. The calming lie he told her had almost convinced himself too. Tentatively, he began to unwind the blood-soaked bandage on his right hand. The tearing apart of each layer of the bandage that had become fused together by dried plasma was the only sound heard on the now silently running shuttle. Layer after layer unbound, revealing a large gash across Brady's blue, blood starved middle knuckle.

Colour slowly flooded back into his hand, and with it, fresh blood seeped from the wound. It started slowly, but gained velocity with each beat of his heart. The woman's discomfort became obvious, watching him in pain as he grimaced, prying apart the laceration to squeeze skin repair resin directly inside.

Brady took a stitch gun from his kit, knowing how difficult it would be to operate with his left hand. Nervously, he positioned the gun over the wound, trying to coordinate accurately. He took a deep breath and gently squeezed the trigger. For a moment, he thought he had made headway on a neat stitch, but his stability just wasn't up to par. He went off centre and the stitches only served to pull apart the wound once more.

Blood gushed from his hand, dripping onto the floor beneath him. The woman leant over and cautiously pressed her hand on his leg. 'Can I help you?'

Her immediate action let Brady know she wouldn't take no for an answer. Not that he wanted to refuse. He was struggling and he would take whatever help he could get. She slid into the empty seat next to him. He could see from her face that his wound and the blood were making her queasy, no matter how she tried to hide it as she looked at the equipment with confusion.

'You know what to do?'

Her lack of response confirmed what he assumed. 'It's okay, you just have to squirt that resin in the wound and then line up this part,' he explained as he gestured to the guide fascia of the stitch gun, 'and run it from end to end of the cut. It does all the work for you.'

Cautiously, she squeezed the trigger, piping hot resin into the freshly opened wound. Brady's nose whistled as he sharply inhaled, gritting his teeth as he handed her the stitch gun. She fixated on his hand and tried to get the gun in place. Trembling, she hovered above the wound as Brady watched carefully.

'Just go for it, you'll be fine.' His voice threw her and she dropped the gun, landing on the ground between Brady's feet with a thud. She bent to retrieve it, looking up at Brady gingerly. With her head between his knees, just inches from his crotch, Brady didn't know where to look.

He felt his stomach knot a little as her head lingered for too long, too close. The information holo across the carriage made for a focal point. The words meant nothing—he wasn't taking them in —it was just somewhere to look whilst she took far too long between his legs. In his periphery, she seemed to be struggling to find the stitch gun. It shouldn't have been that hard, so either she was loitering with intent, or was plain clumsy. Either option wasn't appealing to him.

When she finally returned to meet his eyeline, he could see her nervously fidgeting with the gun. Her hands trembled at the tip for a moment, before she corrected her grip.

'You can do this.' With her out of his crotch, Brady was once more able to make eye contact. She nodded. Her hand was steadier this time and she placed the gun down onto the wound, squeezing the trigger and creeping it across the length with surgical precision. Brady looked down at his knuckle in surprise. The stitch job was perfect.

'See!' Brady said. 'Perfect.'

'Glad I could help. You should get yourself an AmbiSim upgrade, then you could do it yourself in future.'

'I don't touch tech,' Brady stated as he shrugged.

'Oh, you're one of those clean living weirdos?'

'I guess.'

She smiled, coyly. 'You aren't going to start preaching at me, are you?'

'Nah.' He forced laugh. 'It's not like that. I'm—' he began.

'Brady Drummond. I know all about you.' The innocence on her face fell away abruptly.

'What?' He shifted uncomfortably up his seat in case he needed to bug out. 'Who are you?'

'I'm kidding!' Her face softened, smiling coyly again. 'You fight in the Natural League don't you?' She looked around to where she had been sitting.

'Ah yeah.' Brady responded with a laugh to let her believe he wasn't fooled.

'Where did my bag go?'

'Bag?' He looked around as an empty gesture. 'Pretty sure you didn't have one.' He was confused but confident of his answer.

'Really? I must have left it in the other cabin!' She looked puzzled as she handed back the stitch gun.

Brady took the gun and inspected the resin stick. It was low enough to warrant changing. 'Thanks for this though.' He ejected the stick to the ground and returned the gun to his kit.

'I'm just going to...' She gestured towards the carriage she came from before heading off. Brady smiled and nodded as he packed away his trauma kit.

With his kit packed up, Brady sat in contemplation for a few minutes. He had a niggling feeling that he could not shake. The disruption of the shuttle was certainly at the forefront of his mind, but there was something else.

Then it dawned on him. The flow of air as the lady had opened the doors to switch carriages. The shuttles were sealed units in transit. That kind of airflow must have been a breach. He stood and made his way to follow her.

The next carriage was empty. Nothing untoward about that, but he saw the vestibule doors at the other end remained open. That certainly was strange. Brady made his way down through the carriage towards the stuck doors when he noticed movement outside the windows. Something small sped off into the distance, ducking and weaving through the maze of the other shuttle runs.

He watched on as it disappeared between two of the gigantic tower blocks and out of sight. He was used to seeing MediTech security drones whizzing about, but what he had seen was larger, more agile.

He refocused on the open doors as he approached, and noticed arcing on the controls. On closer inspection, he could see the damage, as though they had been struck by something solid. He could feel the flow of air coming from the next carriage, so cautiously, he pressed on.

The air pressure was becoming more prevalent as he neared the next. The doors had shut ahead, but he heard the whistle of air as it forced through the door panel edges. As he opened them to proceed, the gush nearly knocked him off balance. He reached for the sides of the vestibule, grabbing on to a handle to steady himself.

Then he saw it. A gaping hole in the roof of the carriage, two passengers seemingly unconscious below, or worse. He leant over the first, a middle-aged man. He was breathing but unresponsive. The other, a young lady, the same. *What the hell happened?* he wondered.

There was still no sign of the woman who had assisted him, but there was no time to carry on. It was clear to him that someone had entered the carriage, rendered the passengers unconscious and escaped. *Why though?* he thought. *To what end?* For a moment, he wondered about the woman. *No, not her, she must've seen this and ran from it.*

The shuttle was getting close to his tower and there was no way he was hanging about in the carriage on arrival. Quickly, he backtracked through the shuttle to his car. There was bound to be a full investigation on arrival, so he needed to be sure he could disembark and get through security before any lockdown.

CHAPTER THREE

Brady lived on level 78 of the E8-B20 tower.

Eight rings out from the centre and the twentieth in a slice containing thirty. Right in the triple thirteen of a dartboard. The locals referred to themselves as Thirty-Niners. That would've been their score in darts if they hit their tower's location. They were halfway to nowhere, neither flourishing nor languishing. It was the most mediocre of existences in the city.

Just as he had predicted, the moment the shuttle had been scanned the response had been ample. He had made it through the security checks to leave the docking bay just as the investigation team arrived on site. Brady was one of three passengers to have made it through before the docking bay had gone into lockdown. If he hadn't, he would have been languishing in there for at least an hour, probably the rest of the day.

Brady exited the transit hub to the poorly lit parking lot on the outer edge of level eighty. Housed within a gigantic enclosure, it was almost impossible to tell where it ended. Five thousand spaces sprawled for miles in both directions, bays and bays of vehicles, more often than not parked for so long they had mechanically seized. E8-B20 had 140 above the mezzanine. Every ten levels had four lots, and for the first time in his life that scope made Brady feel insignificant.

In all his time travelling around the city, he had never paused to appreciate just how big it was. He had either been anticipating a fight, riding high after a win or contemplating a loss. Physically, he had left the arena, but he was still mentally caged, and Ranley had become an echo chamber.

As he unlocked it remotely, the solace of the Felican SE250 sports car that he'd plugged every credit of his fight fees into since he began fighting shone through in the darkness. It was one of the last internal combustion cars to be made before the full switch to hydrogen in the year 2200, and it cost him dearly. It'd cost him exponentially more to run it since, such was the scarcity of petroleum and the high premium it commanded. He didn't care; it was an effigy to his limited success.

Brady sank into the fine leather upholstery of the driver's seat, turned the key and savoured the purr of the engine. For the first moment since Nikolai's club-like fists had danced around his face, he could relax. Weeks of pre-fight jitters and hours of post-fight anger melted away. Brady turned on the stereo, revved the engine and peeled out of his parking spot, leaving a cloud of tyre smoke in his wake.

Ranley City tower's internal road networks incorporated two four-lane motorways wrapping around each level, one outer, one inner. Up and down ramps splintered off both of them for level switching. The roads were reasonably busy, but the ramps stayed clear. To change levels, cars needed to be fitted with transition authorisation encoding to pass through the barriers.

As always, Brady exceeded the 120mph limit, weaving in and out of the eco cars. He needed to descend two levels, then change to the inner motorway, and he saw his exit ramp ahead. Dropping down a gear, he pressed his foot hard on the pedal, picking up more speed in an effort to beat the car ahead to the ramp. He didn't have to. It would be so easy to slot in behind and remain patient and the chances that the car was authorised to transition were low, but Brady was in need of a win.

He pulled alongside the electric sports car, casting a cursory glance at the driver, a middle-aged man by the looks of it, though it was hard to tell through the privacy glass. The Tamptech Cougar picked up pace. It had Brady's in acceleration, but there was no such advantage over the high-end torque of internal combustion.

They remained side by side as the exit ramp drew closer, but Brady had more left in the tank. His foot nailed to the floor, he shifted to sixth gear and his thirsty engine worked overtime, edging out its electric competitor and pumping noxious gasses in through any open apartment windows roadside. Brady saw his gap narrowing and checked over his shoulder. His rear quarter hadn't cleared.

The entrance was approaching. It was now or never. Brady didn't hesitate, bullying the other driver over to the recovery lane. Brady made it with only a few feet to spare before the lane barrier would have raked his car. He felt the air pressure change rock his car as he went past. He sighed in relief and eased off the accelerator, ready for the sharp drop ahead.

Brady pulled into the four-story car park that served his residential block. His headlights flashed across bays, allowing him to pick out one of the few vacant spaces between predominantly low-budget electric cars and bikes. Most of them had, at some point or another, been broken into or vandalised and Brady could count on one hand the vehicles he had ever seen move places.

He got out of his car, setting the security system with an obnoxious beep that masked the car as a junk heap. The walls of the parking garage were covered in an abundance of graffiti, to the point he wasn't sure if he had ever seen a bare patch of wall. Thirty-Niner tags stood out the most. The first time Brady saw them, he thought he was entering into some kind of gangland. Little did he know it was just local kids playing at tribalism. That was a year ago, when he moved out of Elena's apartment. He couldn't afford the upkeep on a flat three levels up and get his car.

***

Brady lived in apartment E8-B20-1903.

If ever he had fantasies of log fires and rustic living from his childhood stories, the cold, clinical nomenclature of the apartments jarred him back to a stark reality. If the naming wasn't enough, the infinity mirror effect of apartment doors off to either side of the entire length of the six mile long stretch did it. He had once walked from end to end, just to see how long it would take. Three hours of his life, accomplishing naught but making him feel insignificant.

The bustle of residents toing and froing was handled by the travelators; two long belt tracks in the centre of the hallway that sped continuously from one end to the other in opposite directions. Although Brady's apartment was conveniently near an exit, he never used it. As he approached, he hopped over the railing, immediately entering a full sprint to keep from tumbling face first. He managed to control his speed precisely, stopping directly in front of his door. It had taken a few weeks to nail the dismount. One crack in the wall rendering just to the left of his door was evidence of his worst attempt.

Apartment security was tight on these levels. Standard homes came with four-way identification, preventing unauthorised access. Given the moderate lifestyles citizens led, the risk to reward ratio was such that break-ins were all but pointless. Brady pressed his face into the security terminal for the scans; retina, DNA, facial structure and breath print. Matching the profile, the security systems disengaged and unlocked the door.

Brady had lived alone there for just over a year without ever really settling. He had the basic bachelor package installed when he moved in and hadn't changed a thing. A minimalist theme played throughout. It was either that or a slice of old-fashioned Americana, which he couldn't afford. The entrance hallway was bare, aside from the integrated apartment system hub on the wall.

Phone, thermostat, programmer; and, Personal Assistant all in one constantly data-mining convenience.

'Welcome home Brady.' A soft, female voice played out from the system. He had spent hours going through and choosing it out of hundreds of options when he was a child and brought her with him.

'T.V. on. Coffee on, preset two. Play messages.' He relaxed as he instructed his old faithful assistant to begin his homecoming procedure, just as he had a thousand times before.

'No new messages.' The assistant was incapable of judging him for a lack of social life, yet he was certain he heard a little condescension in the voice, regardless.

Brady set his bag down on the floor, took his shoes off and entered the almost untouched kitchen. He grabbed the freshly brewed coffee from the machine and carried on through into the living room. One sofa, one chair, one table, one bookshelf full of trophies and a view of the rolling ocean outside the window, rendered in virtual reality, that almost filled the entire wall. Brady collapsed on the sofa in exhaustion, barely mustering the energy for another command.

'T.V. play news. Mentions; Natural Class league fighting.' The ocean scape switched to the news broadcast.

'The attack on Tower E8-B20 claimed the lives of two citizens with three more in intensive care. Citizens are urged to use caution if they spot any sub-level breaches.' The female newsreader spoke over images of carnage in the aftermath of an attack on a MediTech silicone shipment in one of the outlying towers earlier that morning.

'MediTech Security Forces were on hand to contain the terrorist threat before it could spread any further. Speculation is rife that an upcoming statement from Governor Berg is going to contain details of her plan to launch a full scale invasion into the sublevels to take control of floors seventeen and eighteen to create a fully militarised border on level nineteen of each tower block in the city.'

The segment ended, and the programme moved to a sports set; clips of sporting events in a jigsaw puzzle of individual footage, constantly refreshing and changing behind the two news anchors as the man began to deliver the next piece.

'In the Natural Class Inter Block Fighting League news, reigning champion Nikolai Sciano defeated E8-B20's champion Brady Drummond by knockout. The heavily favoured Sciano retains his overall championship lead by an almost insurmountable forty-seven points over Central Block South's Aurelia Ducass.' The screen switched to show the end of the fight with Nikolai and Brady approaching from their respective corners.

'Controversy marred Nikolai's latest flawless performance when Drummond was found to be in possession of multiple counts of illegal cybernetic upgrades.'

Brady bolted upright, nearly choking on his coffee as the footage showed Nikolai landing the final blow.

'NCIBFL officials have declared they have banned Brady Drummond from future competition.'

'No way!' He slammed down his coffee mug on the table, spilling over the edges on impact as the footage switched to the anchors wrapping up the broadcast.

'T.V... Mute!' The full fallout of what had happened came flooding through. One afternoon had destroyed his career.

Shell-shocked and sat still, he gazed at an inch of the floor in front of him as though it had the answers to life itself hidden within the fibres of the carpet. With a guttural scream of pure rage, he stood in anger, flipping his coffee table and launching the coffee mug straight into the television, shattering the screen. The damage kicked in the screen's auto-repair feature. High current surged through the reactive glass fascia and the cracks merged back into one clean screen.

Once more, he began to truly feel the insurmountable pressure of the city. His breathing grew shallow and rapid. The room began to feel as though it was falling away from him.

Brady remembered Elena's bottle of sake. He had made sure to bring it with him from her apartment when he left. He staggered to the kitchen, feeling his way along the wall, hands taking in the contours of the doorway and through to the kitchen counter. It was two cupboards along on the left. He pawed it open clumsily, grasping for the bottle. He wanted to drink it all so badly, but before he could, he held the bottle close to his chest.

It was all he had left.

***

Brady began to feel the sedation ballistics' effects wearing off, but it wasn't his body. He was dreaming again. Except, he knew what he was envisioning was no normal dream. It felt lucid, to the point he could almost control the vessel he was carried in. Whilst the dreams often varied between a handful of people, he knew this one best. He felt like he had almost lived this person's life, and even knew his name.

Brady could feel how calm Joshua Reynolds was; his host body had experienced it before, that groggy state of confusion was familiar. *Oxalazipam, banned in Europe,* he thought. *Must have been captured there and brought to MediTech's jurisdiction. Hard to know for sure, probably Ranley.* He called up his retinal menu, overlaid against the back of his eyelids. *CHEMICAL LEVELS; BOOST ADRENALINE.*

Joshua's eyes popped open as the surge of adrenaline coursed through his body. Mag-lock cuffs held his wrists and ankles in place on a medical table. He crumpled his chin to get a view of his body, heavily scarred and altered with tech, but nothing new that he could see. He instructed his system, *'Body scan, new installs.'* A mesh overlay mapped out his entire nervous system, but nothing flagged on his retinal monitor. *That's good.* He hoped he had woken before anything had been done.

Realising he was on borrowed time, Joshua began to struggle against the mag-locks. His veins popped, muscles bulging as he sent all power to his arms through his system menu. Not a budge. He knew he would need to get the power to those powerful magnetic locks switched to stand any chance of escape.

He knew exactly what they were after and realised they didn't need him alive to get it. He shut his eyes and activated his electro-magnetic field optical overlay. His vision shifted to a rendering of all the EMF around him and he could see the power surging around the cables in the walls, a grid of electricity mapped out around him. The break point ahead and to his left was excruciatingly out of reach. A couple more feet and he could jack in to the power grid and take control remotely. Joshua tried to wrestle the table over, rocking it back and forth.

It didn't move, just as he knew it wouldn't.

He watched the door slide open, knowing he wouldn't be alone for much longer, and switched to thermal visioning. The figure that walked in was clearly male; he could tell from the shape of the torso. He seemed to pay no heed to Joshua, who relaxed somewhat. He watched the thermal image move to the control panel hooked up to the med table. Joshua knew he had some time to spare. If they knew for certain the location of the chip, the technician in the room would have been a mortician instead.

He heard the thunk below the table as the technician released the locking mechanism that held the table in place and Joshua hoped the mag-lock cuffs were on the same circuit. Subtly, he attempted to free his wrists, but there was still no movement.

The MediTech technician tweaked the controls to his parameters for the job at hand and moved to Joshua. He was clinical and focused, not looking at Joshua's face. He had a job to do, and that was all this was. Checking the bindings, he seemed satisfied the body was secured.

Gauging the orientation of the overhead probe unit, the technician swung Joshua's table ninety degrees, pushing and pulling in slight movements to line his head up with the probe. With Joshua in place, the technician re-engaged the table lock.

Joshua watched carefully as the tech brought the probe unit down to within an inch of his head. He had spent thirty-four years hiding the implant and in that moment, it seemed all to have been for nothing. It was just a matter of time. As soon as that scanner was engaged, he'd have lost everything. Somehow, he had to stop it. The technician, having completed his prep, moved back outside. Joshua was alone and once more handed the briefest slivers of time.

He wondered whether he could tap into the probe scanner and shut things down that way. His eyes closed again, revealing the electrical surges. The scanner was right there, tantalisingly in range and certainly had a connection point he could use, but a calm head told him to re-assess before making any decision. He was glad he did; a further inspection revealed the scanner's layers of security. One attempt at jacking into it would set the entire place's alarm system off.

Hope was ebbing away, like grains of sand in an hourglass, until the moment his head tilted to its side in dejection. The technician's rotation of the table had put him in plain view and within reach of targeting a cable break running in the walls. It was minimal, but the small gap in security insulation had presented the opportunity Joshua needed.

'Signal jack protocol'. His thought engaged the wireless network scanner embedded in his short range communications hardware. He controlled a targeting reticule with his eyes, aiming it precisely over the weak point. The colours changed as it got

closer and rotated, indicating signal lock. His trojan needed seventy seconds to bypass the firewall and another twenty-nine to locate the power controls and shut the room down.

He selected hybrid view, switching to augmented reality.

The power network overlaid a fully rendered reconstruction of the building he was in, pulled straight from the original technical drawings in the data flowing through the network. On the grid overlay, he watched his trojan change the colours of the wiring sections as it took them over on the way to its destination—the firewall server. With it gone from sight, he turned his attention to the door and the corridor outside.

Time passed by and he was clear to continue. No one approached his room as it neared the thirty second mark. He breathed slowly, maintaining his focus. Forty-two seconds down and he spotted a thermal body image heading across his path. It made his heart ramp up, but it wasn't a threat to him. Sixty-eight seconds down, and the firewall was about to be breached.

If they had advanced enough security, he was about to find out. No alarms at the seventy-two point—he was through. Eighty-eight seconds came as Joshua noticed another thermal body image. This one was heading his way.

It moved to reveal another right behind. Not enough time. It was agonizingly close, but they would be on him before his trojan could take down the power.

Joshua had no other choice but to switch off his optics and engage low power to continue running his hack. If he didn't, they would see his power surge clearly on their monitors. He was just in time before the two MediTech scientists entered. They were both armed, but not heavily enough to indicate they were aware of Joshua's escape plan. He counted in his head; seven seconds left. It was a small room and it would only take one button push before it was all over for him.

The scientists got to the monitoring desk with four seconds

remaining. He heard the power-up noise. It was quiet, but he could tell exactly what it was. Two seconds to boot up and negligible time for the scanner to note that he was conscious. He counted out four seconds, his nerves wobbled by the impending discovery. He hit his countdown and struggled to move. Nothing. It hadn't worked. He waited another beat and tried again; still nothing. It hadn't worked and his game was over. *'Nothing left to do but die.'*

One more try. The mag-locks pinged open with ease. He was free. Somewhere along the line he had sped up the count in his head. Adrenaline had skewed his ability to gauge time accurately. He cracked his eyes open a fraction. They were engaged with the monitor desk and had not noticed. A deep breath. *'Now!'*

As Joshua rolled off the table away from the scientists, taking refuge behind it, he called up his combat overlay. The room re-rendered itself with strategic points marked out. Flammable materials he could detonate, gas pipes he could shoot to create diversion and the weak points on his targets bodies. They drew their weapons in reaction to the noise of him crashing to the ground, but it was too late. The room plunged into darkness. Joshua controlled the power.

Two gun shots flashed in the pitch black.

With a thud, a body hit the ground.

Another muzzle flash before the lights came back up.

Joshua held the second scientist in his arms as he silently bled out from the bullet wound in his neck. He pried the gun from the scientist in his arms before slowly lowering him to the floor alongside the other body, its neck twisted the wrong way. Joshua heard footsteps, lots of them, loud and fast, two, maybe three floors above; he had time. His jack was still in the system. That was the one.

'Kill the power.'

***

Brady's head was thumping when he woke up the next morning. Were it not for the relentless banging on the door, he probably wouldn't have woken at all.

Bloodshot eyes peered carefully before he dared move. He was in his own home. That was a good first sign. Passed out in the living room, having nearly made it to the toppled sofa. Empty bottles all around him, including Elena's sake. The T.V. screen was showing the movie channel on mute. Last thing he remembered, it was still shattered. The banging continued, louder. He had to move, though gingerly.

Through blurry and bloodshot eyes, Brady engaged the apartment security panel and selected door view. Outside, he could see his friend Dan Forest waiting, impatiently slamming his fist over and over into the solid door.

Dan was the same age as Brady, but the scars on him suggested his twenty-four years hadn't been as easy. His right eye had been replaced with an optic, and the rest of his body was covered in evidence of bio-enhancements. Brady rubbed his eyes to remove the blurring of a bad night's sleep, just as Dan pressed the corner of his bionic eye, calling up a projected HUD in front of him. He selected his phone app and scrolled through the list down to "Brady."

Despite knowing it was his friend, Brady opened the door cautiously. He could see Dan was alone, but he couldn't shift the sense of panic in his dream. The details were fading as they always did, but he was left feeling as though he knew Joshua.

'So what happened?' Dan barged through the slight opening.

'They screwed me over. I'm done.' Brady cautiously poked his head out the front door to look for anyone else. He had never experienced paranoia before. He didn't like it.

Dan continued through to the kitchen as if he lived there

himself. 'What do you mean? How?'

'I don't know... the whole thing is corrupt.'

'So that's just it?' He opened the fridge without so much as a thought. 'You're finished?' Dan grabbed himself one of Brady's last two beers.

Brady closed the door and caught up with Dan. 'I can't fight in my league if the commission is standing by my conviction.' He declined the last beer as Dan offered it to him.

'But you're clean, you can prove it!' As he fizzed open the beer bottle, Dan continued through into the living room with Brady in tow.

'Who am I going to prove it to? They're all involved mate, there's not a damn thing I can do about it.'

'I don't know, there's got to be something you can do,' said Dan as he scoured the room and the mess from last night.

'I can jack up on bio-tech, screw over everything I believe in, dump on Elena's legacy. How about that?'

'I'm just trying to help. I don't know what else to say.' Dan shrugged at him.

'There's nothing to say. They're dirtbags.'

'So forget them dude, move on.' Dan changed tack rapidly, rounding the sofa and back out to the hallway.

'Move on?' Brady tracked Dan's movements.

'Yeah!'

'Like it's just that easy.' Brady shook his head and lowered it. 'Fighting was all I had. More than that, it's all I am.'

'Don't be stupid, you're not defined by it.' Dan swallowed the last of his beer before setting the bottle down on the floor.

'That's just the thing, Dan. I am. I mean, I was, I guess. I don't even know now.'

'Don't worry about it, Brady. You'll figure it out. Look, meet me later, yeah? I'll ping you the details.' Dan hurried his way back out to the front door, shutting it quickly behind him.

***

A nervous energy enveloped Dan as he jumped onto the travelator and called up his phone app.

'I just left Brady's.' He stayed quiet, waiting for a response.

'Yeah, he's out.' His fingers began impatiently tapping on the handrail.

'He's not taking it well. What did you expect?'

He began searching around to see if anyone was paying attention to him. His head darted to and fro.

'Honestly, I don't know. I haven't seen anything.'

His body began to bob up and down as the nerves had to find a path out.

'How about because if he sees me following him, he may just get a touch suspicious?'

Dan held his face down low as he passed people on the opposing travelator. He didn't recognise them, and that meant they could've been anyone.

'If you want to do it, do it yourself, nobody's going to stop you,' he said and purposefully hung up the call with a sharp tug of his earlobe. The green, in-call tinge on the flesh of his ear turned to red. As the travelator continued to carry him away, he carefully eyed up everyone passing in the opposite direction, one by one.

Up ahead, he spotted someone. They were watching him equally cautiously as they grew closer. Shady looking guy, with a cybernetic trail from ear to mouth. Vision band ocular replacement, black cap pulled down tight. His leather duster jacket could've been hiding anything.

Dan slid his hand into his jacket. He was ready—the other guy did the same. He wasn't looking in Dan's direction, but Dan knew that the vision band gave him a two-hundred and seventy degree panoramic view. Both men slightly withdrew their hands from the insides of their jackets as they grew nearer. Dan twitched.

Too soon. Two feet of separation. Both men snapped their hands out of their jackets. A quick exchange, and a subtle nod. Dan had possession of a small bag of DolaFlex and had handed the guy a credit stick, washed a hundred times through laundering to be untraceable. Dan tucked the drugs away as inconspicuously as his withdrawal-affected hands could.

CHAPTER FOUR

Westarm Steel pumped toxins downwards. They were the sole contractor providing the city with construction beams, operating in multiple locations across the city with one thing in common. They did not care about their impact on the lower levels. Brady stuck out like a sore thumb on the factory floor.

His tight white tank top and jeans contrasted the workers in their full safety suits. He knew he didn't belong there, but it was less to do with his clothing and more about the amount of sweat pouring from his brow and underarms. It was a heat he had never felt; the sheer hell of the combined power of countless furnaces melting steel.

As if the heat wasn't bad enough, he had to deal with the unease he felt around blue-collar workers. He could never work that one out. He had made a career going toe to toe with men and women twice their size and strength, but there was something intimidating about anyone who got their hands dirty with something other than blood.

Brady leant over a railing, trying to look nonchalant as he waited for Adawale, an old family friend. They had known each other since Brady's childhood. Adawale had been a regular visitor to his foster home and had made a specific point of keeping up with his visits, long after his own foster care had ended. Brady felt the friendly slap on his back that was typical Adawale, well-meaning but not well judged for its strength. He had always called it the Ada bite.

'I haven't seen you since the funeral. Why should I help you now?'

'Think of it as helping Elena if it makes it easier for you, Ada.'

'Really? I was just joking, but you're pulling that card on me?' Brady had managed to get his back up with just one sentence.

'It's just about the last card in my hand.' Brady pulled himself away from the railing.

'My heart bleeds for you Brady, it does,' said Adawale. Brady could tell there was not even a moderate attempt to hide how farcical he found the idea of Brady being hard done by.

'It's not my fault you were busted; your choice, your consequences.'

'Words to live by Brady. Take your own advice.' Adawale called on his heads up display, giving him remote control of the machinery in the factory under his care. Brady could see the gauges and dials and the vast array of sliders Adawale had to control. How he managed to remember which did what was beyond Brady.

'You know damn well I'm clean Ada, don't give me that rubbish.' Brady immediately regretted snapping like that.

'Of course you are, Elena's little golden boy.' Adawale swiped the pages of his HUD, revealing more and more controls.

'Don't start with that, I've had a tough couple of days.' Brady's pleading was met with the break of a smile behind the HUD. Adawale pulled Brady in tight for a hug.

'I missed you, little brother,' he said, his words dancing around his laughter.

'Get off me!' Brady grinned whilst pushing him away.

'What I am saying is, my brother, Elena took you in as her last child and wanted a different life for you.' Adawale returned to his tasks.

'Look where that got me.'

Adawale gave Brady a condescending look. 'Yeah, in a nicer apartment than I'll ever have.'

'How am I going to afford that now?'

'It's not about the apartment bro, she gave you another way of life.' Adawale closed his HUD, leant over the banister, looking far through one of the soot coated windows up high, as if he could see beyond the decades of caking.

Brady joined him. 'And now that's over.'

'You still don't get it, do you?' Adawale put his arm around Brady's shoulder.

'Get what?'

'It was never about getting you to follow in her footsteps in the Fighting League.'

Brady turned his head to look at Adawale, still clearly deep in thought. 'So what was it about?'

Adawale broke his gaze from the window and turned to Brady. 'Keeping you clean, brother.'

Brady took a moment. 'Why would she care about that?'

'Look around you, Brady.' He pointed out the workers on site, many of whom looked haggard as the last of their humanity desperately clung on against the oppression of the bio-tech. 'Everyone here is in a race against the person next to them to jump up the tech ladder just to keep their job.'

Brady took them all in. 'That's ridiculous. If you can do your job, who cares?'

'Let me tell you something now.' Adawale turned Brady to face him, grasped both of Brady's shoulders tight, and looked him deep in the eyes. 'There is always another worker willing to go one step further than you to take your job.'

'And what about you?' Brady patted him on his heart in concern.

'Honestly? I wake up every morning disassociating.' This alone elicited a worried look from Brady. 'I have to stare at myself in the mirror first thing every day for five, maybe ten minutes before I can convince myself that I am in my own body.'

'That's brutal, Ada.'

'Compared to half of these people,' he said, and gestured down to the work floor, 'I'm getting off lightly. I hit my limit long ago.'

'But you're still here, bro. You're still smiling and kicking.' Brady tried to lift his spirits with a buoyant slap on the arm.

'At the expense of nine demotions, yes.'

'Hey but you're surviving. Get me a gig here with you. Put Elena's boys back together and we will find a way up and out.'

Before Adawale even had a chance to answer, Brady could see from the look on his face that Adawale didn't agree. 'Leave it with me. I'll talk to the boss. As long as you have the credits, he'll get you onboard. The fact you're fighting fit means you can probably just about last shovelling the slag.'

'What's it like working there?' asked Brady.

Adawale sighed. 'Honestly?'

'Yeah, of course, honestly.'

'It's a hard graft.' Adawale's light expression turned more serious. 'Everyone's working as much as they can to get creds, but it's like climbing stairs on your hands.'

'That bad?'

'Welcome to the real world Brady, you work yourself to death so you don't die working.' Adawale's grin widened, as though it were in the hope it covered his slowly decaying soul. Brady knew him too well to buy it. 'If I'm lucky, I'll be able to afford a proxy work drone to take over a few years before retirement at ninety.'

'It can't take that long, surely?' said Brady.

He watched as Adawale took pause to look around the factory before responding to him. 'How many drone stations you see here? Five, six tops in the entire building. For seven hundred odd workers. Do the percentages.'

Brady took a moment to sweep around the factory as well. Adawale was right, he counted four of them, three of whom had their dormant proxy bots in docking. He noticed the solitary active drone ferrying between work stations, lugging raw material as it went.

'You're doing alright though, aren't you, all things considered?' Brady was floundering to give something positive back to his adoptive brother.

'Yeah, I'm doing good.' Adawale forced another grin as he responded. 'At this rate, I'll be able to afford an apartment on level twenty eight by the time I'm sixty.'

'Seriously?'

'No, I'm just joking, my brother. Probably not even then.' He boomed a great laugh.

'Wow, you aren't doing an amazing job of selling this gig to me!' Brady playfully punched him.

'I'm not the one selling this life. I'm just the sucker buying it.' Adawale put his hands up to surrender.

Brady looked away. 'You gotta wonder what Elena would say if she could see you now.'

'I know exactly what she would say.' Adawale poked him in the arm. 'You do too.'

'I do? What's that then?' said Brady, though he certainly knew what he meant.

'She'd say they won.' Adawale took a pause. 'She wouldn't be wrong.'

'So what, we just take it?' He turned back and flashed him a questioning look.

'Exactly.' Adawale shrugged. 'We just take it. Pay our dues, lump our coal, take our chits.'

'Then why bother?'

'What's the alternative? Drop down below twenty?' said Adawale, evidently trying to bolster his own make-the-most-of-it attitude.

'Can't be that bad!' Brady's brow furrowed.

Adawale sucked air in through his teeth, emitting a squeaking noise. 'You ever been down there?'

Brady knew the noise well; Adawale used it to emphasise

disbelief in something someone had said, and Brady hated it. 'Never.'

'Go see it for yourself. It's not living.'

'And this is?'

'Compared to that, yeah. Anyway, little bro, I have to get back to work. Come back tomorrow and remember this, when Elena taught you how to fight from the age of eight, she wasn't just teaching you how to physically fight.' Adawale ushered Brady away before hopping down steps to a lower platform.

Brady hung around for a few minutes before he left the factory, studying it, taking in the sight of a hundred workers just like Adawale, all gutting it out. His walk was laboured, the sheer weight of the world pushing him down. He had always liked to think of himself as compassionate, but he had to face the fact that this was the first time he had ever really acknowledged just how hard most people had it. And he had to wrestle with the notion that he only truly cared because now it was happening to him.

Every industrial business had its own vacuum loop access points. Fifty tubes ran in a giant loop between the industrial and residential bands. Revolver sections spaced out allowed the personal pods to be boarded and disembarked without disturbing the flowing pods.

Brady jumped into an available pod as soon as it docked.

'Recreational District East,' Brady said as the pod door closed and shot away. The force of acceleration, from zero to one hundred-miles-per hour over three seconds, forced Brady's head back into the headrest. Ahead, the tube rotated to line up with a sharp bend left, heading inward toward the residential zone.

The pod followed the contours and twists perfectly. Each tube was precisely banked to ensure the passengers would traverse the bends at high speed, whilst minimising the lateral g-force. Precision. Anything less would be a tragedy, with pods spinning through the tubes so quickly it would separate passenger's liquids from their solids in a centrifuge. Brady hated the darkness of the tunnels, but they were rapidly approaching. A dark abyss with no end in sight. *Like life,* he thought.

***

Level seventy-eight's East Market Street was heaving with people. Market stalls, as far as the eye could see, took up the space that the crowds didn't. Sellers were pushing all manner of goods, from synthetic food, right through to bric-à-brac not quite good enough for the official stores. Even vehicle sale stalls with interactive three-dimensional models pulled up on a holo-platform.

Whilst every tower itself was a ladder to better living, so was each ten-level section. Level seventy-eight had the premier street vendors for Brady's section. Above eighty, it was all slick shopping strips with all the latest official goods to buy at premier prices. Unlike most, Brady could have afforded to shop in the franchised stores, but he had been taught to avoid them where possible. Elena liked supporting the little guy, even if the credits eventually kicked up to the same place. She had made sure he followed that ethos.

The market street wedged itself between the outer highway and the first residential block. It was there that Brady had carved out his little sanctuary. It was itself large enough to give a sense of isolation, with the gigantic walls either side so peppered in bright lighting and intrusive advertising holo-boards that, when he was there, Brady often forgot there was a world outside of consumerism.

Brady forced his way through a long queue, lining up with fevered excitement in front of a food stall. It was nothing new to Brady. He could guess exactly what they were waiting for. That kind of furore was only ever for real meat. Some lucky stall owner had managed to get their hands on some animal that wasn't quite fit for human consumption at restaurant level and was about to double their usual yearly profit in one evening.

It had been centuries since lab grown synthetic meats had rendered the natural meat industry in MediTech's territories obsolete and unprofitable, yet real meat remained a bragging luxury for the corporate elite. Through those centuries, the quality of the synthesised meat had grown exponentially worse as the generations moved away from remembering what the real stuff was like. Brady was in the rare few who had ever managed to taste real meat, so to him, the synthesised stuff had become no more than fibrous sinew.

Those who scampered to get a hold of the real stuff on the black markets, did so, not because they had a desire to appear above their station, rather their bodies had a carnal craving for something other than filler and chemicals. They were drawn to it.

The desire to get hold of such rarities as real meat often led to full-scale rioting. To protect their investments, the stall owner had hired heavily armed private militia, all kitted out in MediTech's previous generation of Bio-Tech enhancements as a deterrent. Their existence, fully sanctioned by MediTech themselves, gave an illusion of individual responsibility for safety. That's how he knew what was on sale.

Brady began to feel faint, as his vision darkened and narrowed. He was dazed, as though, for a moment he had left his own body. 'Brady!' He heard his name and came snapping back to the moment, but it was echoed, like a voice within a voice. *Hearing things now. What is wrong with me?* He shook it off, his destination in plain sight.

Mio's Bar was one of a few open bars on the market street still in operation. Little independent establishments had mostly been run out of town by the chains and Mio's was probably past due. It was humble; the credits had been pumped into setting up self service taps around the panopticon of a bar to limit the number of staff needed.

It was no busier than usual, so Brady managed to find himself a free seat at the bar. He never liked using self service. There was something about the social interaction with a bar person that he craved. He didn't mind the extra wait for the personal touch, not that he ever truly experienced waiting. His minor celebrity status because of fighting usually let him skip ahead a few places. In the meantime, he sat patiently, eavesdropping on the conversation of the man and woman near him.

'So which upgrade are you thinking about?' said the lady, looking over the man's shoulder as he scrolled through a myriad of Bio-Tech upgrade options on the holo projection in front of his face.

'It's got to be something to boost my dexterity. I can't keep up with the new recruits any more.' He swiped through the shopping page so quickly, Brady couldn't see anything on it with any clarity.

'Going for a promotion?' said the lady.

'I'm just trying not to lose my job at this point.' The man settled on a section of tech, Brady could just about make out some Bio-Tech finger replacements on the screen as he side-eyed to avoid overtly gawking.

'I know what you mean. I had to upgrade my neural processor last month because my numbers were down.' said the lady as she took a bite of what Brady presumed was one of Mio's famous synthesised club sandwiches. Though why they were supposedly famous, he never worked out. Tasted the same as any other synth food to him.

'That's right, you never told me about this new project.' said the man, still fixated on the inventory.

'There's nothing to tell.' said the woman, mouth still full of her bite before she eventually swallowed it down. 'We don't know what it is for, can't talk about it with each other. One guy a few cubicles away from me did, next day, well, we never saw him again.'

'You've no idea at all? How can that be?' said the man.

'Whatever it is, they've chopped up the code and given us all chunks. We are just working through our sections looking for anomalies.' said the woman as she put the remainder of the sandwich down. Brady shifted himself around, just slightly, to get a better vantage to hear without giving the game away.

'But it's some kind of Bio-Tech, right? Maybe they are working on something big.' said the man as Brady noticed him reading through the list of incompatible tech for the finger replacements.

'I presume so. But it's not new. Not with the coding parameters I've seen in my sections.' she said, lifting the sandwich back to her mouth but hesitating to bite. 'It's older than anything I've ever seen.'

Brady's concentration was interrupted when he was greeted by the lone bartender, Mya Prince, within a few minutes. She was tall, slim and attractive. She had to be. The owner, Mio, hired staff based on curbside appeal alone and, whilst she required no uniform, she made sure her staff showed some skin.

'Hey darling, what can I get you?' Mya smiled warmly at him as she slung the cleaning cloth over her shoulder.

'Hiya, can I get a Luckett's please, hun?' He felt awkward calling her that, but he always tried to mirror her little pet names. He knew she used them for everyone, but he liked to pretend they were just for him.

'Bottle or tap?'

Brady fired a wink her way. 'Always tap.'

'Coming right up. First one's on the house. Looks like you need it!' She winked back, coyly.

'First one is always free, that's how they get you.' He grinned at her.

'I've never needed to give anything away to get ya!' She shrugged as she slid him the freshly pulled beer.

Brady chuckled under his breath. 'I bet not.'

He could see her watching him press the glass to his bloodied, split lip. 'So what does the other guy look like?' she asked.

Brady smiled, looking around momentarily. 'See that wall over there?' He pointed at a tall, thick steel wall penning in one of the many power transformers used to run the strip lights.

'Yeah.' Mya seemed to pay no attention to where he was pointing, instead she was curiously scanning the people nearby.

'He was about that big.' Brady downed the drink and hit the glass on the bar. Mya looked confused.

'Another one?' She nodded at his glass and spoke a little more professionally than she had been. Brady shook his head, pressed his thumb to the paypoint on the bar and transferred 500 credits.

'Call it a tip.' He got up from the stool and began heading away from the bar.

He wanted to play it cool with her. He wasn't sure if she knew how many times she had served him over the last couple of years. He didn't know if he had registered on her radar like she had on his, but he hoped. Sure, he would have liked another drink, but that's what she would expect. *Leave on a high,* he thought. He kept his eye on her in the reflection of a clean metal stall side. *If she watched, make your move.*

***

Outside, the air above Central Tower was the cleanest in the city.

Huge filtration systems circled the tower's giant perimeter, ensuring any contamination from the lower levels was filtered out before it contaminated the natural atmosphere. The rooftop complex was bustling with the rich and privileged, all breathing clean air as they enjoyed their freedom.

Bars and restaurants were everywhere, endless choices, all under MediTech's corporate umbrella. It didn't matter if they had no business, it just mattered that they were there, to be enjoyed as and when required.

Maimillion Xiao and Francesca Berg waited to tee off on the 7th hole of one of three golf courses that topped Central Admin Tower.

Xiao could have passed for ten years younger than his age of fifty-three, so rigorous was his self-care regime and immaculate his presentation. Nobody knew exactly how old Francesca was, except herself, but most assumed she was somewhere in her seventies. She didn't look anywhere near, but her reign over MediTech in Ranley city had been going on for almost fifty years, so the numbers spoke for themselves.

She could have played through if she wanted. She owned the course and everything else after all, but the break in play was needed.

'So what did they tell you, Xiao?'

Xiao nonchalantly picked turf from the head of his four iron. 'It was a blip, the technician wasn't sure it was anything.'

'He was sure enough to report it.'

'It's your call, obviously Cesca.' The familiarity with which he addressed her gave her consideration of whether he had become too comfortable, but she let it slide. 'Personally, I'm more concerned with the attack on our network.'

'They are on our radar, I wouldn't lose any sleep.' She politely applauded the shot played by the group ahead. 'That is where this blip, what was his name, Brady, needs to be too.'

'Are we going to chase every question mark we find?'

'That is exactly what we are going to do. Do you know how you find something?'

Xiao polished off the non-existent dirt from his immaculate

ball. 'You look for it?'

'You ask questions. And this blip is a question I want an answer to.'

'We don't know it's a question though, Cesca.' Xiao quizzed her with his eyes as they approached the tee.

'That is exactly why it is a question.' Francesca placed her driver over her shoulders and began rotating them back and forth to stay limber. 'If we knew the answer, we wouldn't be worried. We'd know it either is, or isn't. What it is, as we stand here, is both.'

'What do you mean, both?'

'It both is and isn't,' said Francesca as she placed her ball.

'Fine, who do you want?'

Francesca softly waggled her hips, getting settled into her stance. 'Get Bo.'

'Bo? Really? You're talking about finding one young kid, not decimating an entire community!'

She drew back her club and flowed through her shot with grace and precision. 'No chances.' She had relied on Bo to handle all manner of problems over the years. He had fought on the front lines of wars, single-handedly taking out entire battalions. She had found him as a teenager, an elite athlete, who towered above his peers, both in stature and physical ability. It was his unique physical make-up that leant to his ability to naturally tolerate the levels of bio-tech enhancements that would have killed anyone else. He was her bodyguard, enforcer and pet all rolled into one.

The club had struck the ball perfectly and its ping and trajectory pleased her.

CHAPTER FIVE

High in the rafters of a once splendid hallway underneath Ranley City's ever rising mezzanine, Layne Radchenko deftly leapt from handhold to foothold, traversing the structure like a primate. He could feel his pounding heart begin to subdue and his breathing, despite the strain on his body, lightened.

Layne checked the straps of the backpack he carried again. Those straps were solid, he knew it, he knew it the first twenty times he checked them, he still knew it after another twenty. But the contents were imperative. He had to get them back. Lives depended on the haul inside.

After ten years of scavenging missions to the city since his defection from MediTech Military front-line battalion, Layne thought he had seen it all. But this run had been different. The raid played over and over in his mind, what he could've done differently, how MediTech's security was so quick to respond, right down to the mistakes that Olly, his partner made and whether there was even a shred of hope he made it out alive.

He recalled his first scavenge mission above the mezzanine, the toll it took on him physically to climb the tattered structures of Ranley's early days. It was easier now; Layne let his bio-tech do the work, watching his retinal overlay calculate angles and distances for leaps and bounds that had once petrified him. He'd had the tech for so long that he never questioned the path it would choose.

Life had found a strange equilibrium in the sublevels. Births were a sacred rarity, air and water quality made carrying to term a one in a thousand chance. And yet the population managed to stay balanced. Deaths were countered by the ever ready flow of citizens discarded from above. It was the circle of sub-life.

Most of the residents had been cast out due to their own over indulgence in bio-tech enhancements. Their bodies pushed beyond the limits of electro-mechanical intrusion before they started to shut down. Among the dwellers of the undercity, Layne was burdened with the responsibility of leading raids to take just enough provisions to keep those with a consciousness alive.

He knew he was often the fine line between life and death for the poor souls who lived in the squalor of the undercity. The tech he carried back would not last long. Even with the bag that was lost with his partner, he would've been heading back above deck in a month. Without it, he knew he would have to risk life and limb within a fortnight.

There was an ironic serendipity to Layne's missions. He felt like the constant battle to replace corrupted tech that was both killing and sustaining lives was some kind of sick joke. He could feel the squirming sensation in his own body as his immune system attacked the healthy tissues around his own tech. He always thought it was a crazy notion, bio-tech that had originally been designed as a cure for cancer, was now acting just like it. Convincing the body to eat itself and leave the tech alone.

Countless bodies littered the ground, and to an untrained eye they were corpses, yet Layne knew they lived. Barely. Self sustaining life support machines is all they were; brain dead almost certainly, but the primary rule of the sub levels was life is life. Eventually, they would become fuel for a fire, but until all signs were gone, they remained untouchable.

His upgraded legs coiled like a loaded spring against what was left of an ornate wall before exploding with enough force to launch him like a rocket. As he speared through the air towards a crumbling pillar that would be his route down to the ground, he could see his destination in the distance.

Chunks of wall, salvaged from the buildings that once stood, were propped together alongside thick metal sheeting to fill in the gaps; barbed wire rolls lined the top of the perimeter wall. Inside, at strategically placed points of vantage, stood lookout towers, each one manned by two guards and sporting mounted heavy machine guns.

Layne made it down to the ground with a long run to make it to the gate of the complex. He stripped off the last of his graphene armour from his legs, ravaged by the gunshots during the skirmish he had barely managed to escape. Layne's muscular frame was heavily modified and carrying two significant gunshot wounds. Left shoulder, right thigh. The shoulder wound was clean through and bloodstained, but the thigh wound had no sign of bleeding. The torn skin revealed a fully bio-tech limb, exposed actuators and wiring driving the prosthetic.

His combat retinals plotted out the threats from the bodies between himself and his destination. He knew he was quicker, even carrying the injuries, but it was a relief to be able to navigate them with foresight, regardless. Slower than usual, he began his sprint. His biofeedback reported thirty-nine miles per hour, which he knew was roughly eleven percent down on the usual output, grimacing with each impact of his right leg into the uneven, solid ground.

Layne noticed the laboured movements of the bodies along the path, as though they were drawn to him by some kind of magnetic pull. He knew their instincts to survive drew them his way as a source of tech nutrition. Though he remained calm. Not one managed to get within five feet of him, and before long, his destination was in reach.

He banged on the gate in the distinct pattern of the latest entry code. A few seconds passed before he heard the loud clunk of locks being disengaged, allowing Layne to slide open the heavy, rusted gate just enough to squeeze himself inside.

The complex housed a self-sustained community, with crude

huts for housing, tented areas for trade and governance. A nation alone unto itself. Hundreds of discarded lives going about their business, many flirting dangerously at the point of no return between human and machine.

Layne made his way directly to the medical tent with its dozen beds, around which lay salvaged monitoring equipment that could give out at any moment. Bloodstains and discarded chunks of flesh along with old, broken bio-tech covered the ground. Three beds were empty, the rest filled by people whose tenuous grip on life was rapidly diminishing. One, nothing more than head and torso, had been cauterised at the waist, pneumatic actuators protruding where cybernetic legs were once attached.

He picked his spot at the back of the tent, the bed reserved for him and his team. Always clean, unlike the rest. They could risk sepsis with the general population, but the strike team needed to be on point and the resources to ensure absolute sterilisation were often limited. As he settled into the bed he had inhabited more times than he could count, he noticed Samantha Lynch approach. He had a little flutter in his heart that he knew wasn't down to his injuries. She wasn't conventionally attractive, but over the years of life saving treatment, he had grown quite fond of her.

It had been almost eight years since Samantha repatriated herself from MediTech's surgical ranks to seek to help in the free clinics on the lower levels and a touch over six since Layne had found her and convinced her to dive even lower into the belly of Ranley City.

By the look on her face and silence as she approached, Layne knew he didn't have to say anything to her. He had noticed her briefly looking around for sign of his partner, and could tell she knew it had gone wrong. It was a sense of relief to know he didn't have to explain anything to her, though he would have enough of that soon.

Samantha cauterised Layne's shoulder wound before applying

one of the last remaining dermal gauze patches in her trauma kit. Layne watched as the edges began to assimilate with his surrounding skin. The off-coloured patch shifted tone like a chameleon to match his skin until there was no evidence there was a wound to begin with. Transfixed on the assimilation, he did not notice Benito Cartaleno approach until he felt his hand on his foot.

Benito looked as though he belonged up the top of the city. He was healthy and clean, no sign of bio-tech. He'd never been expelled from above; Benito was a self-governing man at heart and left everything behind in favour of the freedom he could forge for himself in the sublevels. Benito was as close to a leader as there could be down here and, just like the machination he had expatriated himself from, he often confused leadership and autocracy.

'Layne,' said Benito, quietly.

'Benny.' Layne stuck out his undamaged hand, being more familiar with Benito than most.

'How is he?' Benito turned to Samantha.

'He'll be fine. Clean in and out here.' She gestured to his shoulder wound, highlighting the damage to his prosthetic leg. 'But he'll probably need some rebuild here, best-case scenario.'

'Do you have what you need?'

'I can re-prime the hydraulics, maybe get Keenan to patch up the wiring, but he'll lose mobility.'

'How much?' said Layne.

She was in deep thought. 'Twenty, maybe thirty percent.'

Layne shook his head. 'I can't lose that much.'

Samantha took another moment to think. 'Alternative is full replacement, but we just don't have anything like as high spec as this.'

'So what's the best you can do?' asked Benito.

'Maybe a three gen downgrade. Even then, I'd have to take it from someone else and downgrade them even further.'

'Damn it.' Benito looked obviously irritated. 'We need fresh supplies now!'

'It's getting dire.' Samantha's face turned sullen. It was a look she had learned to hide in all her years as a doctor to protect her patients.

Benito leaned in to Layne. 'Were they waiting for you?'

'Hard to tell,' Layne responded cautiously, wary of Benito's questioning. They were often loaded, and he found it tricky to unravel the layers.

Benito perched himself on the table. 'They either were or they weren't.'

'It was all so quick, hard to tell what happened.' Layne knew exactly what had happened. He had taken a team of eighteen to hijack MediTech's latest silicone import. The security detail had been far too organised to indicate anything other than expectation.

'Then doesn't that give you the answer?' Benito stared him down.

'I guess so.' Layne shifted uncomfortably. 'But I'm more concerned with who was there, not how quickly.'

Benito stood, looking puzzled as he began to pace up and down the side of the operating table. 'Explain.'

'Two lots of military. Two captains.' He recalled the entire event, the pain of losing his team. 'One of them knew Olly.'

'Interesting.' Benito stopped his pacing, his eyes narrowed and brow furrowed.

'No, Benny. Not Olly.' Olly had been Layne's closest friend for many years, and wanted nothing to do with any doubts surrounding him. Especially given his loss.

'I knew something was up with him.'

'I'm telling you, it's not Olly, he's the only reason I'm alive.' His face flushed red as Benito's persistence began to anger him.

'Where is he then?'

'We got ambushed by the backup. Olly led them from us. Said he was going to head up a few levels and jump a shuttle.'

'So let me get this straight.' Benito turned and leant in, one eyebrow raised and a slanted grin as he looked beyond Layne. 'You were met by two groups of militia, both with high-ranking officers, one of whom knew Olly, who disappeared afterwards and you honestly buy that he was going to chance a shuttle jump?' He turned his gaze straight to Layne's eyes, straightening his expressions. 'I find it hard to believe you are this naïve.'

'Look, it wasn't Olly. I only brought him in on this one at the last minute. No way he could have had time to—'

'It was either Olly or the intel. Or both.' Benito's tone only served to irritate Layne further, regardless of the interruption.

'Wasn't Olly.' Mya interrupted, as she ducked under the tent awning to join them fresh from her latest shift at Mio's bar. 'And think carefully before you start questioning my intel.'

'Nice of you to join us.' Benito stood tall to greet her.

'I don't put up with Mio's grab-assing to have you question my work and she pays my salary.' Mya met Benito with brief consideration. Layne could see she was more interested in his condition. 'How are you?'

'I'll survive. Any word?'

Mya reached past Benito to Layne, softly squeezing his hand. 'Olly got it trying to jump a shuttle to the central towers.'

'Anyone else make it out?' said Benito, positioning himself to break their grasp on each other.

'Ruby got through too, but we were separated. She's either on her way or—' Layne paused.

Benito jumped in his break. 'Or what? Were you followed down?'

Layne looked up to the ceiling. 'Can't rule it out.'

'I can,' Mya said, pushing through Benito to get closer to Layne. 'Something is going on up there bigger than you right now.'

Benito grabbed Mya and forced her around to face him. 'What do you mean?'

She abruptly shook him off. 'Nobody knows for sure, but the whispers are all about a hunt for someone. Whoever it is, it's bigger than some shipment.'

'What did you get out with?' Benito refocused on Layne as Samantha plugged Layne's leg into her hydraulic pressurizer and topped him up with the neon green liquid.

'Me? My life... Barely.'

'So the entire operation was a waste?' Benito swept Samantha's surgical tools wildly from their cart.

'I'm trying to work here!' said Samantha as she gathered them from the ground.

Benito's gaze snapped around to lock with hers. Samantha turned away, her head down at the floor, looking for a tool she knew she had already picked up. 'How'd you manage to survive, huh?'

'Luck,' Layne said, grimacing through the odd sensation as the fluid entered his body.

'We make our own luck though, don't we?' Benito kicked aside the tools on the floor by his feet, spreading them even further apart. Layne saw the look of muted anger on Samantha's face.

'What exactly are you saying, Benny?' Layne squirmed as the fluid began to tickle his insides with greater intensity.

'Don't play dumb. It doesn't suit you.' Layne could almost feel Benito's heightened tension.

Layne bent his neck to the side, cracking it. 'I don't know what you're talking about!'

Benito sat back down next to him. Too close for comfort. 'Someone here warned them. You just happened to make it back?'

'Jesus Benny, I just watched fifteen of our friends die. I find out Olly has died. You really want to accuse me of this?' Layne shuffled upright as much as he could to try to meet Benito eye to eye.

Mya pulled back at Benito's shoulder to get him away from Layne, but, like a child having their toy taken away, he refused to give in.

'Be that as it may, Layne, you're getting silicone.' Benito was clearly becoming angrier by the minute.

Layne grabbed his arm. 'You're really starting to push my buttons now, Benny.'

Benito took a deep breath. 'Layne, I'm sorry. Look, I know it was nothing to do with you, it's just frustrating. We need to get hold of something and soon. You are the only hope we have.'

'On my own? That's impossible!'

'You mean improbable. What's impossible is our continued existence here if we don't get it,' Benito stated, calmly, composed now.

Benito nodded to Samantha as he disengaged with Layne altogether, allowing her to continue her work. She prized open Layne's thigh wound and he braced as the forceps pushed through.

Layne fought the discomfort the best he could, but his body squirmed involuntarily as Samantha continued peeling flesh and sinew away from the prosthetic to get to the manual override. He knew she needed to isolate it for electronic repair, but no matter how much he tried to let her do her job, the sensation was too much to bear, even with his neural inhibitors blocking out as much as possible.

Samantha pinned him down with one hand on his sternum, her strength belying her size as she managed to hold him in place with ease. She dug the forceps in deeper to a guttural scream that echoed around the chasm of the undercity.

***

Brady ambled through level eighty's entertainment district.

He still recalled the first time he had been there as a boy, fooled by the incandescence of natural lighting installations into thinking he had seen the sun for the first time. Lately he went there for the golf courses and restaurants, but neither of those options were appealing.

At odds with what to do with himself, he was on auto-pilot with a programming error. Most of the shops were quiet, but the restaurants and bars were teeming with activity. Too crowded for his liking, Brady crossed the walkway over to the central plaza. It was a piece of outside, inside. Grass areas, flower beds, fountains, benches and a tremendous sense of irony.

Brady took a seat on a vacant bench, looking towards a strip of particularly popular bars and clubs. He'd been to every one at one point or another, some he remembered, some he didn't. *Funny,* he thought, *they seem so unique and interesting when you're in them. When they have plied you with enough of their liquor to dull your senses and heighten your ignorance.* Looking at them then, in that sullen moment, all he could think about was just how similar they all were.

His melancholy didn't last long before being snapped by a young female jogger stumbling into his lap. He noticed she was attractive. This was the first instinct.

'Oh, I'm so sorry.' She was meek in her response.

'You alright there?' He had an inclination to flirt a little; she was attractive, after all. Perhaps if he wasn't so shaken, he may have.

'Nothing but a bruised ego!'

'Take care out there, you're supposed to be running laps not falling in them.' His eyes closed with the anguish of his choice of joke.

To his surprise, she laughed. Even if he knew she was just

humouring him, it put him at ease. He watched as she jogged away, staring unashamedly, perhaps autonomously, at her backside. Firm, muscly and tightly wrapped in jogging pants. He watched as she turned back, jogging on the spot. Her face looked different. Her demeanour had changed entirely. Brady wondered, *am I about to get lucky?*

'Thanks for the credits!' she shouted to Brady's bemusement. His mind rattled through the permutations of what she meant when it dawned on him. He checked his jacket pocket for his phone. It was gone. Everything he had was on it. His entire credit stack. She held it aloft and blew a kiss before she turned and sprinted away. In a state of shock, Brady took chase.

The runner headed towards the bar zone, easily juking in and out of the crowd. Brady was less subtle in her wake, opting for brute force over agility. His shoulder charges were met with a chorus of outcry, which he ignored entirely.

She led him towards a five-foot-high section of wall separating the bars from the pedestrian walkway and leapt over in full stride as though it were a child's hurdle. Brady attempted the same move, though he already knew it was far beyond his capabilities. Brady found himself scrambling to climb up. He was losing time, he knew it.

From the top of the wall that had taken so much energy to reach, he saw her cross the walkway to the parking side and duck down a tight alleyway between two sections. Brady felt a sense of unease following her into the parking zone. Had he taken even a second to think he would've realised she was goading him into following her, but his brain was locked down in a vault of male bravado and so he took chase.

He turned into the dark alley. It was grotty, and it stank worse than it looked. She climbed a ladder with feline grace up ahead, splintered off sideways before its peak and shot into a ventilation tunnel. He followed suit, though he was much slower up the ladder. Into the vents. Tight, claustrophobically tight. She had flipped on her back and propelled herself along with subtle yet strong strokes, using her hands on the vent shaft. Brady tried the same, but the friction was too strong, and he had to commando crawl. She was making more and more ground.

The ventilation tunnel led them to one of the zone car parks with an uncomfortable, long drop. It was darker than the one serving Brady's apartment and had even more destroyed vehicles and graffiti. She ducked out of sight between two vehicles. Brady ran in, looking around. He had no clue where she had gone. He paused, then took a couple of hopeful steps. No sign of her.

He'd just have to pick a direction and go for it. He began running again, past a couple of parked cars, scattily looking around for her. From the shadows in the dark emerged the monolithic frame of Bo Jacobs. He made Nikolai look like a child.

Brady noticed his eyes first, though, glowing a demonic red with bio-tech optics. As the rest of him became more visible, he could see one entire arm and skull cap made of titanium. He looked like he should have been languishing as a sub-level mess, more tech in him than should be possible to sustain, yet he was functioning on high levels. He extended his bionic arm a split second before Brady could know what was going on. Bo's clothesline hook took Brady into mid-air but Bo didn't so much as flinch.

CHAPTER SIX

Brady was deep in another all too vivid dream sequence about one of his frequent subconscious visitors. There seemed to be a fractured timeline to them and this particular face was ever present in what Brady could only assume were the earliest ones.

Rueben Braunschild II had a perfect view of his project across the Thames from his penthouse suite in the Gherkin building. Both the height and width of the new construction made The Shard look like a molehill next to a mountain out of his window. The huge scaffolding exoskeleton had long been outgrown, serving as a support for the electromagnetic ring that allowed mag lift hover vehicles to propel themselves steadily up to the dizzying heights of the tower construction, hauling giant graphene beams as they went.

Rueben's apartment was immaculate, filled with high-end art, sculptures, and the finest furniture money could buy. He didn't care for any of it. The decorator had chosen everything for him on his instruction to reflect his status in material goods.

He sat in his Jacobean armchair, one of only two things that had any personal meaning to him. It had been in his family since his paternal ancestor, Feizal, was gifted it on arrival to Britain. Feizal had come from The Ottoman Empire during Queen Elizabeth I's reign and built his legacy in the shadows. Behind a secured glass display case was the other; Feizal's diary. It charted his rise from nothing to building a massive financial powerhouse.

Feizal Hafeez's diary started after he had been run out of Alexandria for theft, then was found and taken in by a family near Sofia on the brink of death after wandering aimlessly for almost a year, and nursed back to health. It explained how he worked their farmlands in gratitude and became part of the family, right up to the point he discovered gold deposits in a well in the hills of their farmland.

Reuben was proud of his ancestor's rise from nowhere and he felt a strong connection with the fact Feizal had the courage to kill the family who nursed him back to health to take what he wanted. Not all the Braunschild family had felt such pride, but Reuben believed in survival of the fittest. If that family were not smart enough to realise the value under their land, then they deserved to die. If not Feizal, it would have been someone else, eventually.

Everything about Reuben was a demand for respect. From the single malt scotch that cost thousands of pounds per glass and the crystal cut tumbler he drank from, to the finest Cuban cigar flown in on a private jet for freshness. He was the single richest person in the world and yet felt a driving need to remind everyone.

Prime Minister Phillip Ranley sat on the contemporary sofa across an enormous desk facing him. Rueben had purchased it with the intent of causing discomfort to whoever he was addressing, as another one of his psychological power plays. Phillip had been in that position many times before, enough to realise there was no sweet spot, so he settled for the best he could do and hid it as much as was possible.

'I cannot, in good faith, sanction that kind of action, Rueben.'

'Then do it in bad faith. I really don't care for your conscience.' Rueben's words were stifled by a mouthful of cigar smoke.

'This is too much to ask.'

'This isn't a question Phillip, this is how we are proceeding.'

'You can't expect that of me!'

'Expectations are what you have when you think there might be a chance you don't get what you want. This is non-negotiable.'

'How can you be so callous?' Phillip's eyes widened. 'You're talking about genocide!'

'Genocide? No, when it's vermin', Reuben said, then paused

and drew a sinister grin, 'it's extermination.'

'Vermin? Those are human beings. How can you be so flippant?'

'Look again. Look at they spread and how they multiply and destroy. Isn't that the definition of vermin?' Reuben had a coldness to life, as though he himself was not part of the human race, rather another species viewing it for the first time.

'I'm not arguing that there isn't a case to be made about overpopulation, but this is taking it too far.'

'You mistake yourself, though, Phillip. This isn't really an argument. It's more instructional.'

'I don't know if I could live with such a decision, Reuben.'

'Then don't live with it. That part is entirely up to you. I really don't care either way,' said Rueben.

'How did I let myself get so involved with such a monster?' Phillip postulated.

'See, that's the difference between you and me,' Rueben said. 'You think this differs from the things you do daily that you just see as little decisions? You make them, yet you hide from their ripple effect.'

'That's preposterous. I don't make decisions that kill thousands of people!' Phillip shifted uncomfortably.

'But you do, Phillip.' Smugly, Reuben swilled his scotch around the tumbler, clinking the ice stones inside. 'What's the difference between dropping a bomb or throwing a stone in the ocean that turns into a tidal wave on the other side? They both wreak havoc, but while one of those actions takes conviction, the other takes denial.'

He wasn't particularly interested in the serving temperature of his scotch, but he enjoyed the fact his ice stones didn't melt purely so he could continue to rock them around the glass. He had started doing it years ago as an added layer of what was, in his mind, a calm intimidation, but it had long since become habitual.

'There's a vast difference between directly murdering people and something you do having a knock-on effect,' said Phillip. 'I don't know how you can't see that.'

'Is there a difference between the victim of, say, a gunshot and, I don't know, being hit and killed by a drunk driver?'

'That's unfair!' Phillip said.

'So, you do remember exactly how you got involved with us, then?' Reuben said, satisfied that he had teased out the setup he needed to get to that point.

'There has to be another way,'

'Sure there is. Just beat that bleeding heart liberal in the next election. Seeing as all the polls have her substantially ahead, it's looking pretty unlikely.'

'So why don't you just ruin her career too and be safe either way?'

'Because she is strangely honourable. It's quite irritating, frankly,' Reuben said through a light snort of derision. 'But hey, if you can defy the odds and secure another term, we can systematically clear the construction area of the second tower peacefully.'

'I fully believe, given the proper funding, we can turn the polls around and win this election. Strong leadership for stability.'

'Spare me your campaign buzzwords Phillip, I'm not one of the morons.' Reuben laughed. 'Cohen is set for a landslide and we cannot allow that. It doesn't matter how many smear campaigns we run, she has the youth vote and they are far too savvy for their own good to sway them.'

'But with funding, we can reach them!'

'Reach them with what? A cool hip rap track?'

'No, I mean with some tech.' Phillip shifted in the seat, trying to gain some height. 'Get them messages the way they like to interact these days. Virtual Reality campaigning for one.'

'You don't need to reach them. They are a generation that

knows that the only thing stopping financial decentralisation are dinosaurs like you.' Reuben stood and turned his back on Phillip as he looked out over the city. 'Unless you can undermine the last one hundred years of cryptocurrency based transactions, the only weapon we have against them is fear.'

'So we have to make centralised banking seem cool somehow.'

'You think they use cryptocurrency because it's cool?' Reuben turned back sharply, so much so the scotch swirled out from the tumbler, landing on his clean white shirt. His eyes briefly broke character, showing concern for the staining before he refocused himself. 'Don't be a moron Phil, they use it because they know they have control over it. They use it because it doesn't prop up centuries of our way of doing things.'

'But I know we can move forward with them, not against them. If you increase my budget, I promise I will deliver results.'

'You keep assuming this is some kind of two-way discussion.' Reuben took his seat again, and leant forward over his desk to address Phillip. 'Let me be frank, the only way you get another term is if the people are so scared of changing leadership, they vote in fear. The only way to achieve that is war. So there's the overlap. We drone strike the land I want to clear, I get to build my tower, you get to transition to another term. We both win.'

'But we can think of—'

'Enough! Phillip, the wheels are in motion, you can get started on making it look like it was Russia or...' He paused, then added, 'Well, I'd advise you just get it done.' Reuben's authoritative nature left no room for miscommunication.

'And you think going to war with Russia is a good idea?'

'We won't be going to war with Russia,' Reuben explained as he poured himself a top-up, not offering Phillip any. 'Russia and China want the United States to make the first move. The EU gets angry that they weren't consulted, but ultimately have no choice but to back America. Meanwhile, Russia and China launch retaliation of their own on the EU. America backs out of the whole thing and before you know it, Russia and China are at full scale war with Europe. We get a war on our doorstep that lets me reshape the nation. Russia and China get to have their fight with the EU and our alliance with the US continues.'

'This is utterly absurd.'

'You think it's absurd because pawns just go one step at a time?' Reuben said. 'You can't see the game being played. Just be a pawn, move as I say and don't question me again.'

The two men sat in contradicting silences. Reuben was calm and collected as he sipped at his drink. Phillip, on the other hand, sat still and forlorn.

He was dreaming, yet Brady knew it all. The dates, the moves that had led up to that moment. Not from education. He just knew it all. Somehow. This was the turning of the tide from democracy to MediTech's autocracy.

***

Brady regained consciousness to the sound of loud pulse thrusters humming.

The dreams were getting more and more vivid each time. For years, he had seen them before in one form or another, but since the rifle butt struck his head, they had become more like recordings. He was just beginning to put two and two together when it dawned on him that he had no idea where he was. The concentration he needed to try to open his eyes left no room for the bigger picture thoughts.

As he began to gain his senses back, the first thing he noticed was the force at which his body was being pushed back into the seat. He knew he was moving faster than he had before, which meant whatever he was in wasn't public transport. His eyes slowly peeled open and he could see, though blurry, the inside of a small hover pod. The only time he had ever seen one before was in a news story about Governor Berg's triumphant return from the frontline during the last South American war. He didn't know what it meant, but he guessed it wasn't good.

More faculties came back online and Brady noticed the peaks of towers rushing by. His head felt as though it was welded facing outwards, the g-force too strong to turn, or his neck too weak. Brady could feel someone at his side, a real presence. He began to remember the girl and the chase and then the arm that took him down. He struggled with all his strength to lift himself away from the seat.

'Target is awake,' Bo grumbled in a deep tone, not so much as looking in Brady's direction for confirmation. Both the pod's monitoring software and his own short range combat scan hardware alerted him to the spike in Brady's heart rate.

'What the hell is going on?'

'Doesn't look like he can move,' Bo replied, speaking via his communication implant and ignoring Brady entirely. 'Weak frame can't handle the speed.'

'Who are you? What do you want?'

Being treated like cargo drove home the severity of the situation. He began to question what exactly he had done to deserve such a rapid collapse of everything he knew. The dreams, the fear, the betrayal. Everything spun around in his head rapidly. There was a time when he lived a happy life and it had never seemed so far away. So much so that he questioned whether it was even real. An uneasy feeling grew in strength and churned him up inside. He began to struggle with the dichotomy of whether any of this was real. For the first time in his life, he knew what genuine anguish was, and it drove through every inch of his body like it was caustic.

'Why won't you answer me?!' Brady shouted, needing something to act as a focal point to stabilise himself. 'Answer me!

Who are you? What is going on?' He frantically struggled to try to free himself of his bindings and fight the g-force. His panic caught Bo's attention.

'He's going ballistic. I can't be dealing with this.' Bo reached forward and selected sedation options on the pod's touch control panel. Brady felt his entire body begin to relax and a euphoria spread across him.

Bo's pod weaved around the towers at great speed. Brady felt the lateral G-Forces push him into his seat left and right as Bo took evasive manoeuvres to try to shake the two hover-bikes that trailed him. He could clearly see that Bo had the top end speed, but the other riders had him on acceleration and agility as the race ebbed and flowed with straights and corners. Brady had no idea who this man was, but it was easy for him to sense the frustration that he could not shake his pursuers.

He felt a judder as one bike shot a tethering round into the pod. The diamond-fibre cable was strong enough to hold up to the forces between the vehicles without any problem as the bike engaged reverse thrust to act as an anchor.

The shot came as Bo had positioned the pod perfectly to line up with a long, straight run between towers. It took five minutes to position himself to get such an avenue and would have been long enough to have gained some real separation. Bo's guttural scream of anguish startled Brady.

The bike was far from powerful enough to slow Bo's pod down much, but it was just enough to let the second bike start closing the gap. Brady could hear the extra strain on the engine as Bo punched his pod into full thrust to create enough tension on the line to rip the panel off his pod and get loose, but the thing was built too well. Brady could see Bo fixate on his rear-view monitor as the second rider gained ground.

The pod's combat sensors bleeped frantically as a target lock indicator flashed in unison. Brady felt the power of the blasts' silent impact as it struck the rear, lurching Bo's huge frame forwards out of his seat. *Ion blast, had to have been.*

The instrument cluster blinked rapidly and system monitors flashed countless errors, all in seemingly perfect timing with the penetrating alarm noise. Brady fidgeted, watching Bo as he frantically switched between his attempts to read the situation and trying to solve his obviously faulty controls and the approaching bikes. Another round penetrated the outer shell of the pod with a thud. It wasn't as bad as the first. Old school ballistics. Brady could see the tear in the outer hull in the side mirror display.

The anchor bike was beginning to struggle to contain the thrust power of Bo's pod. Brady could feel the judder. Its engines began to buckle under the strain and Brady knew the window of opportunity was narrowing rapidly. Brady's heart pounded, and blood whooshed in and out of his ear canals, when suddenly it dawned on him. *How do I know they are a better option?*

Brady's eyes widened, watching the chase as best he could in the side display. The two bikes seemed to be manoeuvring into their final approach.

He felt the tether disengage and, for a second he thought they had messed up. The second he saw the lead bike suddenly slam its brakes and fade in the distance, just as the trail bike shot forward, he knew it wasn't. The rush of stale air, almost entirely filtered of oxygen by Bo's premium respiratory system, filled Brady's lungs and held there.

A moment of wonder before silence. Before darkness. The lights went out, the engine died. And next to him, Bo lost function in his extremities. He was paralysed. It could only have been a tailored EMP blast. Nothing else would wipe out all systems in a split second. *These people know what they are doing,* he thought. *No chance this pod didn't have field dampening. They knew the frequency.*

Two rounds burst from the forward-mounted turrets on the

chase bike. The shots limpet mined into the pod and began cutting away at the glass canopy. As incapacitated as Bo was, Brady could see the look of complete shock on his face as he watched, unable to do anything about it. He could see the anchor bike approaching quickly and felt a second tether round strike and claw into the framework of Bo's pod. Brady crunched his face tightly, as there was nothing else he could do. Then he felt it, the absolute force on his body as the rapid descent ended in a split second. He grimaced, as the colour in his face drained.

Brady took a deep breath and let out a wince. He felt a wave of nausea and sudden coldness spread through his entire body. His sight began fading into a blur but he could still make out the flickering of system lights as the pod began to regain power. Through the edge of his ever-increasing tunnel vision, he noticed Bo's fingers begin to twitch. Above him, he could see the plasma burns of the limpet cutters making light work of the canopy. They were nearly clean through.

Then, all of a sudden a loud thud rocked the pod. Brady could just make out the boot of one of the riders through the windscreen, accompanied by the groaning of metal being twisted. On his side, Bo was beginning to show more sign of life. The cacophony of audible alarms began to silence themselves one by one as the systems stabilised. Brady's chill got even more intense. The rush of wind broke through the canopy as the rider managed to lift it fractionally open. His ears began to fill with the horrible rushing of air. Everything intensified at once.

Brady saw the gloved fingertips of the rider as they peeled the last of the freshly cut canopy section away from the pod and tossed it aside. They unclipped their pistol from their leg holster and positioned themself to drop into the pod, but they weren't quick enough. Bo's system had come back online and before the rider knew it, Bo had their leg in his giant vice-like grip.

As Brady remained still, in agony, and paralysed with fear, the rider struggled to get free, dropping their pistol in the process. They quickly placed their free foot onto Bo's shoulder for purchase, giving all they could to escape his grasp, but even limited to the use of one arm Bo was impossible to escape.

Brady could see that the force the rider was putting into their attempt to escape Bo's clutch would throw them backwards and down to their inevitable doom, had they actually managed to free themselves. If he weren't already feeling borderline hypothermic, the realisation that the rider would take a terrifying plummet to their death over remaining in Bo's clutches would have sent chills through him.

'He's got me. Get the target and bug out!'

Brady heard the rider's voice, though faded out by his tenuous grasp on consciousness. He looked up through the gaping hole where the canopy had been at the bike anchoring Bo's pod. He could hear the inaudible muffle of the anchoring rider's response through the engaged rider's helmet comms. Then, he watched as they stood tall on their bike, readying themselves for a move.

They tentatively stood up, perched themselves and readied to leap. Brady noticed small puffs of burning gas from the achilles on both of their legs.

The rider sprang from the bike, closing the fifty metre gap to Bo's pod, just far enough to grab a hold on the rear stabiliser. Brady saw Bo's leg twitch. He noticed a slight alteration in the tilt of Bo's head. He knew the beast was waking from its slumber.

'Hurry!' Brady heard the panic in the rider's voice as they produced a laser blade from a clip on their belt. The intense red beam as it lit up was too much for Brady to take. He closed his eyes but felt the heat and movement of the blade at his waist and shoulders. The warmth was welcome, even as he managed a meek groan at the searing pain of the laser.

He mustered the strength to re-open his eyes, and saw the rider stretching to their fullest extent to reach Brady's ankles, but Bo's grasp put them just out of reach.

'Take this.' The rider thrust the laser blade to Brady. 'Cut your legs free.'

Brady realised the top half of his body was free and though he tried, he still could not move. He grimaced, trying to lean forward, feeling a sharp pain in his ribs. Everything darkened completely for a second, and when he came back around, he saw the second rider scrambling into the cockpit from the edges of the pod.

'Cut him free, just go.' The rider in Bo's grip pulled their partner towards them.

'I'm not leaving you!' The second rider's voice was female. Hastily, she unsheathed her pistol from her shoulder strap, engaged the system and took aim at Bo.

A shot flashed from the gun and thumped its way into Bo's shoulder. A hue of blood mist and pneumatic fluid sprayed from the wound, Bo didn't register it. The rider switched settings on the gun and fired another round directly into the wound. Quiet this time. Bo convulsed, but his grip did not weaken.

His head turned to the rider, anger and determination in his eyes.

The rider ripped a solid metal structural bar from the exposed edging of the pod, twisting to free it from its binding and turned it on Bo. Brady heard the crunch as it struck Bo's cranium, but the man's eyes did not so much as flinch. Over and over, the makeshift baton rose and fell onto Bo's skull. Each blow made Brady wince, but Bo took them all in stride.

'Cut him free and go. There isn't time!' The rider grabbed back the cutting blade from Brady and handed it to their partner.

Brady turned his head to Bo, seeing more movement returning to his free hand. Bo mouthed something to Brady, but he couldn't make it out. His jaw and lips moved slowly, not pronounced enough to be decipherable.

Before he knew it, Brady felt the rider hoisting him out of the seat. The agony pushed out a weakened groan as his ribs were laid over the riders shoulder.

Brady could feel the rider hoisting themselves up the tether line as he watched, eyes dipping in and out of focus. Eyelids closing and opening. He was watching a flick book play of the demise of the rider. Each frame, Bo had gained more mobility. He could see the rider being lifted by their throat with one hand. Then he heard the clink of the tether line release.

Below him, he watched Bo snap the rider's neck like a chicken, and heard the woosh as the line flew downwards. The pod had no power. It, Bo and the corpse of the rider began to plummet as Brady finally lost consciousness.

CHAPTER SEVEN

Joshua sprinted through a sterile corridor. He hadn't been back to the MediTech facility since his escape 43 years ago. He looked good for a sixty-year-old and moved even better.

His eyes flashed with an intense red hue as his ocular scan looked for body heat signatures throughout the complex. He had two bodies in a room to his right, clear in the room to the left. Neither one interested him. He was on a tight schedule and they didn't matter.

He pressed ahead towards the end of the corridor, taking time to scan each room. Most were clear, a few had a body or two inside, but he carried on ahead towards four bodies as though he were a moth drawn to a flame. That was his destination. He was focused on it.

A set of double doors blocked his path at the end of the corridor. Against his better judgement, he tried the button. Predictably, the doors remained shut tight. He noticed the adjacent retinal scanner and surveyed it momentarily before turning to run at full speed back up the corridor.

Joshua didn't break a step as he shoulder-charged through a door leading to two heat sources. His hands caressed the grips of his two Kavetech Combat Interface .52 handguns. He loved everything about them, foremost how they communicated with his biometrics via full fingerprint touch interface. Every time the guns integrated with his combat implant, creating a fully symbiotic killing machine, it was like the first.

As the pistols engaged with his ocular implants, his eyelids closed and the strategic combat rendering of his environment picked out his entire strategy for him. All he had to do now was decide which order to hit each target.

Before either of the MediTech technicians inside realised, the room had been breached. Joshua had fired a slug into the nearest man's chest. The impact kicked the body flying backwards into the equipment shelving behind. Joshua slid under a long table, his momentum enough to carry him all the way to the other end. He popped back up with gymnastic agility.

He was right next to the second technician. Close enough to lock him in a sleeper hold before he knew what hit him. Joshua had to be careful of applying too much pressure. His bio-tech enhanced muscles could easily have snapped the man's neck. To be on the safe side, Joshua set the combat tactic to non-lethal so his CPU could adjust power sent to his arms to compensate for the fragility.

Joshua carried the unconscious body down the hallway with one arm as though it were a light bag. At the double doors, he hoisted the technician into position to scan his eye. The security system passed stage 1 and presented a breath implant sensor. Joshua quickly put the man into the Heimlich position and compressed the diaphragm, expelling enough breath to unlock the second stage security.

'Nothing personal.' He let out a sigh, before twisting the neck of the technician and casting the body away. With the doors unlocked, he entered the pitch black room.

He disengaged from his guns and holstered them, switching his ocular implants to night vision. He was inside a cold storage for cadavers. Most of the tables were occupied, predominantly bagged up, but a couple were fresh enough to be on display, waiting to be examined or picked apart.

Up ahead, beyond the rows of morgue freezers he could see the doors to the laboratory. Switching back to heat sensors, he clearly saw three bodies beyond. Three more joined them. He could see them manoeuvring into an offensive formation. They were expecting him. He could feel it. He switched back to night vision and began systematically inspecting the contents of each body bag.

After searching four bags, he found one much flatter than the rest, with an almost completely destroyed body inside. He took a moment to consider an alternate plan, one that wouldn't require chemical cleaning of his combat suit, but nothing sprang to mind. Fighting against his stomach, he climbed in on top of the carcass. It had been out just a little too long for his liking. He could feel it defrosting to the touch and releasing a gut churning stench of decay.

Joshua swallowed his nausea down deep and took a grip of one pistol, zipping the bag over him up to his midriff. He unclipped one of the four flash mines on his bandoleer and threw it down to the floor in front of the laboratory doors. He grasped the bag's zip with his left hand and aimed the pistol in his right hand at the lab door. Firing a single shot, Joshua took one deep breath outside the bag before quickly zipping himself up and shutting down his eyes and ears.

Within seconds, the lab doors opened and two Meditech high security guards entered the mortuary. Perfectly timed, they splintered away from each other to take up positions of cover behind tables. The expectant onslaught did not come, and that confused them. The senior guard gestured to his squad to keep eyes peeled, directing one to break from cover to scan the room. Before he could move, a single beep broke the plan.

Joshua detonated the flash mine, exploding it with a tremendous flash of radiating heat. The explosion rang through their ears and overloaded their night vision and the power of the mine had created enough of a blast to take them off balance and out of cover. The sensory overload had given Joshua the distraction he needed to unzip his body bag without being noticed.

Joshua bolted upright, both hands on his handguns, and systematically took out the M.H.S guards. He took them out based on proximity, closest to furthest away as the second wave of three burst into the room. They fired blindly through the radiating light of the device on the ground, rounds flashing as they hit metal. A few came close, but never really threatened Joshua.

He rolled out of the bag and took cover behind the table. His combat overlay had his targets pinpointed, and he didn't need to break cover. He extended a gun beyond the table. Using his inbuilt targeting system, he fired a burner round into the head of the point guard. It entered the skull and immediately incinerated, setting the head ablaze from the inside.

It was a more gruesome way of taking someone out than Joshua really liked, but over the years of playing cat and mouse with MediTech he had learned that going up against multiple enemies, the more of a shock the first kill was the easier it made taking out the others. Aghast after seeing their colleague burn from the inside, the two flanked guards presented no problem; a couple of standard rounds into their chests, and they dropped like flies.

Switching to heat sensors, he saw the remaining body mass cowering in the lab. He confidently stood and casually walked in. He had picked his way through MediTech's Central Tower to get to this point and it was the first time in the last three hours he could breathe naturally.

He scanned the area and switched off his ocular implants before slowly approached the cowering lady. Elena was battered and bruised after hours of torture and hooked up to monitoring devices. The drugs in her system had a strong sedative effect that was only just beginning to wear off as Joshua approached her.

'Elena!' He was happy to see her in a much better condition than he had expected. She looked up at him, barely recognising the face she had worked with for the last thirty years. Elena tried to speak, but the muscles in her face were too limp to manage anything aside from a stream of drool and a gurgle.

Joshua knelt beside her and took her in his arms, lifting her up to prop her against a cabinet for stability. He looked her in the eyes and smiled. He knew everything he needed to know. She was alive. It didn't matter if she couldn't speak.

'I'm going to get you out of here.' He clamped her face between finger and thumb to ensure she looked him in the eyes. 'If anything happens to me, it's up to you to get the implant to safety. You are with me, right?' Elena nodded ever so slightly, just enough for Joshua to know she was in agreement. He took off his jacket and helped her into it as he heard smashing glass above his head.

Particles of glass showered down into the room, and six mag-lift pads dropped through the ceiling to the floor below. Joshua ripped his bandoleer off and threw it at the wall on the other side of the lab. He took both guns, aimed one at the bandoleer and one up to the ceiling.

MediTech militia were the best they had. Fully augmented soldiers, with combat software so system-heavy they lost their personalities. Five of them descended into the room, steadily sinking as the mag-lift pads' power dwindled. They took shots from Joshua's gun as though they were being hit by spit balls.

Joshua fired an incendiary round at the bandoleer, setting off a tremendous explosion. He shielded Elena from the blast, his back absorbing the heat and debris.

Joshua knew there was no way out other than the hole he had just blown through the wall. The rapid-fire shots he directed at the rappelling militia squad were nothing more than a distraction. If it were just him, he imagined he would have been able to take them out, but there was no way he could do that and keep Elena alive.

Joshua grabbed hold of Elena and pushed her towards the hole in the wall. He positioned her perfectly to guard from the onslaught of bullets fired their way before throwing her outside to face the sheer drop of two-hundred floors, activating his jacket's automatic parachute deployment as he did.

Joshua's blood and pneumatic fluids sprayed Elena, and he watched as she cast her eyes over his body. He recognised the angry face, though he had never seen it quite so intense. She didn't have to say a word to him. If she'd known that was his plan, she would have stopped him.

Their eyes locked as they descended, windows flashing past at great speed. Approaching terminal velocity, Joshua's jacket kicked in, firing out its stabilisers, righting Elena into an upright before deploying the parachute. Her descent slowed rapidly, and all she could do was watch Joshua overtake her. She mouthed the words *I love you* as she watched the gap between them grow. And the gap between him and the mezzanine shrink.

***

Brady shivered as he regained consciousness.

He wasn't sure if it was the temperature or his blood-loss. He had certainly never felt anything like as cold as he did. Maybe he shivered as a reaction to seeing his grandmother in his dream. It had felt a lot different from any of the other dreams. More visceral, more personal. As he began to regain sensation in his body, he could feel the bullet wounds that had torn through Joshua. He could still smell the bodies.

It took Brady a few moments to readjust to where he was and he could still feel the cold. The smell of the corpses faded away to be replaced with a damp, musty aroma. It was unlike anything he had ever smelled before. As his eyes adjusted to the light, he began to piece together his surroundings.

Everything around him was at odds with itself. High-tech

installations the likes of which he had not seen outside of the Fighting League stood as a stark contradiction to what he could now see as cavern walls. Mineral deposits chased around him like a web of spider veins, and he could feel the moisture in the air. In the distance, a constant soft dripping noise was like a metronome.

'Hello Brady.' He recognised the weathered male voice. Brady snapped his head left to see a shadowed figure leaning against the wall. It slowly moved forward towards him. Brady's face widened as he began to make out the person emerging.

'You! Who are you?' he said, his voice trembling.

'My name is Joshua Reynolds, but what's more important is that you are safe.'

'I know you. I saw you die!'

'Die?'

'Yes. But, wait. You looked older.'

'Then perhaps you have seen my future?'

'Okay, what is going on here!' Brady moved away from his previous line of questioning as the realisation of his situation hit him in the face like a ten tonne hammer.

'I know you must be champing at the bit to get answers. Believe me, I was too—'

'Too? What do you mean, too?'

'You are scared... probably confused, but I'm going to explain everything.' Joshua attempted to placate Brady who had, on attempt at moving, discovered he had been tethered to a support post and hooked up to a cranial monitor.

'You want to start with why I'm tied up like a prisoner?'

'Only for your safety. You're not in any danger.'

'Okay cool, so let's get to the part where you let me go.'

'I can't let you out, Brady.'

'Why not?' his eyes concentrated intently on Joshua. 'You said I'm safe, right? I'm starting to feel a lot like I ain't safe at all.'

'I'm not choosing not to. I just can't.'

'Give me one reason why not?'

'I mean, I physically can't.' As Joshua explained, he walked towards Brady, passing through one of the high-tech pieces of machinery and his lower body flickered as it re-established its form once he cleared it.

'Woah-woah, what are you?'

'You saw me die, right? Isn't obvious? I'm a ghost!' Joshua wryly grinned as he spoke. Brady took a moment to compose himself. His gut instinct was to let the building anger out in a scream at the top of his lungs but, despite Joshua's promises he did not feel reassured that he wasn't in imminent danger.

'Okay seriously, you need to start explaining what is going on here, now!'

'The truth is, I'm not a ghost, but I am dead.' Joshua approached, taking a non-existent seat in front of Brady. 'I have been since, well, minutes before you were born. Whatever you think you saw about my death, you're probably not mistaken.'

'Right, so you're dead and I'm alive? I'm here, you're not.' Brady's brow furrowed at the preposterous notion being presented to him. 'You can walk through objects. I can't escape these bindings. Great. But I have a question for you,' he said, pausing to create an extra punch to his follow up. 'Do I look stupid?' He was getting more and more agitated by what he was beginning to assume was some huge prank taken way, way too far.

'I don't understand how to answer that question.'

'Really? I feel like given the circumstances and all the many, many questions I have, that's probably the easiest one to answer.'

'I don't understand how to answer that question.'

'Yeah, you understand me just fine.'

'I'm sorry Brady, I don't understand.'

'Okay, stop trying to avoid answering the questions and have a damn conversation with me,' Brady snapped.

'I am sorry. I do not understand.' Joshua's holographic

projection began glitching with flashes of code where the pixels making him up broke down. Brady's attention was taken away when he heard the creaking of a heavy door and he looked over to see a young lady, maybe late twenties, enter. Brady immediately noticed her appearance. She used make-up and tattoos like an artist uses paint. She was an ever evolving and varying tapestry of her own design.

'He's a hologram, Brady.' She had a confidence about her that stopped just shy of being intimidating to Brady.

'I'm guessing by the fact you had to open the door, you aren't?'

'Let's focus on you, I think,' she said as she looked over the cranial monitor on Brady's head. She had leaned in to him to get there and he felt a rush when she brushed against him. So much so, he didn't notice Joshua's holo projection disappear as the cap came off.

'Wait, who exactly are you? What is going on, and where am I?'

'Just one second,' she said, as she tweaked the monitor settings.

'Hang on. The big guy in the pod. Where is he?' Brady began getting agitated again as the rush of hormones dropped back to a manageable level. 'More importantly, who is he?'

'That'll be Bo Jacobs. MediTech enforcer extraordinaire.'

'Wait, this is MediTech?' Brady panicked, fearful he was inside a secretive MediTech underground kill lab. 'You don't look like MediTech.'

'Oh, I'm not. We rescued you.'

'So who are you?'

'My name is Ella,' she said, still tweaking the cranial monitor. 'I'm part of the same organisation that has been taking care of you since you were born.'

'I'm sorry, you are looking after me?'

'I mean, Elena did most of the work.'

'Elena? What the hell do you know about Elena?'

'I think that's better coming from Joshua.'

'Okay, and do you want to have a crack at explaining him?'

'Sure,' she said. 'He's in your head.'

'I know he's in my head.' Brady grew more annoyed by the fact he was none the wiser to anything. 'I've been seeing him in my head for years.'

'No, I mean, he's literally in your head. Well, enough of him is so we can create a version of his consciousness anyway.'

Ella placed the cranial monitor into the docking station on the server control desk. The screen reeled through thousands of lines of code as the device re-synchronised with their systems. As it finished its process, an audible tone alerted Ella to the completion of the procedure and she removed the device.

'Just look.' Ella entered a code onto the cranial monitor, bringing it back to life, and replaced the crown on Brady's head. As soon as it was engaged with him, Joshua's projection fired back up, fully rendered and animated.

'I don't understand the question,' Joshua said. Brady examined the holo, putting the information together that it was somehow projected from his mind and coming to the incorrect conclusion that he had some level of influence on it. He concentrated, trying to move the image of the man who had haunted his dreams.

'Joshua, skip the question,' said Ella. 'Return to previous enquiry, reference point minus seventy-eight seconds. Logged output; Whatever you think you saw about my death, you're probably not mistaken.'

Joshua's holo recalibrated quickly before continuing. 'Well, if you say you saw me die, then you know how my story ended, Brady. That was your beginning. We had pretty similar starts in life except you had Elena. I didn't.'

'Elena was an agent of ours, solely responsible for keeping you hidden,' said Ella as she began pacing.

'Hidden? What exactly do I have to be hidden from? And who exactly are you people?'

'We are AntiFa,' said Joshua.

'You say that like it means something to me.'

Ella paused her pacing. 'It stands for Anti-Fascist.'

'I asked who you were, not what your belief system is.'

'It stopped being a belief system when Alfred Braunschild became President and forced like-minded people to unite,' Joshua said, as Ella passed straight through him.

'Whatever. You fight fascists. What does that have to do with me?'

'MediTech are fascists, and we've been hiding you from them,' said Ella.

'Please let me explain.' Joshua smiled at Brady. 'When I say I was just like you, I meant it. You and I are one of many, not the first and probably far from the last.'

'One of many what?'

'To answer that, I have to start at the very beginning.'

'I wish something would start making sense here soon!'

'What exactly do you know about MediTech?' Joshua crouched in front of Brady as Ella took a seat on the top of a desk and watched on.

CHAPTER EIGHT

Brady suffocated under the aftermath of a thousand heavy words that hung in the air, refusing to dissipate. Every single word of their explanation had stunned him more than any punch in any fight he had ever been in. Slumped down against the cavern wall, somewhere between the bombardment of information and the fact he had been pulled from pillar to post for the last forty-eight hours straight, he was tired enough for Ella to have released his bindings.

Joshua's holographic projection paced back and forth between salvaged sofas from years gone by. Brady was unsure whether the visage was finally out of things to say, or whether it was stuck in an endless loop, such was the meticulous repetition of pattern. Ella was leaning against the far wall, eyes glued to Brady. She was calm, but alert. She had watched him for most of his life, apparently, and aside from the fact he knew she was there this time, it was no different.

Brady finally mustered the energy to stand, though it felt like he was lifting the weight of the world up with him on his shoulders. Ella reacted subtly. He noticed that she shifted forwards onto the balls of her feet, as though readying herself to react if required. After a lengthy puff of air out his cheeks, Brady broke the silence.

'So let me get this straight," he said. 'This chip in my brain, it was designed to regulate brain response to implants so my immune system won't start attacking itself?'

'Essentially,' Joshua replied.

'And this technology was discovered when they cured cancer?'

'They work the same way, yes. Cancer tricked the body into thinking it was the healthy tissue and the defences against it were the parasite. So when they found they could switch the body's responses to not be duped, they realised this would work for invasive implants, too.'

'But I don't understand why they would cure cancer, then withhold the cure for tech poisoning.' Brady rubbed the back of his head. He didn't know exactly where the implant was, but he wanted to feel like he could touch it.

'I feel like we're going around in circles now,' said Ella, ever more infuriated by the repetition it had taken to get to this point.

'Oh, I'm sorry, this must be so confusing for you.' Brady looked at her with contempt, struggling to keep secret the fact he found her striking look appealing.

'Look, I know this is difficult for you to hear—'

Brady scoffed. 'Difficult is an understatement.'

'Okay, I appreciate that. I'm sorry.' Brady noticed Ella's face soften as she let out her exasperation in a breath. 'Curing cancer kept people alive. They, in turn, bought new technology to improve themselves.'

'That's my point. If they gave everyone access to this technology, people would buy more tech. Or am I missing something?' He winced a little, finding a reactive point of sharp pain near his atlas. *There?*

'Again, it's more complicated than that. Just because they could, doesn't mean they would.' She shook her head. 'Most people can only afford low levels of enhancements, and those that want to push themselves beyond their means resort to black market, maybe salvaged tech. That doesn't put credits in MediTech's account.'

'More importantly,' Joshua said, 'they don't want citizens to be on an equal footing with themselves. If this technology went public, they could be facing the idea of presiding over swatches of super soldiers.'

'Right, so if you have had it in your possession for two generations, why not replicate it and get it out to everyone?' Brady stood up and shook off the pins and needles in his left leg.

Ella laughed in disbelief. 'What about being in a cave here makes you think we have a sterile ultra-high spec laboratory and the equipment to produce, what is no doubt, the most advanced piece of microchip technology the world has ever seen?'

Brady took a moment in deep thought before continuing. 'Okay, so sell it to the EU or hell, even the Russian-Asian alliance.'

'Why? So they can create armies of super soldiers and wage war?' The way Ella looked at Brady as she spoke angered him and made him feel small at the same time.

'If MediTech is so bad, I don't see the problem.' Brady shrugged, then tested his foot to see if it had woken up.

'MediTech is terrible, yes, but the collateral damage to civilians would be astronomical if they launched full scale assaults on MediTech cities. Which, they undoubtedly would,' said Joshua.

Ella walked through Joshua's form to a bench, before sifting through some of the debris on it. 'Not only civilians. We don't want to get MediTech's soldiers killed in droves.'

Brady walked to the opposite side of the room from Joshua. When he turned back to face him, he noticed a fading of the projection. 'What? Joshua, I've seen your memories don't forget. Seems like that's all you did.' He walked back towards Joshua, seeing the image sharpen as he got closer.

'There's a big difference between doing what you have to do to survive, or complete a mission, than sending waves and waves of cannon fodder to wipe out everything that moves.'

Brady played with his new discovery, backing away and moving towards Joshua's image as it dimmed and brightened. 'Is there really any difference aside from the numbers? Kill one man in your way. His family feels the same as they would if you'd killed a thousand.'

'Brady, we aren't here to get bogged down in the ethics of warfare. We have to do what we have to do, but we are not prepared to risk the ramifications of full-scale domestic war. We just aren't.' Ella picked up, then thumped down a slab of debris onto the desk.

Brady stopped his pacing and turned to Ella. He took a moment to pause for thought, seeing her tensed body language as she leant on the desk.

'Okay, forget that.' He calmly approached Joshua and tapped on his head. 'So this thing is inside of me, and you're inside of it?'

'Yes and no,' Joshua replied. 'This that you're seeing is just an AI representation of who I was. The implant was in my brain, yes, and has a latent memory of me and things I did, but it's not like I actually exist anymore.'

'So if you want to take MediTech down, why don't you just go public with this information?' Brady turned between Joshua and Ella.

Ella looked up to the ceiling, then around to Brady. 'Who would believe it?'

'Well, you're expecting me to.'

Joshua moved into Brady's view. 'But you know it's true. You've seen my memories. Even if you hadn't, you can't deny you feel the familiarity with what we are telling you. Like déjà vu, right?'

'What's to say you haven't just programmed this into whatever you put in my head, though?'

'I suppose that's possible, but what on earth would we do that for? What would be the point if all of this was some elaborate trick?' asked Ella.

'Can't you just download the memories from the MediTech guys who had it and then expose them? Play them out like holovids?'

'Why have we never thought of that?' Ella grinned and shook her head. 'You're a genius!'

'Ease up Ella. I'm sure I asked the same question when I found out.'

'Come on Josh, even you weren't that naïve.'

'It's not that simple. Wish it were. We can't get anything off the implant. Security protocols on it are way beyond our ability to crack.' Joshua motioned for Ella to ease up.

'Wait, if you can't get information from it, how do you know what happened to Joshua?'

'Throughout my time here, we uploaded my thought patterns to this AI construct's server. It's interacting remotely with the implant right now and recognising me within it, so I can recognise myself within it.'

'Okay, and are you doing that with me now?' Brady walked to the server stack, carefully studying it.

'Yeah Brady, we are stealing your soul.' As Brady looked back over to her, he just caught the end of an eye roll.

'Ella, please.' Brady could just make out Joshua mouthing something to Ella before he turned to face Brady again, but couldn't see enough to decipher it. 'It's honestly not like stealing your thoughts.'

'It sure feels that way.'

'Brady, every feeling you have about this is exactly the same as I did.' Joshua nodded softly and smiled.

'What's your point?' Brady tested the clear panel covering the server stack, running his fingers down the seam. He pushed lightly, but there was no give.

'It has to mean something that I'm now standing here passing on the torch and not telling you to run a mile.'

'You're not standing here, though, are you?' Brady noticed Ella pacing back and forth, taking deep breaths. He took the opportunity with her eyes off him to peer around the back of the server stack.

'Well, no, but that's not really relevant, is it?' Joshua moved towards the stack. Brady watched from the corner of his eye when he noticed that whilst Joshua kept trying to get nearer, his legs maintained a walking motion but his body did not get any closer.

Brady came back around to the front of the server, carefully watching Joshua's stuck walking motion. 'You said yourself you're just a program. What's to say you aren't programmed to not tell me to run?'

'That's what I'm trying to explain. The AI construct is just the shell. It's designed to recognise my old thought patterns, and that allows it to interface with the imprint of my memories on the chip. There's no way to corrupt how I come across.' Joshua seemed unaware that he was in a walking loop without any progress.

'Okay, for one second, let's just assume I'm not a computer scientist.' Brady made his way from the server to take a seat in the vacant chair.

'In the simplest terms,' said Ella, 'the brain puts out electrical wave patterns that radically alter when agitated by external stimuli.' As Brady began to glaze over, she paused. 'All we are doing is taking recordings of how your brain waves react to situations. Right now, we are seeing how your brain reacts to stress. Once we've also recorded how it reacts to other situations, that's it.'

'And then what?'

'Then we have the imprint of what your thought processes look like. Nothing more than that.'

'Okay, but to what end?'

Joshua finally managed to break from his walking loop and made his way to Brady. 'One day you might be in my position and hopefully you'll be able to reach out easier than I can. This artificial intelligence idea was mine, so I didn't get to record my own initial reaction. You'll have that advantage over me.'

'That's not what I mean.' Brady stood from the chair. His chest finally felt a little lighter, like the belt around it had been loosened a notch or two. 'You said yourselves, you can't get the information out there and you can't replicate this implant. All you can do is hide it.'

'So that's what we are trying to do. Our best-case scenario here was if they never discovered you.'

'Exactly. This whole thing is a complete waste of time and, way more importantly, my life!' Brady grabbed the seat and hurled it directly through Joshua's projection. As it crashed into the servers that housed his construct, his form scrambled. Brady looked carefully to see if any damage had been done to the cabinet, but they remained unscathed.

Ella lunged towards it. 'What are you doing? Joshua is on there, you idiot!'

'Easy Ella,' Joshua said, the pixels once more knitting together to form a solid image, but his voice was wrong. 'I'm fine. Besides, the torch is passing. I'm no longer important.'

'He will never be half the man you were!'

'Rip it out of my head and let me go, then!'

'Calm down, Ella. We have no idea what sort of man he will become,' said Joshua.

Brady flipped around to Joshua, his face contorted with anger. 'What do you mean, man I'll become?'

'I'm sorry, it's a turn of phrase.'

'You know what? How about I'll become whatever man I want to become? Better yet, I already am a man. Who are you to dictate what parameters should be set for me to achieve being a man? Hell, anyone?'

Ella sighed. 'He already wants to run from his responsibility, Joshua.'

Brady matched Ella's sigh with one even more apparent. 'I'm getting really fed up with people thrusting responsibility at me and expecting me to shoulder it or I'd somehow not be a man. I'm a man, therefore I'm a man and I'm my own version of it and that's enough.'

Ella stared blankly at him for a while. He met her gaze. 'He's got no fight. This isn't going to work.'

'No fight? I've been fighting since I was thirteen. It's all I've known and now I find out the whole thing was thrust on me.'

'It was to keep you safe, Brady.'

'I hate fighting. I hate it! You trained up these fists to hurt and I can't stand it.' He bunched his fists up, looking at them as if they were someone else's when he noticed the wound he bonded together had almost disappeared. 'You did this?'

Ella nodded. 'We had to. There was a tracking implant under the stitches.'

'And what? You've got rid of it? Excellent, I can go then?' Brady took a step to the door.

'It's not that simple. You're on their radar now. Biometric scans will track you all over the city. Anytime your face appears on their surveillance, they will be on you.'

'So I'll change my face and my biometrics.' His steps began to slow.

'How will you do that? You think there's a surgeon out there that isn't on their payroll?'

Brady turned back. 'You have a surgeon, clearly,' he said, gesturing to the incredible work on his hand. 'Get them to do it. Rip the chip out of my head, stamp on it and let me go!'

Ella balked. 'You want us to destroy technology that has the potential to save millions of lives and end their tyrannical rule?'

Brady laughed hysterically. 'You want me to carry this thing and be, in your own words, hounded for the rest of my life until they eventually find me and kill me?'

Joshua moved towards Brady. 'No, now we want you to take the fight to them.'

Brady span back to Joshua. 'Oh, so offer myself up on a plate so they can cut me open and serve me up?'

Joshua's holo appeared to freeze for a moment, as if calculating the perfect response. 'There is no other choice. Remaining incognito was plan a. Plan b is, unfortunately, this way.'

Brady turned back to the door, leant on it and buried his face into his arms. 'Go with plan c, then. Get it out of my head and give it to someone else and let me go back to my life.' He hesitated. 'Not that it was ever really mine, was it?'

'We can't just do that, Brady,' said Joshua.

'Why? Don't want to put someone else's life in danger? Just me?'

'It's not that. If it's not implanted at infancy, before the brain has developed, it can cause serious damage.'

Brady backed away from the door, before slamming his fist into it, hard. He grimaced, but tried to play off the pain. 'Isn't that convenient?'

'It can be done, but the host would need to have a very specific alpha and delta brain wave frequencies or they will turn into a hyper-anxious mess,' Joshua said.

'Brady shook his head. 'So go back to destroying it if you can't use the damn thing anyway!'

'We aren't destroying the implant, Brady, so just stop.' Ella let out a quiet grumble.

'Ella!' Joshua tilted his head in her direction before addressing Brady. 'Brady, we can't let it be destroyed. If we don't have it, we have nothing. They will win.'

'You know what?' Brady looked around. 'I don't really care.'

Ella approached him with fervour. 'You'll care when they rip it out of your head like it was a nut in a shell. They will stop at nothing to get to you, so either you become what they can't kill, or you run for the rest of your short life.'

Brady turned with his back to the door and slumped down to the ground against it. He stared at the cold ground in front of him. 'Just get it out of me.'

Ella approached him and knelt down. 'Even if we did, they wouldn't know that. And hell, if they did, they will still kill you. You know too much. But not before torturing you until you give them our location.'

'I don't even know where I am. How could I tell them?'

'You really have no choice, Brady.' She tried to meet his eyes, but no matter how much she positioned herself to, Brady avoided her.

'Look, just alter my biometrics and face and let me go back into hiding. Let me take my chances,' said Brady.

'What are you going to do? Just turn up at your apartment, see your friends, new face, new tags and think they won't notice?' Ella grabbed him by his arms. He quickly shrugged her off.

'I'll go elsewhere. Everything I knew was a lie, anyway. Who cares?'

'And you don't think a nineteen-year-old just rocking up out of the blue with no history won't turn heads?'

'So what the hell do I do?'

For the first time, Brady noticed a genuine softening to her stare. 'I'm afraid you've no choice but to work with us, Brady. You have to trust me. In time, you will thank us.'

'You had me living a life of your choosing and you expect me to trust you?'

Brady waited for a response. He watched as she switched from maintaining eye contact to complete avoidance of it. As her eyes tried to engage the analytical and creative parts of her brain, Brady weaved his head left and right in an attempt to meet her gaze once more. Finally, she settled and refocused on him.

'You think anyone out there has autonomy? No, they are all

just pawns in MediTech's long game. If it weren't for us, you'd just be another cog.'

'But I would have been oblivious, and that sounds pretty good to me.'

'Work with us and you can be a spanner in their works. You can do something other than live and die in their machine.' Her tone had shifted. Brady heard the lowered confidence as she continued to argue with, what he felt, was a losing battle for her.

'You make it sound like it's such a privilege, having no choice, being your patsy.' His shoulders grew broader, his stance just a little taller.

'You honestly think you're the only one who has had their life railroaded? You don't own forced obligation.'

Ella screamed and stormed away, pausing as she passed Joshua. 'I can't.' She continued back to the table, leaning over it, her head dropped low.

'Don't try to play me like I'm anything but a glorified courier in your eyes!' He tracked her movement away, and began to step forward to close the gap, knowing she was on the ropes.

Brady was going to push his advantage when he saw Joshua step in his way. 'If you want to see it that way, then that's what you were. Now you have the opportunity to be so much more.'

'What? Like you? Some kind of super soldier, a one man killing machine?'

'You get to be the last remaining pawn on the board. You get to advance to their king so they focus on you and don't notice the setup happening on the back lines.'

'Are you for real? You think telling me I can march forward to my death so you guys can organize an attack is selling this to me?'

'Who said anything about death?' said Joshua.

'What else is a pawn for?'

'All you have to do is get to their back lines and then you get to be whatever you want to be. You can become anything.'

'I can't get over how blasé you are about this.' Brady chuckled. 'It's one thing coming from you, but her? She has no idea how this feels. Your life just ripped from you on pure chance of who your parents were.'

Brady noticed Joshua's head glitch a little before he spoke. 'Brady, Ella—'

Ella flipped around violently. 'System access override two seven gamma!'

With that command, Joshua's holo disappeared. Brady looked back to the server, immediately noticing that all lights had been extinguished. Before he could question anything, he felt the impact on the back of his shoulder as Ella barged passed him. He was knocked off balance more than he would've expected from such a small woman.

'Fine, think things through, but please try to look at the bigger picture here. Those guys are monsters and if you can be a part of bringing them down, this will all be worth it, I promise you,' Ella added, noting the shift in Brady's mood. 'I'll leave you with Josh to gather yourself up.'

'Shut me down. He needs to be alone.'

Ella looked quizzically at Joshua, whose gaze reassured her that he knew what he was doing. Reluctantly, she shut down Joshua's server and left Brady alone.

He took a moment to look around, not ready to trust that he was actually alone before venting out everything that had just been thrown at him through puffed-out cheeks and pursed lips.

Outside, Ella failed to notice Brady quietly following her out of the room as she walked along the corridors of the resistance's compound. The walls housed exposed cables haphazardly thrown together to power the complex and run their intranet service safe from the MediTech mainframe. The caverns had been clad in brickwork walls long ago and centuries of patching were all that stopped them reverting to their natural form. Ella headed to what was once a heavy duty security door but had long since given up its ability to withstand any form of pressure.

As she shut the door behind her, Brady crouched. He looked between the two directions of the corridor, one seemingly heading to nowhere, the other where Ella had disappeared. His face scrunched as he made his decision, before cautiously heading to the door she had just shut.

'Any news on Bo?' said Ella.

A male voice answered. 'Hey Ella, um, no. Basically vanished. Recon team reported some structural damage but no body.'

Brady's heart rate was increasing as he leaned into the door to hear better.

'So what we thinking? Medi or salvage?' said Ella.

'Way too soon for a salvage op. Can only be a Medi recovery. Too quick, too clean to be anything otherwise. How'd it go with the sleeper?'

'I had to shut it down for now. He's resisting more than Josh did, but I'll give him some time to think. Just have to hope Elena planted the seed. But it shouldn't have happened this way.'

Brady's breathing grew more rapid. *Can't linger here much longer,* he thought.

'I know we dropped the ball on it and lost a good man because of it. But the kid's going to be alright, you think?'

'I don't know. More time with the Josh program and we will see,' said Ella. 'But this was a major missed opportunity. Who knows what information Bo had in his systems? That's the kind of information that could turn the tide.'

'We must've missed them by minutes. There's no way they could've got there, cleaned up the site and got him clear before we were on scene unless he was tracked.'

'Well obviously, that's why we've got to scramble quicker. Scramble a hover to check this out. Either he put that dent in the side of the generator or someone's been joyriding.'

'You want me to send out a bike to look at a dented generator?' asked the unseen male.

'I'm not interested in a dent. I'm interested in whether anything was torn out of him by the impact on that. We cannot be leaving stones unturned.'

Brady had listened to all he could. He was beginning to panic, and had to move. As quietly but quickly as he could, he headed in the other direction, carefully trying not make heavy footsteps.

Heart racing, breathing hampered by the panic and his crouched position, he noticed the lights fading the further he got. The unknown up ahead, the fear left behind him.

Suddenly, he heard the sound of a door being operated. He froze. Nowhere to go. Up ahead, someone half emerged from a room.

He could hear his heart thumping in his chest. Eyes wide open, he watched.

Brady got lucky. Whoever it was went back inside. But there was no time to breathe easy. His pace quickened. Less emphasis on quiet, more on speed. There had to be a way out somewhere.

He made it beyond more doors twisting and turning to follow the line of the corridor. Each one he passed, the dimmer the lighting and the colder it became. Then he saw it. The dead end.

Brady crouched in the darkened corner, carefully eyeing the far end that he'd come from. He studiously looked over the panels on the walls, eyes darting back every so often to check for signs of anyone appearing. His fingers ran over the panel gaps, trying to find a weak point.

Beyond the whining of electricity running in the old cables on the walls, he heard the faintest of footsteps. He was caught between two ideas, staying perfectly still and just using sheer force on the wall panel. He knew there were doors, numbers of them, twelve, thirteen maybe. Including the room he'd just escaped from.

Brady counted down the doors as the steps grew louder. Nine left maybe. Seven of them far enough away that he could remain unnoticed. They passed another one, down to six. Brady began to feel uneasy. He hadn't been spotted yet, but time was running low. Five more. He readied his excuses at the point the figure became clear. Maybe they didn't know who he was. He couldn't rely on that, and had to have something feasible together in time. They were getting close though. He held his breath the best he could.

Brady was just formulating his excuse for what may just pass muster when he heard a door's security panel beep and slide open. Brady could breathe again. But it was close, way too close for comfort. His only chance now was fading fast. He turned his attention back to the panels and managed to slide his fingers into a gap.

Summoning all his strength, he managed to bend it open a fraction. He couldn't go at this like a bull at a gate. Too much noise would surely alert someone to his presence. It was quiet in the building and the heavy wrenching of a panel would easily carry to the nearest set of ears. Especially if those ears were enhanced. Carefully, he continued to increase the gap, ensuring he wouldn't rip it free. That was going to be the easy part. Squeezing himself through sharpened metal, not so much.

CHAPTER NINE

Xiao peered through the observation window, looking over Bo's lifeless body that lay on the operating table in MediTech HQ's Bio-Tech lab.

Xiao had been working as Francesca's head of foreign and domestic affairs for thirty-three years, ever since he defected from China. The adrenal implants he had relied on keeping his nerves at a perfectly calm balance during the time he spent behind enemy lines gathering intel were making short work of overriding what, for anyone else, would be a gruesome and tense moment.

Lab technicians bustled around the body, fetching and carrying equipment and surgical tools for the two surgeons, desperately trying to bring the behemoth back to life. One of the technicians rushed to the surgeons with a tray of laser cutting implements. Xiao watched, as they immediately began suturing a wound that had been oozing a viscous hydraulic fluid and blood mix.

Xiao turned his attention to another tech, as they focused on reading data being uploaded from Bo's remaining functional bio-tech as two more technicians frantically readied replacement parts. Full optic system, carbo-weaved spinal column, nano-fibre prefrontal cortex and an entire bionic right arm, complete with interwoven weapons systems, all being arranged on trolleys around the body.

His attention was drawn away and into the observation room as Francesca's holo projection appeared next to him.

'Francesca,' he said.

'Xiao. What is the progress?'

Xiao double checked the operating room. 'Everything is in place as far as I can tell.'

'It better be. I can't afford to find another.'

'We have his brain wave patterns on record, Francesca. Any search for a suitable replacement would at least be expedited.'

'And the time taken to train, modify, meanwhile, this sleeper of hers has woken.' Xiao noticed an arm appear at the side of the holo, presenting Francesca with a cup. She took it and had a slow sip. Xiao used the break to watch the operating theatre again.

Below him, the operating table pivoted one hundred and eighty degrees, leaving Bo's body facing the floor. On what was now the top, a mesh of tiny square sections flipped away to leave a precise gap in the table material that revealed Bo's spine.

As the surgeon's laser cut his flesh and sinew, a technician sucked away the debris, revealing the spinal column, crushed and contorted by the impact. Guiding an extraction arm, one of the technicians carefully positioned it to take hold of the more intact discs as another carefully monitored his readouts.

'If my—' Francesca paused, blowing the heat from her drink. The waft of hot vapour dissipated at the edge of the holo display, turning to broken light particles. 'If she gets him up to speed before I can ready another enforcer, well, I don't need to tell you what could have happened if Mr Reynolds had been left unchecked.'

Xiao, still calmed by his adrenal tech, took time to continue watching the operation.

The extraction arm moved delicately, belying its large and cumbersome appearance. Pincers deftly positioned themselves with precision before slowly clamping onto solid bone or titanium, depending which disc they got hold of.

Carefully, it retracted the spinal column; the surgeons worked quickly to disconnect wiring and plugs from the column as it tentatively came out of his body. Every piece of tech in Bo's body ran through the spine and the operation to remove all the connectors in time was clearly intense. Xiao noted one of the surgeons periodically looking up to him. He could see the moisture on their visor build, their breath fogging and abating on the Perspex.

Xiao knew as well as they did, there were no second chances for medical professionals in MediTech HQ. They were there because they were the best at what they did, and if they failed, they would no longer be the best. He had lost count of the professionals who, following a mistake, had never been seen again.

'Xiao?' said Francesca, snapping him from his concentration on the operation.

'Sorry, just watching the spinal extraction. What were you saying? Oh yes, well I'm sure it won't come to that. The surgeons appear to have it in hand,' he said, turning back to the operation.

Eventually, the old spine was free, and the surgeons set about installing the new one. It went in easier than the old one came out; they had more time to position the connectors correctly and wire it in. Xiao knew he was a long way off from being rebuilt, but they had made a solid start.

With the new spine in place, the tech on vital sign duty switched his display from Bo's readouts to an exploded diagram of his brain. The prefrontal cortex was the only section showing signs of damage, which amazed Xiao, given the obvious impact to Bo's skull. His carbo-weave skull plate had done a better job of protecting the brain than could have reasonably been expected.

'And you are sure it was her?' said Francesca.

'Hover bikes, two assailants. Certainly fits their M.O.'

'And both managed to escape with the target?'

'It's safe to say one did not make it. Viscera surrounding Bo's body suggests he took one down with him.'

Xiao watched on as the surgeons placed a regenerative mesh over Bo's prefrontal cortex. He was excited to see the results of this new technology. Tissue derived from the Axolotl MediTech had been researching for centuries, trying to unlock the secrets of their tissue regeneration. Controlling their natural habitat in South America had been one of the positive sides to the war.

'And they hid him in plain sight.'

'They are clearly getting more brazen, Francesca.'

'And now we know, they will be ghosts.'

'How do we go about catching ghosts?'

'You tell me, Mr Xiao, espionage is, after all, why you are here.' Francesca's holo immediately disappeared.

'Indeed. I'll send my recon team—' Mr Xiao noticed she had already gone, leaving him with a sense of confusion. Abrupt departures weren't out of the ordinary for her, but her tone had been questionable.

The surgeons closed up Bo's skull with a graphene plate, fusing it to what remained of bone before layering a dermal patch over the top. The neutral colour took a few seconds to match his dark skin tone before becoming completely unnoticeable.

***

Brady felt the cold begin to chill his bones as he struggled through the dark, narrow tunnel. He had lost track of time. Maybe an hour, maybe two. Feeling his way around the wall, he rounded a corner. And for the first time in however long he had been stuck, breathing the musty air, a thin, square boundary of light shone to him from the ceiling. That was his way out.

He felt the cold of the metal step leading up to it and carefully climbed up to the hatch. He paused for breath, mustering up the energy to lift what he assumed was a solid hatch that hadn't been operated in who knew how long. One hand reached up. He gritted his teeth and pushed. Nothing. He could feel the metal. This would take everything he had.

Brady positioned himself on the top rung, crouching under the hatch with a shoulder pressed up to it. A few more deep breaths, in and out. As he pushed, he let out a guttural scream, calling his body to give more than it had.

The hatch groaned with the initial push. Then movement. Heavy as hell. He had to dig even deeper. Even then, it was no guarantee.

Within the frame of a large Russian Air Assault vehicle, Brady struggled to lift the hefty hatch door from the underside. The hinges cried out as he tried so desperately to create enough space to escape, lifting with his shoulder and grimacing under the strain. He managed to raise it enough to manoeuvre his body through the gap. It took all his strength just to get that far and the crushing weight of the hatch forced his remaining breath out in one push.

His shoulders were free. That gave him just enough of a boost to wriggle his arms underneath himself into a push-up. With a final, all-out effort, he raised himself and the door into full extension. The hard work was done and Brady held his push-up position, taking the weight of the metal. He psyched himself up, drawing in deep breaths and letting them out in sharp puffs as he readied for the make or break moment. A little dip, one explosive lift, and go.

The hatch dropped heavily, catching his trailing leg at an awkward angle. He let out a cry of pain, yet instinctually grabbed his leg and pulled it free. The weight pressing down on his shin as he scraped it through was excruciating, and he bellowed in agony. It was like a dulled knife blade carving his muscle away from his bone all the way down to his ankle. It was bad. He knew it instantly.

Brady scrambled around the wreckage for anything he could use to fashion a splint. He dragged himself between piles of debris, unable to stand as the agony grew with each passing minute. He managed to overturn a huge chunk of siding panel to find a partially intact skeleton. Clothing had been stripped, no

Bio-Tech around, but evidence that the body had at one point or another been salvaged. As he studied the bones, he noticed the marks and gauges where Bio-Tech had been prised out crudely.

He had seen MediTech forces strip bodies before. This was too crude for them. Even AntiFa seemed more savvy than digging out implants with knives. His interest was piqued. If it wasn't MediTech or the resistance, someone must have made it outside the wall. A thought sprung to mind that perhaps it had been a survivor of one of these skirmishes, but it quickly faded. Studying the damage, there was no way anyone could have survived such devastation.

And then he saw it. An old, barely noticeable trail of dried hydraulic fluid leading beyond the wreckage. Whoever recovered the tech had left their mark. That would have to wait, though. His leg was of higher priority.

Finding two suitable pieces of graphene debris, Brady tied them tightly to either side of his leg with some loose wiring. The yank to get the cables tight enough to provide adequate support was overwhelmingly painful. He yelled in sheer agony, then it dawned on him that they had almost certainly noticed he had escaped and could be breathing down his neck.

Teeth gritted so hard he could feel the nerve endings in his gums, he looked back at the hatch to make sure nobody was tailing him. He was clear for the moment, but he knew it was only a matter of time.

At the back of the vehicle's chassis, he noticed a free-standing arms cabinet, stripped bare of its wares. It was still heavy enough to make opening the hatch from below impossible. He struggled to his feet and, dragging his splinted leg, he slowly limped over. He knew the only way to get it to position was by pushing it over. The noise would more than likely alert everyone below, but it was his only chance to get away.

The cabinet tipped over with relative ease, but the need to put weight on his injured leg to get it to move was so intense, blood rushed from Brady's face. Pale and cold, he stumbled over, catching himself on an old table. The cabinet had landed with an almighty crash. If he had pursuers anywhere near, they would have been in no doubt as to where he was, but his ballast would buy him plenty of time.

As much as he wanted to remain still until the agony passed, he knew he had no choice. Waves of nausea washed up and down as he teetered on the brink of consciousness. He fought his body's desire to quit and mustered up the strength to stand and follow the trail of hydraulic fluid. If it led him to whoever had left it, it would be the only chance he had of survival.

Brady's injured leg dragged behind him as he slowly followed the trail. Ever fading, he knew it would end soon. It led him out of the carcass of the crashed ship and across the barren ground towards the walls. With each step, the trail grew weaker until it faded into nothing. He had a direction; he hoped that would be enough.

Above him, light winds blew up fine dust from the swathes of wasteland that circled Ranley City's exterior walls. The walls were immense. As tall as the eye could see, looking straight up from the bottom, and two hundred yards thick.

He noticed that the land was not just barren, but chemically scorched. Nothing had grown there in centuries and it was clear nothing ever would again. The barren land stretched off for miles, further than he could see.

Ahead of him, the walls were strewn with armaments, huge high-calibre gun turrets, fully automated, jutting out like a mesh of spines. The evidence of their efficacy lay all around the outskirts. Shells of destroyed assault vehicles from countless attempts to breach the defences were a stark reminder of the price of war.

Gargantuan tanks, hulls of flight craft, both large and small, all in various states of decay. The shells of the vehicles were a timeline of centuries of assault vehicle design, each one as ineffective as the last. Many were marked with flags from the various nations that had opposed MediTech's global domination. Chinese, Japanese, Russian, Brazilian and Argentinian made up the vast number, but smaller nations had also sent reinforcements. They had one thing in common: they all lay defeated and dormant.

The city wall ahead acted as a wind trap. Dust swirled in a vortex against it. In one moment of calm, Brady noticed something out of the ordinary. Something leaning against the wall. He couldn't make it out from that distance, but it was the only abnormality he could see and, although the dust soon hid it again, it was his beacon.

As he got close enough, he could finally make out exactly what he had hoped it to be. A ladder fashioned from old structural supports and debris leaned up against the wall, terrifyingly tall. He couldn't make out where it ended, or what it led to, but he had no choice. With the remaining strength in his upper body and one good leg, he began his ascent.

His energy ebbed away as though someone had opened a tap in his back and left it running as he struggled to haul his weight upwards. Each rung brought more pain, but his adrenaline kept him going.

As the dust swirls eased momentarily, he could just make out the end. It rested at the opening of a gun turret, and though he could not make out an entry point, the knowledge that one must be there spurred him on. The higher he climbed, the less impact the sand had until he could determine his position relative to the ground. It was clear to him that the gun must have been lower than the city's exclusion zones.

The guns at that level were relics of long ago. Unlike the functioning defences higher up, they were once manned turrets, long abandoned since the capping off of the city at level ten. Strategically, they had little to offer against attacks on the city. The newer guns could target to pinpoint accuracy from much further afield, so wasting resources on gunners was pointless.

Brady peered cautiously into the gun port. The room beyond the wall was dark and musky. It was apparent it had been abandoned long ago, just as Brady had hoped. There was a slim gap between the gun and the wall. He positioned the top half of his body through, then, grabbing hold of the railings on the gun he heaved himself through and rolled off the cannon, slumping onto the ground with a thud. He was tired and in pain. Having taken more from his body than it had to give, he curled up into a ball in the underside of the huge gun and closed his eyes.

***

Back in AnitFa's compound, Ella studied the livefeed from the camera on a hoverbike, as it shone its bright headlights on the dented transformer that was struck by Bo's head.

The sound of the hover engine barely disguised the relentless cacophony of industrial noises emanating from the towers mechanics. It was all mixed with the muffled, echoey sound of loud music. Ella was unsure whether it would've sounded any better without the other noises which danced around the chaotic notes.

Ella's fingers controlled the touch display, contorting the image, zooming in, out, rotating and panning. The exploded viscera of her former colleague sickened her to her stomach, but she pushed through. Then she spotted a patch of blood and fluid that seemed out of place with the rest.

'Get me closer,' she said, before the hoverbike's engine increased thrust, propelling the bike towards the transformer. Deftly, she manipulated the image as the bike neared. She paid close attention to a small chunk of body tissue that had snagged on a sharp corner. As she zoomed in the image further, she could make out a small pattern of nano-circuitry tracks.

'There!' said Ella. 'Extract that and run bio-analysis. I need—' She was cut off by the sound of a door bursting open.

'Brady's disappeared!'

Ella turned to the bearer of bad news, eyes wide with panic as she saw the young man at the door. He looked nervous, she could tell as much. 'Get back to base. He's gone.'

The hoverbike rider replied over comms, broken by static and interference. 'Who, Brady?'

'Of course Brady!' said Ella. 'Report back ASAP. Forget the analysis. This is more important.'

'But I'm right here. This DNA might save lives!' The voice over the comms crackled worse this time.

Ella slammed her palm against the speaker on the desk. 'We need to find him before they do!'

'He's likely — the complex —' The interference was getting worse. The reply was broken. Words missing.

Ella groaned in exasperation. 'Change comms. Repeat.' The communication feed clicked, then became stable.

'He is probably still in the complex.' The communication was cleaner and crisper this time.

'What if he isn't?' Ella's head dropped. 'If he's made it out, they are going to find him. We can't risk that happening.'

'If he is out, I'll find him first. I'll make sure of it. I'm not letting all our work go to waste.' said the young man in the room.

'It's not just the work. He doesn't deserve what would happen if they find him.' She took a deep breath, her eyes closed, and she turned from the display. 'He doesn't deserve any of it.'

CHAPTER TEN

Brady began to stir as the morning light broke through the gun port and slowly illuminated the room.

It was small in there, just enough room for a couple of technicians to perform maintenance on the artillery that had been long abandoned. A narrow path running from the gun port to the hole where a door once was had cleared the dust and cobwebs that had accrued over centuries where foot traffic had been.

Groggy, Brady peeled his eye lids apart. For the briefest of moments between sleep and awake, he forgot his situation and the pain he had endured. Then he felt the sharp, pulsating pain in his leg. Like a pin prick that radiated outwards, until almost the entire left side of his body felt it.

Doing his best to block out the pain, he took a moment to familiarise himself with his surroundings. He remembered how he got there and why he had been running. He studied the gun jutting out of the wall, a forgotten relic of a defence system no longer needed. He took in the mess in the room and how the pathway had cleared the bare minimum for whoever was using it to do what they needed. And he considered the door. A destroyed frame leading into darkness and mystery.

What was it, two days since the fight? No, must be three, he thought. The last of the light had been fading when he got there. It was rising again. *Ten hours on the light cycle, gotta be.* It didn't dawn on him that for the first time in his life, he had witnessed the sun setting and rising.

He knew there was no chance that his pursuers didn't have an alternate route to him. It was nothing more than dumb luck that he hadn't been found already, which meant only one thing. *No more time to waste*. He had to move. Slowly, he pulled himself up to his feet. His teeth gnashed and he groaned as he tried to put any weight on his injured leg.

The narrow, dark corridor outside led in both directions. To his left, Brady could see nothing but darkness, but he could hear noises. Too faint to make out. Light penetrated to the right side and illuminated a stairway heading upwards. His home was somewhere above.

Dragging his trailing leg across the ground, he slowly made it to the stairs. At the top, he could see the silhouette of a thick barred gate. Fearing the worst, he pulled himself up the steps, regardless. As he neared them, he pleaded for good fortune. *Please, give me a break.*

Through the bars, he saw the flickering lights of fire dancing off the damp on the walls.

'Hey!' His voice was croaked and broken. He didn't have the strength to muster up much more than a timid yell. If anyone was there, they wouldn't have heard. He grasped hold of two bars and tried to open the gate, first pushing, then pulling, but it refused to move. The dim light was barely enough to make out the bars themselves, so he felt around for a locking mechanism. His fingers caressed a loop for a padlock, but the lock was missing. 'Seized. Brilliant.'

He considered the ways he could force it open, but came to the conclusion that they all required him being in peak physical fitness. He only had one more option; back the other way through the corridor.

Every laboured step brought him closer to the noise. He knew it was just as likely to be his doom as it was his salvation, but he didn't have any other choice but to press on. It grew louder, though he couldn't tell what it was. Movement for sure, but not the hustle and bustle of civilisation that he recognised. It was subtler. More ominous than the civilisation he was used to, the constant traffic of thousands of people, each rushing to get somewhere, each hurriedly telling someone the story of their day. This noise carried no voice and no humanity. Yet the closer he got, the surer he became that it was alive.

Brady followed the curvature of the narrow corridor, the noise still growing as darkness began to be diluted by the familiar, faint glow of neon light up ahead. He pressed on, grimacing more and more as the blood rushed down his leg. He dare not look at it, just hoped he wasn't bleeding to death anytime soon. Neon grew stronger. They seemed concentrated as though the light was being funnelled in through a narrow gap. He began to hear the movement. A shuffling of sorts. Almost echoing that of his own movement.

The noise and light grew louder and stronger. He thought for a moment he heard a voice, but couldn't be sure. If it was, it was faint and short-lived. Then there it was. A small section of floor had been burnt out with a laser cutter. The edges were too precise for it to have been done by anything else. Brady quietly got down into a prone position and crawled forwards carefully. His splints dragged across the ground, scraping and twisting. No matter how he moved, his leg was being contorted in ways that only exacerbated his pain.

As Brady peered over the edge of the hole, his face dropped. He saw corpses in various stages of decay piled up, one on top of another, from the ground, almost to the hole itself. Had to be a good fifty-foot drop. He couldn't even begin to fathom the amount of bodies that made such a pile of misery. Almost instantly, after he saw, he smelled a rotting decay unlike anything he'd had the displeasure of smelling before. It turned his stomach, so much so, he had to swallow to stop from vomiting.

He was amazed, both by the sheer volume of bodies, and at the sight of the undercity. He tried to picture everything as it would have been when it was first built. He wondered what lives were played out there and how long ago that might have been. Old signs with brands he had never heard of and rusted out car bodies he didn't recognise.

It took him a minute to process what he was seeing, but when he did, he noticed something else. A man once, maybe. Staring right at him but not seeing him. There were more. Moving slowly, seemingly without purpose. Just moving. Brady watched them, utterly unsure if they were aware of anything at all.

Some picked at carcasses, ripping limbs apart and delving their hands into rotten cavities. It was hideous, yet he couldn't look away. *Are they eating these bodies?* He continued to observe them; they weren't consuming any flesh, just picking it apart. Brady had never seen anything quite so horrific in his life and had no idea how to process it. What he did know was that going through them was his only way out.

Brady composed himself whilst looking at the pile of corpses that would soon break his fall. *You can do this. You can do it. Just do it man, just... Just go!* He psyched himself up, drawing himself ever closer to the edge. He was still being watched, but it was as though it was the stare of a painting, the eyes feeling like they were following him, yet remaining perfectly still. He began to take a deep breath to steady his nerves, but instantly regretted it as his lungs filled with the putrid stench of a thousand deaths. Quickly, he blew it back out. No more time to waste. It was do or die. And he hoped he wouldn't die. *Not here, not like this.* Not to become another carcass picked into pieces by the husks of men and women.

He heaved himself clear of the hole. Aimed himself at the peak of the pile, but off the mark. He landed into the rot with a thud. Bodies moved and the peak began cascading but the creatures didn't so much as flinch. He tumbled down with countless bodies, lost in the turmoil. One minute he was on top, the next he was covered by decayed flesh. A hundred thoughts ran through his mind about what his next move would be. He could stay deathly still if he wound up under other bodies. They probably wouldn't notice him before he could make a break for it, but a break was going to be hampered by his injury. If he wound up exposed, he'd have to take his chances swinging with whatever strength he had left.

Eventually, the cascading slowed to a halt. He was exposed. He rolled himself off the pile, then shuffled on his back to get some separation between himself and the closest creature, the one who had been watching him. It didn't move an inch. *Is it dead? Definitely human... At some point.* No time to dwell, as the others weren't. They had spotted him moving. They were narrowing in. Brady counted his blessings that they moved as slowly as he did in his diminished state. He could just about stay ahead if he moved now, but hesitation would undoubtedly be his downfall.

No time for pain. He'd have to take his weight and try to run. Ever closer they came, transfixed by his fresh body like he was prey to their predatory instincts. The sheer force of will to survive this nightmare was enough so he could block out the worst of the pain, barely. The faces of the husks of humanity as they narrowed in spurred him on. Rotting, missing eyes, soulless beings that once may have been his neighbours. He might have gone to school with some of them. Hell, he might have become one of them, still might. He ran. Hobbled, but ran.

There were so many more of these damned creatures than he realised. As he increased ground from one, he neared another as if they were appearing from thin air. He kept going through the weave of troughs in the corpse piles, passing husks left and right, men and women, and worse, children. Humanity decaying in front of his eyes. Pity and fear overwhelmed him, unable to take his eyes off the children, not looking where he was going. When he did, it was too late.

He was heading towards a dead end, a giant wall of metal

scrap, and penned in on either side by bodies. He slowed his pace. He shouldn't have. That brought the realisation of his pain back. He fell to the ground, unable to go on. All he could do was roll onto his back and shuffle slowly up to the metal wall. At least the right way up, he could go down with a fight. Men, women, children, it didn't matter; they weren't really human any more.

Brady felt the cold metal against his spine; he had nowhere left to go. *This is it. This is how I die.* He was resigned to his demise when, out of nowhere, he heard the clanking and grinding of metal on metal. The scrap metal panel was rising. He fell backwards as it lifted above his head, no longer supporting him.

He looked around, still stricken by panic. He saw another husk moving much faster. Sprinting, in fact. *Bring it on.* He reached up, stretching to grasp hold of the base of the lifting wall to haul himself upright, then letting go, he readied his stance. Fists in front of his pale face. He prepared a left hook, twisting his body onto his injured leg, knowing his balance would shift to his good leg to draw at least some power. One solid hit might get it down. But the husk pulled up short. Brady looked through his guard. It was no husk. This one was alive.

***

Dan approached Mio's bar. It was empty, except for Mya as she cleaned the bar and pumps.

It was quiet all around. Too early for the morning crowd and a little too late for those coming off the night shift. In this one hour, the entire entertainment district was a ghost town. Every bar, club and inch of street were empty, save for the clean-up crews. And there was a lot of cleaning to be done. Night shift workers were always the worst, rowdy and messy, and always leaving a trail of destruction behind themselves. Dan could see Mya, meticulous to the little details, making sure each pump shone like it was brand new, lining up bottles so that every label was exactly parallel to the shelves.

With her head down, focused entirely on cleaning the last drip tray, she did not notice him taking a stool in front of her.

'Hey Mya.' She jumped, startled by the voice and seeing Dan as he bent his head down to catch her eye.

'Dan, you scared the heck out of me.'

Dan scoffed. 'Why so jumpy? Rough night?'

Dan grinned as Mya took a few deep breaths, drawing in and pushing out with her hands before going back to her cleaning.

'It was okay until you showed up.' Mya raised her head and eyebrow to Dan. He could see the little judders in her body as she tapped her foot.

He desperately tried to think of a retort, but nothing came. 'So... You catch Brady's latest fight?' Dan noticed Mya's body calm, but she looked disappointed in place of the movement. He fidgeted, then gave her a smile.

'I saw some highlights. Not that he had any. That guy was a beast.'

Dan leaned in. 'Right? I've never seen our boy so outgunned.'

Mya dropped her cleaning rag on the bar in front of him, 'What are you doing here at this time in the morning anyway? Shouldn't you be unconscious with your latest conquest?' Dan leaned back away, feigning indignation.

'I've come to see you, gorgeous. Why else would I be here?'

She scoffed. 'Is that so? And what can I do for you?'

He grabbed her hand, stopping her from cleaning. 'Well, you can start by letting me take you out for dinner tonight.'

'What makes you think I'd let you do that?' Dan grinned as she leaned towards him, softening and widening her eyes.

'You know a good thing when you see one,' he said, winking at her.

'Do I now?' He watched her softened features sharpened again.

He smiled, cheekily. 'Come on Princess, I'm not that bad am I?'

'I honestly don't know how bad you are, Dan.' She pulled her hand away quickly. 'How bad does your girlfriend think you are?' Mya tossed the cleaning rag over her shoulder and placed her hands on the bar in front of Dan in a display of resolution.

'It's Brady, isn't it? You've got it for him?' Dan looked away sharply, over-exaggerating for affect.

She smiled. 'You know, if I thought you were being serious, I'd bite.'

He flashed his gritted teeth to her. 'If I thought you'd bite, I'd be serious.' Dan winked at her. 'What's up with the boy, though? I saw him earlier and—' Mya abruptly stopped. He could see she was getting an incoming call on her comms when her left eye glazed over with a green hue.

'What's going on?' said Mya softly through her comms. Dan craned his neck to try and hear anything, then caught Mya's eyes in the reflections of the glass backing behind the bottle display. He settled back down quickly.

Dan noticed Mya's face drop. 'What? When?'

She got quieter, but he could still make out her response. 'Are you sure it's him?' They caught eyes again in the mirror and Dan saw as she cut the call.

'I've got to go.' She hurried out from the bar, taking off her branded apron.

Dan stood, ready to leave with her. 'Everything okay?'

Mya scanned her retina on the security console at the side of the bar and stepped out as shutters came down around, closing it up. 'Something's come up. I'll talk to you later, okay?'

Before she could move, Dan grabbed her and pulled her in for a hug. He felt the rapid beat of her heart against his chest. Dan slipped his hand into his back pocket and pulled out a tiny tracking device, pretended to straighten her collar and hooked it into the material.

He released her half way, looked straight into her eyes. 'Alright, you know where I am if you need something.'

'I'll see you.' She hurried from the bar, leaving Dan alone. He watched as her pace got progressively faster until she had broken into a sprint, exiting the entertainment zone to transit. Dan gave it another few moments before placing a holo-call. Ella's face projected onto the shutters of the bar in front of him, her eyes wide in anticipation.

'I think I've got something.'

'Meet me at the usual place,' said Ella.

'On my way.' He hung up quickly before placing another call. The image in front of him shifted to a scrambled face.

'What do you want?' The voice was modulated to sound like a robot.

'I think I have something. Can you hook me up?'

'It depends on what this something is.'

'I think he's with a friend. You can follow her signal, but I had to alert AntiFa. I'm on my way to meet them. I haven't told them I've got a tracker fitted, but if you don't hook me up now, I'll give them the signal too.'

'Fine. Meet me in ten minutes. If you are messing with me, you know how this goes.' With that, the call ended and Dan immediately left the area in a full-speed sprint.

CHAPTER ELEVEN

The long needle of an adrenaline shot pierced through Brady's chest and he woke with a convulsion. Though blurred, he could just about make out a mechanical arm retract, taking the needle that had woken him with it.

He found himself on a rudimentary operating table among the tents of the undercity slums. He had little time to orientate himself before he saw something that made the weight of the world lift away. Mya, standing over him. She looked more beautiful than usual. He felt safe, despite his surroundings and everything that had happened.

'Mya?'

'Hi Brady,' she said.

He looked around frantically. 'Where am I? What's going on?'

'You're in the undercity. You're safe.' He felt her hand softly placed on his chest. His heart, already quicker than normal, raced even faster.

Brady tried to sit up further, but her hand, though placed gently, stopped him. 'What are you doing here?'

'That's something I'll have to explain later. You need to rest,' she said.

Brady suddenly remembered what had happened to his leg. He looked down. What he saw made him shift uncomfortably on the table.

'What happened to my leg?' he asked, as he realised the lower part of his leg had been replaced by a cybernetic limb. An old one at that.

Brady could see the sad look on her face. 'We couldn't save it.'

'I can't fight with this!' Brady stopped breathing for a moment as he remembered his career was over anyway. Then sucked in a huge lungful of air to play catch-up.

'I'm sorry hun, we tried.' As she said that, he saw her scoot his new leg over to make room to sit. He saw it, yet felt nothing.

Brady took a moment to gather his thoughts. In the last week, he had lost his career, his identity, now his leg and, at times, his grip on reality. He stared vacantly at his new limb, contemplating just how much had changed, not only about himself, but how he viewed the world and why very little of that remained relevant. He had not been unconscious for long, but to him, it felt as though he had just woken from a fifty-year coma.

He sighed, heavily, then looked Mya in the eyes.

'Last thing I remember, I was cornered by some kind of zombie.'

She smiled at him. It was sweet, but he couldn't help but feel a little patronised. 'Our sentry saw you out there, brought you in,' she said.

'Our sentry?' Free of her hand on his chest, he sat more upright. 'What do you mean, *our*?'

Mya gestured around. 'Our community.'

Brady took his time to observe his surroundings. Hastily scrambled together, the medical facilities left a lot to be desired. Dirty, full of archaic technology, most of which had some form of rudimentary repair keeping it ticking over. The beds around him were all full of people at death's door.

The more lucid he became, the more his senses were overloaded. The smell almost burnt his nostrils before it turned his stomach. Rotten. Stale. The cacophony of noises alone were almost a sensory overload. The driving sounds of the heartbeat of an industrial city above reverberated around the echo chamber of the undercity, like a concert hall with every instrument out of tune. It grated on him.

It was all too much. Brady tried to drown it all out the best way he could, refocusing on Mya's friendly face.

'Wait, are you guys with Ella?' he said.

She looked puzzled. 'Who is Ella?'

'Ella, AntiFa.' He saw from the look on her face, she had no idea what he meant. 'No?'

'AntiFa?' said Mya.

Brady's brow furrowed. 'Okay, you're not with them. You aren't MediTech, so why are you guys after me?'

'After you? MediTech and AntiFa are after you?' She scooted up the table, closer to him. He felt her hip brush against his.

'Yeah, apparently I'm number one on their hit lists. Or hide lists, or, actually, I don't even know.' Brady watched Mya processing.

Her concentration was broken by the screeching of an alarm. One of the life support systems on a bed opposite Brady began flashing red almost in unison with the convulsions of the patient in the bed. Brady could see their face, which was lifeless, yet the body lurched and contorted.

Mya jumped to action, sprinting towards the exit of the medical tent. 'Crash in bed fourteen!'

She was about to exit when the tent flaps burst apart and a young male ran inside, nearly running directly into Mya, but she managed to side step him just in time. He was dialled into his task, ignoring everything else and making his way directly to the bed. Mya followed him, keeping a distance.

He threw his bag on the table next to the convulsing patient and immediately attended to the monitoring equipment which continued in its trauma response. His fingers fumbled on the touchscreen, sliding parameters left, right and centre. Brady wondered if he really knew what he was doing, seeing him slide settings one way, then the other, as though he was just hoping for a miracle.

Brady sat further upright, watching on. The body convulsed

again, more violently this time. It wretched, spewing forth foaming, purple bile. Brady assumed the attendant had done something wrong, but he couldn't know for sure.

The attendant reached into his kit bag, pulling out a stomach pump and quite violently began to ram the extraction pipe down the patient's throat. Brady was glad it wasn't him. His stomach turned a little, squirmed at the thought of something being rammed down his oesophagus in that manner.

The pump engaged with a laboured whining sound and the clear pipe became purple. Within a few seconds of the bile being extracted it turned to pure blood red. The attendant looked troubled, and unaware the pump reservoir had filled to spilling point. Brady thought about letting him know the bile and blood was sputtering out over his boots, but figured he had bigger things on his mind.

Instead, he gestured to Mya, waving a hand and nodding to the reservoir, but she was too fixated on what was going on in the bed to notice him. She looked concerned, but calm at the same time. Brady felt as though he should have taken solace from her calm demeanour that everything would be fine, but the scene playing out in front of him was too gruesome to ignore. If he was betting on the outcome, he would've put it all on black.

The sudden shift in alarm tone, from frantic to solid, let him know he would've won that bet. The body became still. The bed apparatus reacted before the attendant, lowering two arms down to the patient, one with a needle, just like the one that had awoken Brady, while the other held breathing apparatus.

As the attendant realised what was happening, he panicked, racing against the robotic arm to remove the stomach pump tube, but he was too far behind. The breathing apparatus tried to push itself into the patient's face, but the tube prevented it. Still, it began to hiss as it pumped oxygen into the air. Brady watched Mya join the attendant, grasping the face mask and lifting it away to relieve the pressure it was placing on the tube. That allowed the attendant to extract the last part of the stomach pump, tossing it to the ground, finally noticing the spillage on the floor.

Mya manually manipulated the mask onto the patient's face as the needle hovered, ready to strike the chest. She stepped back, having secured it. All they could do was wait and see.

The needle struck down solidly, piercing the breast bone. Brady saw the plunger lower as it shot the liquid in the body. Mya and the attendant watched on in anticipation, but there was no response. The life sign monitor remained flat and the beep remained constant.

Brady vacantly stared ahead, falling into a trance. Other people rushed into the room and hurried to the body. One mounted and tried CPR. Everything seemed to be in slow motion, yet simultaneously sped up. They bustled around the body, seemingly like hummingbirds, all shouting at each other, but all Brady could hear was a white noise. Then, he heard his name. Faintly. And again. Louder each time.

'Brady!' said Mya, as she leant by the side of his face. He snapped out of it. She was the only person left. The bed opposite was empty.

Brady stared at her for a moment. 'I—' He ran out of words immediately.

She smiled softly. 'I know.'

He looked at her, puzzled. 'How can you be so cool about it? That was brutal.'

She placed her hand on his arm. 'Unfortunate truth of life here. We see it almost every day.'

'What do you mean, every day? And who is we?'

'Brady, I think I have an idea of what's going on with you. You have to trust me now. Can you do that?' She looked into his eyes with sincerity.

Brady was confused. 'As much as I can anyone at the moment.'

She gripped his arm tightly. 'This must all be an absolute minefield for you. I can't make you trust me, not yet, I know. But what you said about AntiFa, MediTech, please, just don't mention that to anyone else. Promise me. Not yet, anyway.'

'Look, whatever you think is going on, you're wrong. Trust me on that.' He pulled his arm away and shuffled himself up against the headboard.

Mya stood up, and he could tell she was deep in thought before she answered. 'What do you think I do?'

'What do you do? As in, for work?'

'Sure.' She dragged a chair from one bed over, scraping the floor as it moved.

'You're a bartender.'

'What do people do at bars?' Mya took a seat close to Brady.

Brady shook his head. 'Drink?'

Mya leaned closer, speaking quieter. 'They talk. It's been my job to keep my ears open.'

Brady raised one eyebrow. 'You're saying you're a spy?'

'That may be a stretch far, but essentially, yes.' Mya sat back in the chair, crossing her legs. 'Let's just say I've heard enough to piece this together.'

'Okay, so what have you heard?'

'It's more what I've seen when I've been watching you.'

'Watching me?' He sat upright, swinging his legs down to the side of the table. 'Why were you watching me?'

Mya moved forward on the chair, blocking Brady's space to stand. 'I know it looks bad, but it isn't.'

'Looks bad? You have no idea! I'm getting really sick and tired of being told I'm being watched.' He moved to stand, but Mya placed her hands on his knees, using gentle force to keep him from getting anywhere.

'Of course you are, hun. But I had no idea why anyone was watching you, not until now. Can you please believe me?'

He studied her face, looking for any sign of insincerity, but he could find none. 'I don't know, I guess. But what do you think you know?'

'I've heard rumours up there for years that MediTech has been looking for someone with stolen military tech. Right after your last fight, it all ramped up.' Brady slumped back down and she took the pressure off his knees. 'Now, the fact our medics found some kind of implant in your brain they couldn't make head nor tail of, and the fact I haven't seen you around for a while, puts it all in perspective.'

Brady sat in contemplation for a moment; he could see Mya patiently wait for him and felt no pressure to rush his reply.

'So what difference does it make if I tell anyone? If you can put those pieces together, so can anyone else.'

'Nobody else knows I've been watching you.'

'Wait, so why did you say they called you here when they found me?'

'Brady, please believe me when I say the reasons I and anyone else have been watching you are vastly different.'

'Well tell me.'

'I've been keeping an eye on you because of what you do, not who you are. And people here know you, they know of you, anyway.'

'What, because I'm some no-name fighter from the low leagues who got one shot at the big time and blew it? You expect me to believe that?'

'People here gamble on sports like it's a profession. They know the vital statistics of amateurs from sports you've never even seen before. There's nothing else to do here. They obsess over it.'

'Still, doesn't explain why they would alert you.'

'Like I said, they know everything about every athlete in the city, including which towers they represent.' She put her hands on his thighs and leaned in slightly. 'They called me because I work yours.' Her hands squeezed Brady's thighs and smiled sweetly. 'I was only ever feeding back how you were looking for their betting. I promise you, it's that simple.'

'That...' He tried to think back through all their exchanges, recalling the amount of times she had asked him how he was feeling in the days leading up to his fights. 'Okay yeah, that makes sense.'

She smiled. 'Because it's the truth, Brady.'

'So, really I was just a job to you? All that talking. It was because you had to?' He could see she looked hurt by his suggestion.

'No of course not!' she said. He could see her looking down at the ground, solemnly. 'Okay, maybe at first, but I do really care for you, you know?' Brady reached out his arm and placed his finger under her chin, gently raising her head again.

Brady looked into her eyes and felt the chemistry. He had hoped for a moment like this for a long time, but never imagined it would happen under such circumstances. He put his hands on top of hers. As much as he wanted to take hold of them, he removed them from his legs and stood. The new lower leg prosthetic held him off balance, not bending at the knee as his other leg did, and he wobbled before holding himself up on the table of monitoring equipment he was linked to. Mya reached to steady him, but he brushed her off, ripping the monitoring leads off his body immediately after.

Each piece of adhesive hurt as it tore off, but the pain was easier to take than the pain he felt where his prosthesis met his hip. That was agony, like a hot knife slicing. Even in pain, he could see Mya looked hurt by the manner in which he brushed her off.

'Sorry, I just want to do this on my own,' he said, reaching for her arm. Not for support, but to comfort her. 'I don't understand why, if you say I'm safe here, I need to keep this to myself. So obviously I'm not. I need to get out of here.'

'You are safe, but I honestly don't know how people here would react if they knew you were carrying something MediTech coveted so highly. Whatever it is.' Mya took a seat, understanding that Brady needed to work out his new limb on his own terms.

'You don't know what it is then?' He paced slowly along the edge of the table for support, back and forth as he learned how to flex his knee. With each step, he grimaced and snarled, feeling the edges of the prosthesis digging in.

'Not exactly.' Mya began pacing with Brady, close enough to catch him if required.

'So why would you worry about what anyone else would think?'

'Things are tight down here, Brady. Sometimes people do whatever it takes to make sure their family can survive.'

'How do you mean tight?'

'Put it this way, for a lot of people, there's a fine line between being inside the compound and being out there as one of those, what did you call them? Zombies?'

He could see a genuine sadness on her face. For the first time in a while, he felt compassion for someone other than himself. 'So tell me about them.'

'We call them husks. That's what happens when a body overloads on tech. The mind shuts down and they become... That.'

'Why isn't anyone helping them?'

'There's nothing that can be done for them. When they go that way, MediTech strips them of whatever is useful and casts them down here.'

'That's barbaric!'

'That's MediTech. That's what they are. They use us up and spit us out,' said Benito as he entered Brady's medical tent.

'Who are you?'

'Name's Benito. Used to live up there, now I'm down here free of their oppression. So are you now, my friend.'

'Friend?' said Brady, sizing up Benito. 'I'm not your friend. Look, I appreciate you patching me up and all, but I don't know you from Adam.'

Benito strode confidently up to Brady. 'Maybe not yet, but you will. Everyone knows me down here. Everyone needs me down here. You need me too.' He extended his hand.

Brady looked down at Benito's hand, contemplating whether to shake it. 'Can you get me home? That's all I want right now, just to go home and forget about everything. If you can make that happen, you can be my friend.' He decided against the courtesy.

Benito withdrew his gesture. 'I'm afraid that's not possible.'

Brady looked over to Mya. 'And why is that?' The subtle widening of her stare reminded him not to give anything away.

Brady noticed Benito looking suspiciously at Mya. 'Someone has corrupted your DNA tags,' said Benito. 'You don't technically exist as yourself anymore.' He gestured for Brady to take a seat on the table.

Brady scoffed. 'What do you mean?' He had begun to feel sore from his altered gait and wanted a seat, but was hesitant to make it seem like he was placating Benito.

Benito sat on the table. 'Please. Sit.' Brady took Benito's lead, which felt more an invitation than an instruction after seeing him sit. 'We don't know who, but someone has reprogrammed your ID to give no readout.'

Brady turned his head over his right shoulder, towards Mya, away from Benito's line of sight, and winked to her. 'Why would anyone do that?' He turned back to Benito, forcing a puzzled look, all the while, realising. *Ella!*

Brady noticed Benito reach into his jacket and produce a crude-looking cigar. He bit off one end and spat it to the floor, spitting out wisps of tobacco as he spoke. 'I don't know.' He placed the cigar in his mouth and drew out his lighter. 'But you'll set off every security system they have up there if you try going home.' He waved the flame across the end of the cigar, ensuring the entire surface was lit as he puffed in and out to get it going, billowing puffs of smoke out through the corner of his mouth.

Transfixed on the cigar, watching the billowing smoke, Brady wondered. He had never seen one before. 'Is that...?' He watched as Benito slowly ribboned smoke out of his pursed lips. 'I thought they were banned?' He coughed, failing to avoid the final cloud of smoke that Benito purposefully built up and exhaled towards him.

'Nothing is banned here, Brady.' He placed his arm around him. 'You have seen what you presumed to be ugliness out there.' He offered the cigar to Brady, who declined. 'In time you'll appreciate that beauty exists under the surface.'

'So why are you guys hiding away from those things out there if it's so beautiful?'

Benito laughed, inducing a slight cough with the smoke still in his lungs. 'We aren't hiding from them.'

Brady made an overt gesture to their surroundings. 'The scrap fortress says otherwise.'

Benito tapped off the ash from his cigar. 'Separation isn't the same as hiding, Brady.'

'Okay, what I'm getting at, is why not just get rid of them? You have weapons, right?'

Mya stood and walked to the opening of the medical tent. 'We need them.' She looked outside. She seemed to be in a thoughtful moment. 'We need them for the same reason they are out there tearing up flesh.'

Benito stood, discarding the three quarters that remained of his rapidly burning cigar. 'They are creatures of instinct, Brady. That instinct was the last conscious thought they had. Salvage tech to replace what they thought was corrupted.'

'Wait!' Brady got up, momentarily forgetting the prosthetic. 'What do you mean you need them for the same reason, then?'

'Brady, take a walk with me.' Benito nodded at Brady's leg. 'Try out that new leg of yours.' Brady was shepherded towards the exit of the tent, noticing his steps weren't in phase. The prosthesis had a quicker response time than his own. 'Stop thinking it's different.' Benito's instruction made sense. Brady had been acutely aware of trying to move his leg. As soon as he let that thought go, he managed to get into a better rhythm. With each step, he came closer to walking normally.

Outside, Brady was aghast at the sheer number of medical tents, all lined up in rows and columns. Benito led them through the centre gangway in silence. Brady didn't know where to look. The amount of tents was overwhelming. His eyes darted around looking for something to take his mind of that thought. Then he looked up. He noticed the structural supports. The pipes and cables hanging loose. Then he forgot about the body count as an even more overwhelming thought struck him. *All that life above, being supported by so little.*

But even that thought only lasted so long before his attention turned back to the tents. He could see inside most of them, all with bodies nearing the verge of collapse, being tended to by people not so far off it themselves.

As Brady was deep in thought, Benito broke the silence. 'Those husks are the only things keeping us alive down here.'

Brady stopped dead in his tracks, putting two and two together. 'Hang on, are you saying you take tech from them to save these lives?'

Noticing Brady had stopped, Benito turned around. 'Exactly.'

'So why not just kill them all and take it now?'

'Do you know how long bio-tech lasts in a deceased host?'

Mya, who had held back a step or two to be ready to catch Brady if he stumbled, caught up. 'Days. Sometimes hours if it's really high-spec.'

We salvage what we can from them and put it to good use.'

Benito pointed out a larger tent, filled with stripped carcasses. 'But we never know what we are going to get.'

'My other job up there is to listen out for any talk of specific tech being shipped, from where, to whom,' said Mya.

'Mya gives us leads on where to get up above. I put a raiding team together.' Benito gesticulated towards the ceiling. 'Send them up and if they don't get killed by MediTech, there's a slim chance they might get their hands on what we need to save someone's life. That's how fine the survival line is down here.'

'So why are you here? You're both healthy, right?'

'Some of us would rather struggle to live free than be part of the nightmare up there,' said Benito.

'Some of us were born here. And others...' Brady could see the forlorn look on her face as she paused. '... followed loved ones who had no choice but to escape.'

Brady reached out to her. 'Everyone knows it's bad down on the lower levels, but I didn't realise it was this bad.'

Benito scoffed. 'Brady!' His hand slapped Brady's back with a sting, making him grimace. 'This is the undercity. The lower levels are paradise compared to this.'

Brady remained fixated on Mya, seeing her struggle to hold back tears. 'They are just waiting rooms for here in reality.' It was easy to see that this was personal for her.

Brady's concerned look made way for one of confusion. 'What about all the humanitarian efforts that MediTech sanction?' He noticed Mya's tears and reached out an arm in comfort. 'Aren't they helping?'

Benito led them out of the medical tent complex to a large opening, in the centre of which was his three-story home and gardens. Amid the ramshackle construction of everything else around, his home existed in isolation. Classic stone craftsmanship passed down from generations of Benito's Tuscan family roots, all built on top of a huge graphene-lined security bunker. The gardens surrounding the house were reminiscent of the Italian hills, miniaturised and fed by under-soil irrigation and suspended lighting. Benito grew vines, olives and tobacco, all walled in by ornate stonework-fronted graphene walls, periodically sporting automated defence turrets. It was a bastion disguised as a bathhouse.

Leading towards his underground villa, Benito playfully nudged Brady with his elbow, snorting a laugh. "Fake philanthropy, makes it look like they care.'

'Everyone thinks going there helps. They feel good about themselves and move on.' Mya grabbed Brady's arm to stop him. 'They go down once a month, maybe every two months. Everything looks the same, so as far as they are concerned, it's keeping people alive. What they don't know...' Brady saw the make-up smears from her tears as they ran down her face. 'When nobody is there, MediTech sends teams to clean house and bring in the next on their ferry of the damned.'

'But they are up there killing people at will, chucking them down the disposals and nobody bats an eyelid. They don't have to bother with such a ruse, surely?'

'See Brady, it works on two parts.' Benito turned Brady to face him. 'Firstly, it gives the illusion that it could be worse, so everyone above counts their blessings.' His eyebrows furrowed. 'And worse, they have a constant supply of cannon fodder for their frontline troops.'

Brady balked. 'What? If they are so sick, what good are they as soldiers?'

'For the frontline, they are perfect. They kit them out with neural inhibiters, targeting optics, arm them and let loose.'

'Oh, come on, you expect me to believe that?'

'It happened to my father.' Mya looked away and struggled to speak through her sobbing. 'That's why my mother came down here, me in tow.'

Brady closed his eyes at the realisation he had put his foot in it. Awkwardly, he considered whether to reach out and console her, but couldn't quite bring himself to. As he stood uneasily, the silence was broken by a burst of gunshots echoing around the cavernous undercity.

Panic set in among the residents. The enclave burst into life, and hundreds of people panicked, running for Benito's sanctuary. Those that had it in them to fight grabbed weapons and found cover as a last line of defence.

Before Brady had a chance to comprehend what was happening, Mya had taken off like a shot, running head first towards the sound of the gunfire as Benito shepherded Brady towards the gate of his compound.

'Mya!' Brady shouted for her to stop, but she ignored him entirely.

Benito shoved Brady towards the security gate, slamming him into the solid steel bars. 'She can take care of herself. We need to get you safe.' The gate security scanned Benito's face and opened up, just in time for the two to bundle inside ahead of the stampede of citizens herding themselves to safety.

The crowd bundled through Brady, knocking him to the ground as Benito led the charge towards the bunker entrance by the side of the house before he realised Brady was nowhere to be seen. Brady watched Benito as he fought against the current, jostling his way through the crowd until he found him. Benito picked him up by his arm, threw it over his shoulder before hoisting him over his back and carrying him back towards the shelter.

CHAPTER TWELVE

The inside of Benito's bunker was simple, but huge. Seating for around two hundred people, basic supplies for short stays. The only other thing of note was the monitoring station near the entrance.

Brady scoured the screens with Benito. All the feeds together covered a huge area outside the compound. All but one seemed to show the same level of husk activity that Brady had observed earlier. But in one of the feeds, he spotted Mya.

On the outskirts of the compound, Mya leapt from the ground to the perimeter wall, clearing fifteen feet in an effortless bound as her bio-tech calves sprung her upwards. Reaching the wall, she deployed hundreds of tiny barbs from the palms of her hands, gripping into the sheer surface of the wall, allowing her to scale it like a spider. Brady and Benito followed her movements, from screen to screen.

Hauling herself to the top of the barricade, she crouched to assess the situation. Brady spotted one heavily armed man. He held a position behind a destroyed support pillar. Three bodies lay in his path ahead of him, four more behind. Twenty feet separated him from the barrier, with one defender left, crouched behind a slab of duracrete that once made up the foundations of a sewer pipe.

Brady watched intensely as Mya reached behind her back and withdrew two heavy handguns. He was amazed that these weapons had been so cleverly integrated into her jacket, and their appearance was a complete shock. The MediTech 700 he recognised as standard issue in her left hand. In her right, a crudely fashioned custom weapon with a grappling hook jutting from the barrel. She took aim with her right, way above her head, and the grapple fired towards the beams above. It dug firmly into the solid duracrete before splaying out for grip.

He could see her watching the attacker carefully, monitoring him dipping in and out of cover as he and the remaining defender exchanged shots, working out the timing. When she was sure of the pattern, she waited for him to deliver the three shots and duck behind cover. At the exact point the third shot left the attacker's barrel, Mya engaged the grapple motor and launched herself up into the air, swift and unseen.

Brady tracked her movement the best he could through the screens. As her trajectory took her above the assailant's head, her left hand aimed the Seven Hundred down at him. She fired off three rounds; two hit the ground by him, the burning bright blue-green smoke of phosphorous rounds lighting up the screen, making Brady and Benito squint as the audio feedback of the shots could be heard loudly in the bunker. The third struck the man in the shoulder. As his ultra-grade armour absorbed just enough of the bullet's force, it couldn't quite penetrate his skin, though the phosphorous burning was enough to stagger him from his cover.

Brady watched as, with the target exposed and burning, the last of the defenders immediately rose from their cover and laid down a blanket of heavy assault fire. Shots ricocheted off the armour doing no damage, but the sheer power pushed him backwards, flushing him out even further. More bursts of fire kept him off balance as Mya detached the grapple from her gun and plummeted towards the ground. Brady's eyes widened at the thought of the fall.

She landed deftly, her legs absorbing the impact without a problem and, amazed she survived the fall unscathed, Brady let out a sigh of relief. He watched on as Mya didn't hesitate to open fire, popping steady rounds of phosphorous into his chest as she advanced towards what was now a huge ball of flames. As she neared her target, she discarded both guns, broke into a sprint and launched a fly kick straight to the centre of his torso, sending him reeling backwards to the ground. Quickly, she closed in, kicking the assault rifle from his hand.

'Who sent you?' Brady heard her shout as loud as she could to be heard over the agonising screams of the man, as he desperately tried to remove his helmet. The unbearable heat of the metal on his scalp was clearly too much.

The man screamed, 'Go to hell!' in Russian as he tossed aside the melting helm.

'You first!' She picked up his burning personalised Kavtech high-power assault rifle and attempted to fire an execution shot to his head. The gun did not respond to her trigger action. 'Bio imprinted!' Brady heard her shout through the audio feedback. Dropping the rifle, Mya took her Seven Hundred in hand, grabbed a round from the magazine from her belt and loaded up. She took aim at his heart at point blank range, shielding her eyes with her offhand and readying her stance to absorb the heightened recoil.

Brady and Benito watched her squeeze the trigger carefully. The bullet impacted in his chest, immediately exploding, ending the man's agonised screams and sending her backwards at the same time. Brady looked away, the ruthlessness of her actions shocking him.

***

Benito, Mya and Brady stood over the burned-out armour-plated body of the attacker. The metal of his armour had fused to his skin. The flesh that could be seen no longer resembled anything more than charcoal. His body and surrounding area were coated in a fine blue powder, remnants of the copper sulphate that had been used to put out the flames. Brady watched on as Benito, with his hands inside thermal-resistant gloves, slowly began to undo the clasps of the armour.

He pulled away sections of fused Kevlar and flesh. Watching him pick apart the corpse turned Brady's stomach. If he was looking for anything that could be used to identify him, Brady thought it would be slim pickings. Fried pieces of implant technology he managed to find were charred beyond recognition as Benito worked his way from the torso up to the head as the corpse continued to billow with smoke.

Brady noticed Mya inspecting the man's assault rifle. 'Bio-imprint on his rifle.' She looked back to Benito. 'I know these. Locked to fingerprints.' She tapped her head. 'And transponders, two-step authentication.'

Brady turned to Benito, and could see him deep in thought. 'It'll be cooked, too,' said Benito.

Mya discarded the gun. 'Transponder will, but they insulate the comms so the transponder doesn't mess with the frequencies. Should be fine.'

Benito looked up at Mya as he took hold of the head. 'Give me a hand,' he ordered, clamping hold of the skull on both sides and nodding to the torso.

Brady watched on as Mya knelt beside the corpse. His stomach, already quivering, began to churn at the thought of what was to come next.

Mya grabbed hold of the corpse's shoulders, took a deep breath and looked Benito in the eyes.

'Good to go?' said Benito.

Mya exhaled. 'Ready when you are.'

Brady watched on, through the corner of his eye, not wanting to look, but unable to look away.

Benito nodded to Mya and took a firm grasp of the corpse's cranium, both hands gripped so tightly that Brady could see his knuckles turn white.

Benito sharply twisted the head, his teeth gritted.

Brady looked away in horror, but he could not escape the gut-wrenching noise of the bones snapping and charred flesh tearing.

Before he could stop himself, he looked around to see Benito tearing away the tendrils that kept the head attached to the body. He had seen some gruesome sights before, but this was too much. Quickly, he turned away, hunched over forwards and with a heaving, hawking, retching sound, vomited pure bile on the ground.

With his stomach a little settled, Brady looked back at the corpse.

Benito reached his fingers inside the head through the neck cavity, searching inside like it was a blocked drain before he pulled out a piece of hardware, half cooked, half shrouded in insulation, unharmed by the intense heat that had cooked everything else. 'Here.' He tossed it to Mya.

Brady watched Mya place the implant on the ground, hitting it with the butt of her pistol, just hard enough to crack the insulation. She slid back a flesh cover on her wrist, revealing a small display under it. Where most citizens had moved to integrated system monitors in their ocular tech, Mya's old-school touch panel was like a blast from the past. The kind he used to see on his teachers. She activated the scanner and passed her wrist over the small implant.

Benito stood, discarding the head like a chicken carcass after the meat was gone. 'Anything?'

Mya studied her display; she looked confused. 'I've got a read, but there's no ID.' She motioned for Brady to come over. As he did, she showed him a list of recent contacts she had downloaded from the chip.

He looked over the data. 'What am I looking at?' he said, confused as to what she was expecting from him.

She pointed at an entry marked *"X,"* and expanded the entry details. 'See there, under conference additions.' She highlighted the additional contact entry under the call details for X. Brady recognised the comms ID immediately.

His eyes widened in disbelief. 'Dan.' He mumbled it under his breath as his gaze darted back and forth, as if the answers were in front of him.

Mya clicked the screen off. 'Are we sure?'

'E eight, b twenty, nineteen forty-two, f, o, r, e, d.' Brady nodded as he recalled Dan's user ID from memory, matching what they had seen on the display. He was cautious to not let Benito hear clearly what he was saying.

Mya shook her head. 'I needed to be sure.' She brought her boot down on the device with great force, shattering it. Brady could see Benito struggling to comprehend what the two were mulling over.

'What's going on?'

Angry at the thought his best friend had betrayed him, Brady found the nearest solid structure and punched it. He let out a wail of pain. 'That son of a bitch.' He put his face in his hands and screamed.

Benito grabbed Mya's arm. 'Tell me what is happening.' He looked her straight in the eyes. 'Right now!'

Mya struggled free of Benito's grip and hurried over to Brady, throwing her arm around his shoulder. 'Let's not jump to any conclusions.'

'Brady threw her arm off. 'Not jump to any conclusions?' he scoffed at her. 'Some kind of crazy assassin comes after me and I shouldn't jump to conclusions?'

Mya raised her hands and backed away. 'We don't know he was after you.'

Benito stepped between them. 'Someone tell me something!' Brady could hear the frustration in his voice spiral.

Brady looked to the rafters. 'I'm sure it's just a coincidence.' He shook his head and laughed.

'I never trusted the guy.' Brady saw Mya peer around Benito to him. 'But we can't just assume the worst.'

'Answer me!' Benito nearly deafened Brady as his voice reverberated around the echo chamber of the undercity.

'You want answers?' Brady engaged with him, his eyebrows furrowed in anger. 'My best friend has just sent this guy to kill me.' He kicked the corpse solidly with his prosthetic leg, unaware of the power it had, sending the body flying.

'Brady!' Mya rushed in front of him. 'Calm down.'

'Who knows you are here?' Panicked, Benito looked around to try to find any other threats. 'If you have compromised us—'

Mya pushed Benito back. 'Not the time Benny!' She gestured for him to give her a moment. 'Let's find out what he knows before we decide to do anything stupid.'

As Mya looked at him, Brady could sense for the first time she was genuinely nervous around him. His face was red hot, hand he could feel the muscles tensed. Brady's stomach churned; nausea and anger, in equal measures. He had trusted Dan since childhood; the betrayal was as overwhelming as it was surprising.

Brady wondered how much he was feeding Benito's anger. He could sense his agitation, and anytime he looked towards Benito he was jittering frantically. As Benito began to storm off, Brady could feel just the slightest lift in the pressure that had been crushing him.

'I'm going to make sure everyone is okay!' said Benito, quickening his pace. 'At least one of us cares about the wellbeing of our people,' he muttered under his breath, just loud enough to be heard, before turning the corner of a large pillar and out of sight.

Still seething, Brady contemplated his response to Dan's betrayal. 'I'm going to kill him!' With his face filled with rage, he stormed off, completely unaware of which direction to go.

'Wait!' Mya chased after him. 'You can't do anything rash.' She positioned herself in front of him, blocking his path. 'It'll get you killed.' Brady tried to push her backwards, but she was too strong for him.

'I can't stay here.' Frustrated by being weaker than her, Brady gave up. 'Benito was right, I'll get everyone else killed.' He crouched down, almost fetal in position. 'What has happened to me, Mya?' He fell backwards into a seated position, tucking his knees up to his chin, then tapped his prosthesis and shook his head in despair.

Mya crouched down slowly. 'It's okay, we will figure this out.'

'How is it okay?' Brady gazed into the distance. 'They are going to hunt me down and kill everyone in their way.' He looked her in the eyes as his own began to well up. 'Everyone down here is suffering enough without me bringing the weight of MediTech down with me.'

Mya took Brady's hand and held it gently. 'He wasn't MediTech, babe.' She looked over at the corpse. 'If it was them, they would have sent an entire battalion.'

'Whatever, does it matter who it was? I'm still putting you all in danger.'

'We can handle this sort of thing.' She looked back at him, smiling. 'We're built to.'

'What about those guys?' Brady nodded towards the bodies of those who'd died defending the compound. 'They're dead because of me.'

Mya sat next to Brady, close enough that he could feel her warmth. She shuffled nearer, putting her arm around him.

'And they will be mourned, but nobody was expecting this. For all his faults, the one thing Benny can do is keep us all safe when he knows what he's up against.'

Brady began to calm as he leant his body into hers. 'You heard him. Why would he waste lives protecting me?'

'He'll come around. Right now, he's just scared for us, but he knows you're a fighter.'

Brady chuckled. He thought it was subtle enough that it would go amiss, but it piqued Mya's interest. He could see her look at him, studying him. The eye contact she made with him was enough to flush him out. If they had been playing poker, Mya would have just taken all of his money.

He felt her hand gently pull his face around to hers. 'If you know something,' she said, her finger stroking his cheek, 'you need to tell me. I can't help you if I don't know everything. You know you can trust me, right?'

He looked away, unable to maintain eye contact and dismiss her pleas. 'I can't.'

'You really don't trust me?' He looked back as she asked and Brady could see real hurt in her eyes. The way her brows furrowed, the way they softened.

'No, I do. Of course I do.' He placed his hand on her thigh, feeling intense chemistry, thinking to himself, *not the time*, so he moved it up to her shoulder. 'But I can't pull you further into my mess.'

'I can't get much further in.' She took hold of his hand and moved it back down towards her thigh. 'Whatever he is doing, he knows I'm involved now.' She had been lightly flirting with him for almost a year, but that was professional. This felt different to him.

Brady pulled his hand away. He couldn't deal with the feelings of wanting her, not in that moment. 'I know what it is.'

Mya's eyes widened. 'The technology?'

'It's a prototype. Regulates brain activity.'

'To do what?'

'I mean, I'm not sure of the details, essentially stops the body eating itself when the bio-tech starts taking over, I think.' Brady noticed the husk activity increasing in intensity up ahead. Getting up hurriedly, he dragged Mya with him. 'I think we need to move.'

Mya quickly assessed the threat. 'That intensity of gunfire scares them off.' She took Brady's hand and led him back towards the compound. 'But this prototype sounds like it could end the relentless torrent of their creation.'

'What do you mean?'

Mya doubled their pace. 'If that's what it does, I don't know. I think we need to tell Benny.'

'I thought we couldn't trust him?' Brady said, as he struggled to keep up.

'I trust him completely. No matter what he says, his first concern is always the protection of our people.' She weaved, leading in an odd pattern. 'Careful, mines.'

Brady, afraid of stepping on anything, traced her steps as if he were her own shadow, arm stretched out to keep a grip of her hand. Yes, but you said he may give me up to keep them safe, right?'

She continued a specific pattern, avoiding the mines that Brady could not see. 'If it was just some expensive piece of tech, sure, but that sounds like it could end the suffering of millions of people. He's not going to give that kind of technology away.'

'From what I understand, there's nothing that can be done with it. People have been trying.'

Mya gestured it was safe again as they closed in on the compound walls. 'What people?'

'The people I escaped from.'

'Who are they?'

'AntiFa, apparently.'

Mya paused. 'AntiFa? Are you serious? I thought they died with, whatever his name was, Joshua?'

Brady whipped his hand away from hers. 'You know Joshua?'

'I know of him.'

'What do you know about him?'

'Just that he fought MediTech.' Brady noticed Mya in sudden deep thought, as though she were calculating a difficult maths problem. 'He was some kind of superhuman.' Mya called up her system scan on her wrist display, programming in a close range scan. She began passing her wrist around her body, starting at her ankles.

He looked at her, curious about her actions. 'Are you okay?'

She continued scanning up her legs and around her midriff. 'Just had a thought. I saw Dan right before they let me know you were down here.' Twisting her arm, she tried to get a reading on her back.

'You think—' Brady was cut off by the beeping of Mya's scanner as she passed it around the back of her neck.

'That little...' She unzipped her jacket, took it off and handed it to Brady. 'Tracker.'

He watched as she began unbuttoning her shirt, feeling awkward in the moment. He was about to look away from her when he noticed her torso and the scar tissue around it. She was blasé about being watched, but picked up on the fact he had noticed.

She began bundling up her shirt before placing it on the ground and stepping back. 'We've all been in the wars.' From one of her trouser pockets, she pulled out a miniaturised stick grenade, pulled apart the two sliding sides and tossed it onto the shirt, stepping back and pulling Brady away with her. 'We aren't all super heroes like Mr Drummond.'

As the grenade detonated, creating a localised explosion, Brady handed Mya back her jacket. 'Yeah, so that was the prototype.'

'How do you mean?' she said, zipping herself back up.

'He had it before me. I've got his memories in my head, or something anyway. Other people's too.'

Mya's face dropped. 'I'm sorry, what?'

'Apparently I'm some kind of MediTech database. So that's fun.'

Looking behind, Mya spotted a couple of husks closing in on them. 'Okay, fill me in on the way back. There's a scientist in the compound who may have some insight into the tech, but let's not share this memory side with anyone just yet.' She hurried Brady towards the compound.

'What about Dan?'

On her wrist display, she entered the remote code to open one of the compound's secure doors. 'We'll come up with a plan for him.' She ushered Brady forward as the door opened. 'We'll just give him enough rope to hang himself.'

Brady studied the walls carefully as they approached the door. 'I don't know why you think these walls are going to stop anything.' He hammered on the thin metal sheet next to the security door. Among the sections of reclaimed material, patchwork quilt of unfit-for-purpose boundary, the door was like a heavy duty padlock on a piece of wet cardboard.

Mya pushed him through the door gently. 'That's just a facade. Underneath, the walls are pure Kevlar composite.' Inside, she turned Brady's attention to above his head. 'See that?' She pointed skywards at a suspended canopy. 'If we are ever under real threat, that comes down. From the outside, the whole compound looks like one big pile of debris.'

Mya led Brady towards Benito's villa in silence. He walked closely, not for support. He had finally got the hang of his new leg.

CHAPTER THIRTEEN

Dan's modular apartment was a mess. Remnants of food containers and dirty clothes littered the floor. His sofa looked like it hadn't been cleared in at least a year, and doubled as his bed. It would have taken him minimal effort to tidy up enough for the switch to the modular bedroom option, but even that was too much for him.

Though Dan had managed to amass enough credits to afford a windowed apartment, something thousands of people would have given anything for so they could have the illusion of sunlight, his shutters remained closed. The only light came from his wall display as it flashed a notification that if he wished to continue watching, he must request continued playback. Dan was slumped on the floor, leaning against his sofa on the precipice of toppling over. His face was as pale as a white sheet and his body shook with minute tremors. He was awake, barely.

His daze was broken by an incoming call. He had calls at home set to synch with his apartment's infotainment centre, and the volume set way up, so the ringing deafened him. He snapped to and answered, hoping it was good news. Struggling to find the energy, he squeaked out a tepid 'Hey.'

Nerea Moreno's voice boomed through his speakers, 'Put me on holo.' Her image appeared in front of him. She stood outside the Buena Cena restaurant in the dining district of level one hundred. It was a moderately affluent dining district, but she was dressed as though she were attending the finest restaurant in the city.

Her attire was a world apart from what he was used to. Usually clad in scruffy black, like she was permanently coming out of a

Lords of Djent concert, the fine dress was jarring.

She was a child of one of the last influx of immigrants allowed into Ranley during the last shortage of high level scientific workers. Her parents had emigrated from Spain, under the promise of high salaries and excellent working conditions. Nerea was seven when they arrived and twenty-one when her father broke under the strain of long hours and dwindling pay, and purposefully crashed his car with mother and child in tow. Nerea survived, her mother had not.

Failing to hide his disappointment, he feigned a smile. 'Oh, hey baby.'

Immediately, his opening line riled her Latin temperament. 'Don't you hey baby me.' She remembered she was in public, so brought her volume down a little. 'Do you know where I am?'

Dan tried to shake some life back into himself, and rubbed his face with both hands trying to buy himself time to think, but came up with nothing, 'No, should I?' He looked around the apartment floor, grabbing some of the closer detritus and attempting to hide them.

Nerea pressed her tongue forward into the back of her lips, forcing her lip piercing outwards, trying to stifle the anger she felt before responding. 'Unbelievable, la única cita organizamos en seis meses y estás demasiada absorta en ti misma para recordar siquiera, aquí estoy en um antro que reservaste llamado "Buena Comida", que, por cierto, no tendría que anunciarse como tal si realmente la tuviera. Y tú—'

Dan watched as the translated text appeared floating in front of Nerea as she switched from English to Spanish: *the one date we organise in four months and you are too self-absorbed to remember, here I am at some dive called Fine Dining, which, by the way, would not have to advertise itself as that if it actually was and you--*

Her pacey Spanish tirade alternated back to slower, calmer

English as the frustration subsided with the release. 'What is wrong with you?' Noticing how pale and sickly he looked, her anger took a back seat to concern. 'Are you sick?'

Dan scrunched up his eyes in the hope it would make his symptoms disappear. 'No, I'm just exhausted.'

'Don't lie to me. I can't help you if you lie to me, Dan.'

'I'm not lying babe, I just fell asleep. It's been a long week.'

'Why are you lying?' She shook her head in exasperation. 'You are sick, or you are on drugs. I am not stupid, I can see.'

Dan didn't know how to respond for a moment as his faculties struggled to keep up. 'Really? I'm just waking up. I've been non-stop for a week, doll.'

Nerea's eyes widened with anger once more. 'Don't call me doll! I hate when you call me doll! I am not a doll!'

Dan backtracked immediately, realising he was not sharp enough to sustain a fight. 'I'm sorry. Just give me one second. I'm putting you on hold.'

'Don't you—' Her holo projection froze as he put the call on hold.

Dan looked around frantically. Sliding his arm under the sofa, he pulled out a small box. Inside, his last hit of DoSe amphetamine. Dan was on the precipice of tech-poisoning and had been getting progressively worse for the past year. DoSe was the only thing keeping his body running as a bio-organism.

He looked at the auto-injector, painfully aware of the ramifications of not having one to fall back on and how it would balance against letting Nerea know he was vulnerable. He didn't love her and he knew she didn't love him, but he was acutely aware of how she would throw herself at him in an effort to help. As deep as the hole was in which he found himself, he could not drag her into it. His mind made up, he plunged the injector into his thigh, delivering the last rush of life he had.

As his functionality accelerated, he took the call off pause, immediately seeing Nerea, her face ready for a fight. 'Baby, I'm sorry. I had to go get some water on my head to wake up.' He smiled at her, hoping the refreshed sparkle in his eyes would placate her.

'Your hair is not wet.'

Just for a second, his cheerful facade faded, revealing his frustration that she did not believe him. 'I just splashed my face, I didn't wash my hair.' He doubled down, so determined to not let her have the upper hand, he even began to convince himself he wasn't lying.

Nerea gesticulated towards the sky. '¡Dios mio!' she said before bringing her attention back down to Dan. 'I can't do this anymore. I can't watch you blow yourself up with whatever is going on and try to hide from me.' She took a deep breath, steadying her emotions.

Dan was torn between two thoughts. 'Baby, no, we can talk about this.' He tried to buy himself time to work out what was going on in his head. He had wanted her to instigate a break-up for a few months now, but the moment he felt it coming, he wanted to hang on. He was like a child who'd lost interest in a toy until the moment someone tried to take it away. 'Come over baby, I'll make us some dinner.'

'You think I'm so stupid?' Her eyes rolled in time with the tut she let out. 'You're not going to talk me out of it.'

'No, not at all.' He said, smiling, 'I'm not going to talk you out of anything, I promise,' he said, and winked, 'but we should do this in person if that's what you really want, no?' As he got to the end of the sentence, his accent subtly mimicked the remaining twang of Spanish she had.

'Okay, fine, but only because I am no coward.' She hung up on him, leaving him to stew over his position. He had about fifteen days' worth of hormonal normality, then he would slump.

Dan had managed to get the single shot from his dealer for

providing his contact the information on Brady's whereabouts, one up front, twenty more when they had what they wanted. He had expected the delivery of the remainder of the drugs an hour ago, but the dealer didn't show. A sense of dread hit him. *If they didn't deliver, what happened to Brady?* He hadn't acknowledged it until that moment, such was the crushing despair of the doldrums he had been in since he crashed a few hours after he had seen Mya.

He worked through the scenario of resorting to black market synths, but given their two-day half-life and astronomical price tag, he knew it wasn't a viable solution for anything other than one-off desperation. His level of medical insurance wouldn't cover pharmaceutical vending machines, nor did it afford him access to a practitioner who had the authority to prescribe it. His contact was his only hope. He called Xiao, poorly codenamed as "X" in his contacts.

Dan had been given the ID of an underling, but had managed to use backdoor tracing to get a direct point of contact to Xiao himself. He knew it was a risky move, but he was beyond caring.

***

Mr Xiao ignored Dan's incoming call. He was presenting findings on his investigation into the latest Russian-Asian alliance's incursions into MediTech airspace to the military commanders of all territories. In attendance, sat in prime positions on the huge half-moon table, curved around Mr Xiao's podium, were Ranley's Airforce and Naval commanders along with Francesca. Holo projections of the commanders from New York, Los Angeles, Dallas, Chicago, Montreal, Winnipeg, Edmonton, Johannesburg, Melbourne, Brisbane, Perth and Wellington cities.

Behind Mr Xiao, huge holographic displays of strategic maps slid and rotated, with flashing pings of enemy activity and reams of data, from airspeed or knots, to ballistic range and trajectory. Xiao had the focus on the eastern seaboard of North America, pinched to zoom in on the central of three radar pings as he held the patience of the room whilst waiting for the incoming call to drop out.

'I'm sorry about the pause, ladies and gentlemen.' Turning his attention back to the display, he double tapped the radar ping to explode the technical data. 'As we can see, the bogey is a new Chinese Chengua V eighteen.' He called up the rendered model. 'Modified Russian Meerkats. Fusion propulsion, graphene body and a range of weapon systems, including short range electromagnetic pulse blast. We need to be aware that, unlike the seventeens, these have now developed directional EMP for tandem deployments.'

Xiao selected the flight path playback, and the ping began charting the movement, going quickly from offshore to the northernmost point of California. As it neared, the distance to threat number decreased, all the way from 3000 down to 1580.2 before rapidly heading back out to sea.

Xiao paused the playback. 'For those not paying attention, the bogey returned at the one thousand, five hundred and eighty point two. Zero point two miles outside of our current defensive capabilities.' He turned back to the display, selected the overlay of the defended zone and rewound the flight path until the two were almost overlapping. 'This is how close they came, which we all know is not a coincidence. They are letting us know they know. What we don't know is how they have learned of the increase in defensive distance so soon after the upgrade.' He overlaid the old defensive radius, a full fifty miles shorter. 'Three days this has been in place, and they are out there mocking us that the news has reached them already.'

Francesca stood abruptly. 'Cut to the chase, Xiao. There's a mole somewhere on our grounds and you all need to get your houses in order. Mr Xiao is going to explain our three-point plan to flush them out.' She paused, giving enough time for anyone in attendance to let their poker face slip. Seeing nothing she thought bore further notice, she slowly sat, gesturing for Mr Xiao to continue.

'Thanks Miss Braunschild. First and foremost, the plan is to work together. We can't be sure this is a problem only for Los Angeles and yourself, Francesca. Just because you are the first city to roll out the upgrade, doesn't mean we are pointing fingers here.' He shut down the map projections and pulled up a map of interconnectivity between cities, with thousands of nodes, all joined up in every manner of direction. To the untrained eye, it was a mess.

Xiao began rotating the map, trying to find the best angle to make his point, when his personal comms once again alerted him to another incoming call from Dan, throwing his train of thought. 'Excuse me again.' He shook his head in exasperation and embarrassment, holding the room's attention once more with a single raised finger. The call notification continued, growing in intrusiveness with each flash and ping. Xiao cancelled the call, but Dan rang back immediately. Three more times he cancelled, three more times Dan called back as Mr Xiao grew more and more impatient and frustrated. 'You'll have to excuse me for one moment.' He left the podium and began for the door out. 'I'll just be a few minutes, so talk among yourselves.' He faced Francesca, hands together, and bowed. 'I'm sorry Miss Braunschild, this may be an update.'

Dan finally got through. The scrambled image floated in his living room as he perched impatiently on the arm of his sofa. 'About time!'

Mr Xiao had extricated himself from the briefing room and found a server room, free of technicians. The buzz of the servers, he hoped, would prevent him from being overheard. 'How did you get this comms tag?'

'Don't worry about that, I need those amps.' He was hitting the peak of the up from the amphetamine. 'One up front, the rest after, you said.' His speech was frantic, his mouth drying.

'After the payload was in my possession,' he said and grimaced upon hearing Dan's teeth beginning to grind as the bruxism from the DoSe amphetamine phase began. 'And I neither have that, nor the patience to deal with your tweaking right now.' He peeked through the narrow window in the door to make sure nobody was nearby before raising his voice. 'Do not, ever, call me like this again, and do not mistake my abruptness as a sign that there will not be ramifications for the fact I do not have what I want.'

As Mr Xiao rejoined the briefing room, he could feel the inquisitive eyes of Francesca and the others burning a hole in him. 'Miss Braunschild, apologies.' In truth, they were no more invested in his return than they would be under normal circumstances, and the spotlight he felt was only intensified by his own guilty secret. 'Something I ate, I believe.' Xiao feigned stomach cramping, holding his gut and closing his eyes, though it was an effort to hide the reaction he had upon realising he had shared the last two meals with Francesca. Having ordered the same dishes, he panicked that he had given something away.

Francesca pondered for a moment, fingertips of both hands bridged together as her elbows rested on the surface in front of her. 'Must have been the stroganoff.' She paused, waiting for the response. Like Pavlov's dog, her audiences were conditioned to laugh at her jokes, no matter how poor. And they always were.

Those in attendance remained awkwardly quiet for a moment, none sure whether her comment was because she knew he had recently eaten stroganoff, or whether it was a poor attempt at a joke aimed at their Russian enemies. Ultimately, it was the naval commander of Melbourne that decided to gamble on it being a joke and broke the deadlock with a laugh. The uptake was slow to begin, but as more and more realised Francesca had intended her comment to be humorous, the room eventually filled with the crescendo of false laughter.

***

Still staring at the terminated call notification, Dan's eyes widened, and though his pupils were dilated from the DoSe, the reaction was a result of knowing Brady had clearly evaded capture. *What is it he knows?* Wrought with nerves and the amphetamine coursing through him, his leg juddered up and down on the ball of his foot. *Of course he knows... but what if he doesn't?* His mind raced. *X is going to kill me? What if X and Brady both try to kill me?* Each thought piggybacked on the last, leaving no room between. *Does Nerea know? Wait, Brady can't know it was me. Unless...* His face scrunched tight. *Mya! What if Mya found the tracker? She'll know it was me. So Brady knows. Everyone knows, man. What do I do?* The thoughts circled around and around, repeating and growing in pace, tormenting him like sharks circling.

CHAPTER FOURTEEN

Benito reclined in his wingback. The piece had been brought over by his great grandfather from Italy and Benito took great care to keep it looking good. The leather around the frame was perfect, well-kept and original, but this was a chair made for sitting on, not looking at. Benito had replaced the leather on the upholstery once already, and the mismatch was noticeable. Cow leather was a long-forgotten material to anyone aside from the elite, but Benito had done wonders with rat skin leather.

He tracked Mya's movements as she paced back and forth in front of his living room fireplace. Benito had reclaimed all the materials used inside his house, including the marble he had repurposed into his fireplace. Her mind swam in questions, examining why she had failed to see Dan had been a threat and how Benito would take the news about who Brady really was.

Benito leaned forward. 'This better be worth the wait.' He watched for Mya's response, but she was so far in her own world that she didn't hear. Feeling somewhere between embarrassment and indignation at being ignored, Benito settled into the armchair, creaking as he put his weight back into the leather.

He watched as Mya moved to his bookshelves and fingered the spines, taking as little actual interest in the titles as he had in ever reading them. He hadn't opened a single one since he had taken possession of them and wasn't sure, given their age, that the spines would be supple enough to not break even if he were interested in their contents.

'Did you say something?' she said, tearing herself away from the distractions and facing him.

Benito snorted in derision. 'Nothing I haven't said already.'

'Sorry, miles away. What's taking so long?'

Benito stood, and the leather worked itself back into its natural position. 'Doc takes his time, but he's thorough.'

On cue, the carved wooden door opened as Brady walked in. Benito watched him, carefully taking in every detail of Benito's living room as though he were in a museum. For the first time since the surgery, he had worked out how to walk in synch with his prosthetic. Benito saw Mya smile. Though, it didn't last long when she saw the seriousness on the face of Doc Fisher following Brady in.

The Doc had abandoned his official duties almost forty years ago after returning from the front lines of Central Africa. The callous manner in which the battle weary had been treated jaded him enough to risk the ramifications of abandoning his post, which, given his insight into the military tactics employed, carried a death sentence.

In the years since, Doc had cultivated the drinking habit that afforded him the courage to extract himself from the city and take up home below. He worked slow because that's the only way he knew how to compensate for the nerve damage the drinking had done. The one facet of his job he had never learned how to handle was delivering bad news. Benito knew this from Doc's avoidance of eye contact. The signs were always the same.

Mya closed up to Brady to whisper, though Benito could hear clearly enough. 'Everything okay?' Brady nodded to assure her.

'Someone say something.' Benito bent, leant and pivoted to try to catch the Doc's line of sight, who evaded him with ease. 'Brady, what's the deal? As he asked, he turned his attention.

'Bad news.' Brady's feigned look did nothing to fool Benito. 'I've got three months to live.'

Unimpressed, Benito stared down Brady. 'I need some answers soon before I lose my temper and I make that prediction accurate.'

Mya gestured for Benito to ease up. 'Doc, what have you

seen?'

Benito fixated on Doc as he brought up the notes on his HUD, flipping pages with blinks of his eyes, right forwards, left back. He scanned through multiple pages, finding his first point of interest. 'I cannot be certain, but I believe we are looking at some form of interaction between the hypothalamus and the outer membrane which is regulating the body's responses to pathogens,' He moved forward through a few more pages, looking for the next note.

'Doc.' Benito grabbed Doc and pulled him to face him directly, allowing no chance for evasion of eye contact. 'Let's pretend I'm not a medical practitioner and be clear with me.'

Doc pulled himself away. 'Mr Drummond has, in layman's terms...' he said and backed away to create some distance, 'a device regulating how his immune system reacts to foreign bodies.'

Mya placed her arm around Brady's shoulder and shepherded him towards the exit. 'Let's leave them to it. I think you could probably use a break.'

Benito watched as they left. 'Don't go far.'

'Like I have a choice,' Brady said.

'We will be in the tub.' Mya opened the door for Brady and showed him through.

Benito turned back to the Doc. 'Carry on.'

'Normally, in a first-time amputee, we would see an immune response to fight the prosthesis where it joins the flesh, but Mr Drummond's immune response is nowhere to be seen.'

'So, if he doesn't have a functioning immune system, he actually is dying, or what?'

'Far from it. There appears to be nothing wrong with his immunology, per se. It's actively being regulated to accept bio-tech without recognition.'

Benito's face blanked. 'I don't understand Doc. What does any of it mean?'

The Doc switched away from his report. Benito could tell he was beginning to relax. 'Whilst I was in the system, there were reports about prototype technology that had been developed centuries ago which eliminated the body's response, which causes tech-poisoning.' He paused, holding Benito's attention. 'I think that is what we are looking at.'

Benito pondered the meaning of what he was being told. He was caught between two predominant notions. One, that the tech must be worth enough to fund extensive help for his flock, the other, whether this technology could be used to cut out the middleman. 'Are you sure?'

'As sure as I can be. I've never seen a body just sit back and allow itself to be invaded.'

'Does he know?'

'I can't read minds. Let's just say he didn't seem surprised when I told him.'

Benito considered the fact both Brady and Mya must have been aware. It explained their behaviour towards him. 'So what's the play, Doc?'

'I'm not sure what you mean.'

'What can we do with this?' Benito walked to the fireplace and stared in. 'Can it help us?'

'In what way?'

'Can we replicate?'

Benito allowed the Doc time to come up with an answer without pressing.

'MediTech couldn't even replicate it.' The way Doc nervously responded made Benito suspicious, but now wasn't the time to press. 'Even their latest immunosuppressive technology wasn't perfect. I fitted a few, but they were bandages, not cures.'

Benito turned away from the fireplace. 'So what? This is a one-off?'

'As far as I can tell, it was a happy accident.'

Benito inhaled a huge breath. 'So this is really valuable to them?' He knew the answer already. The real question, he asked himself, was whether the payout would be worth the damage it could cause.

***

Down in Benito's first basement level, Mya had taken Brady to the bathing room. The hot tub water bubbled and popped around his neck as Brady fought the urge to fall asleep. The hollow wall surroundings had been set to replicate a tropical island, and Brady let the sounds of the lapping ocean lull him into deeper relaxation. Chirping of bird song seemed to speak out his name and tell him to let the warmth of the water take him away.

Mya perched at the edge of the large hot tub, her trousers rolled up and legs dipped in up to her knees. 'I'm not a lifeguard, you know.'

Brady snapped out of the relaxation that had dragged his chin underwater, choking and spluttering up the amount he had nearly swallowed.

Mya laughed. 'What did I just say?'

Brady coughed, trying to shift the tickle in his throat. 'I think I just fell asleep.'

'I know you did, hun.'

'I think this is the first time I've felt relaxed in days.' He sat upright, lifting his torso out of the water and noticed Mya looking over the bruises and lacerations. He smiled at her to let her know he was okay.

'Must be my influence,' she said, playfully giggling.

Brady attempted a suave wink, but it came off more like an involuntary spasm. 'I'm not saying it isn't.' His voice croaked.

Mya playfully kicked water up at Brady. 'Well, at least some good has come from my post.'

He looked up at her. 'Oh yeah, I keep forgetting I was just a job to you.' Instantly he realised that he could've come across patronising so lightened it with a chuckle.

He felt the lightest of clips around the back of his head. 'Don't be mean,' said Mya.

'Me mean? I've just been through hell and you're out here hitting me.' He looked back at her and stuck out his tongue.

'You know you weren't just part of my job, right?' she said.

'I know, I know. I still don't get it though. How can anyone afford to gamble here?' He sunk back into the water, fully submerging himself for a moment before lifting his face out again.

'They can't afford not to. How do you think we afford anything?' She rested her foot on his head lightly.

'Are you going to drown me if I get the answer wrong?' Brady let her foot sit there. She had no pressure on him.

'Maybe!' She raised an eyebrow.

'Why don't we assume I got it right, but you just confirm it for me.'

She lifted her foot away. 'Everyone gambles on the black market just to earn enough credits to buy the basics that we can't forage for. We pool together and once a month, I or another one like me goes and buys up all we can. It's never enough, but it's something.'

Brady lifted himself out of the water to his waist and walked to Mya and, standing between her legs, he placed his hands on her thighs. 'So you really are an angel, then?'

For a moment, they stared at each other, not saying a word. Brady could feel the tension rise to the point he could not take it. Clearing his throat, he broke eye contact and moved away. A quick glance back and he could see Mya looking confused.

'I'm no angel,' she said.

'Sounds like it to me,' said Brady, as he settled into a seated position opposite Mya.

'I just do what needs to be done.' She stretched out her leg, but Brady was just out of reach.

'That's more than I've ever done.' He lifted his prosthetic foot up to hers, placing them sole to sole. He had forgotten about his leg, and when he saw the juxtaposition between the two he withdrew it again.

'You'll get used to it,' said Mya, smiling at him.

'The leg, or not doing anything?'

'You can do something about one of those,' said Mya as she shrugged.

Brady reached forward and grabbed her ankle. He looked at her for a moment, and could tell she knew what he was about to do, and he was just waiting to see how annoyed she would be. She didn't react. It was Brady's cue. He pulled at her leg, dragging her into the water with a soft splash.

They two were close. Chest to chest, looking at each other but not moving.

'I didn't mean that.' Mya chuckled playfully.

'I know what you meant,' said Brady. He edged closer.

The tension built. They locked eyes. Brady's heart began racing. His stomach felt like it was in a spin cycle. But he wasn't going to back down this time. He took her by the waist, giving it a moment to see if she would pull back. She didn't.

Brady was about to pull her close when he heard the creak of the door opening. Looking up, he saw Benito with little but a towel wrapped around his waist.

'Well well, Mr Drummond.' He sauntered over, eyeing up Mya. 'Or should I say, enemy of the state?' As he reached the hot tub, he leaned over the edge and placed a hand in the water. 'What are we going to do with you?'

Mya tracked his movements. 'So what did the Doc say?'

Benito smiled and shook his head. 'Oh no angel, you first.' He cupped his hands together in the tub and threw the contents into Mya's face. 'You know I don't like secrets.'

Brady felt uneasy, not knowing whether Benito was messing with Mya or dead serious. He saw her tense up, ready to react, but clearly she thought better of it. 'And sometimes we need to wait for all the evidence before we spread rumours.' She wiped the water from her face, over-dramatically flicking it away as though she were disgusted by it.

'It's not really her secret to tell, anyway.' Brady raised himself out of the water, holding back his shoulders to enlarge his chest.

Benito chuckled, looking him up and down like he was nothing. 'You know, I'm not sure about you.' He stood tall, mirroring Brady.

A lopsided smile drew across Brady's face. 'I guess the feeling is mutual.'

Mya stood to interrupt. 'Enough!'

Both Brady and Benito smiled. Brady found her authoritative stance overriding their bravado amusing. He relaxed himself, sitting down on the lip of the tub, and began running his finger over the seam between his thigh and the prosthetic knee and lower leg. The Doc had done the best he could with old tech, but the skin tones were vastly mismatched. He was still impressed with the join, as his fingertips traversed between his own skin and the grafted synth-skin. Tactilely, he struggled to notice the transition.

Benito made his way to the room's control system, awakening the interactive holo-display and changing the background setting from tropical paradise to Tuscan hills. The projections changed all around, right up to the edge of the swimming pool, giving the illusion of an infinity pool peaking over miles and miles of olive and orange groves and succulent vineyard, all sinking away then climbing again towards a picturesque hilltop town. Directly in the centre of which, the peak of the town church's bell tower rose tall above the other buildings.

'Where are we now?' Brady asked, taking in the new view.

Benito gazed out towards the town, unfolding his towel and tossing it to the tiles. 'Home.' He checked the knot in the chord of his bathing trunks. 'Sinalunga, specifically.' He sighed heavily, taking up position at the edge of the pool. His toes curled around the edge of the tiles, the water rippling over them before he dove in. His entrance wasn't neat, the splash big enough to bridge the gap between pool and hot tub, reaching both Brady and Mya.

Brady was confused. He waited for Benito to finish his submerged swim of one full length until he casually paddled back, facing the ceiling. 'This isn't home?'

'This is where I live, sure. But that is where I'm from.'

Mya shook her head. 'You were born here, Benny.'

He reached the edge of the pool and leaned on the side, just enough to support himself. 'My heart will always belong there.'

'Your parents were born here,' she said.

Mya turned her attention from Benito back to Brady as he slid back into the tub and submerged himself.

'It doesn't matter, it's in my blood,' said Benito.

Brady rose from the water, and squeezed the wet from his hair as he slicked it back over his head. 'So why don't you go back?'

Benito looked at him, clearly puzzled. 'I can't just go back.'

'Well, obviously not there. It's not there anymore.'

Benito pulled himself out a bit more. 'What do you mean, *not there*?' Crossing his arms on the pool's coping, he rested his chin on them. 'You don't buy that line, do you?'

'Are you telling me you believe it still looks like that?' Brady gestured to the rolling hills and bountiful yield of fruits.

Brady heard the alert of an incoming call on Mya's comms panel as she stood out of the hot tub. 'I'll leave you boys to it.'

Benito snapped his fingers to get her attention. 'Woah, don't go anywhere.'

Brady could tell she was irritated by his demeaning gesture. 'Layne's calling.'

Benito kicked off from the poolside, shooting backwards through the water. He shouted, 'Bring him back here.' Mya nodded and left.

'I bet none of that is there now.' Brady lifted himself out of the hot tub and, stepping wet footprints across the tiled floor, headed to the pool.

Gently propelling himself on his back, Benito distanced himself from Brady. 'There's no wasteland out there, kid. It's all smoke and mirrors.'

'How's that possible?' Brady asked as he prepared himself to dive in. 'Ever heard of World War Three? The nuclear fallout?'

Benito laughed. 'It didn't happen like you think.' He watched as Brady dove in, splashing heavily and sending a wave his way.

Brady carried on underwater as the displacement lapped over the pool edge, disrupting the holographic rendering. As he neared the three-quarter length mark, he could feel himself struggling to hold his breath. But he was determined to match Benito's underwater length. He kicked furiously, without rhythm as he tried desperately to reach the end. He felt his chest tighten as he reached out to feel the wall, then surfaced with a gasp. The holograph settled with the calming of the water, but as Brady held himself on the edge, he interfered with it from knitting together. The image of the edge of the infinity pool bowed across his torso.

'How did it happen, then?' He did his best to hide the struggle he had just been though, gently pushing away from the edge and treading water, allowing the holo image to settle.

'Do you know how big the world is?' Benito grinned at Brady, gently swirling his arms back and forth to keep himself steady. 'There wasn't enough nuclear payload to turn the whole thing into ash.'

'I've seen the footage.' Brady began to get on top of his breathing again, the tightness in his chest fading.

Benito scoffed. 'You believe we are in Italy right now, too?'

'Oh come on.' Brady spread out his body and laid back, allowing buoyancy to keep his mouth and nose above water. 'What would they have to gain by faking a scorched earth?' Some water breached his mouth and he gently spat it back out in an arc.

Out of the corner of his eye, Brady could just see the look on Benito's face. 'Of course, it's much easier to control a population when they have freedom of movement.'

'You honestly believe they went to all this effort to build these cities just to stop people moving around?'

'Of course,' said Benito. 'That and stopping the spread of information from outside the colonies.'

Brady reverted back to treading water. 'So you're telling me there's land out in the European Union that's undisturbed by the war?'

Benito pointed to the walls. 'I'm telling you there's more than likely land on our own doorstep that's undisturbed by war.'

'That's ridiculous,' Brady said as he began swimming back to the edge of the pool.

Benito began following, switching to breast stroke. 'You think that's more ridiculous than penning everyone in before these nuclear strikes started happening?'

Brady reached the side and hauled himself out, sitting on the side with his legs still in the pool. Water ran off his body and pooled where he was sat. 'They saw the threat coming, I guess. Isn't that what intelligence is for?'

As Benito reached the side, he grabbed on, holding himself in place. 'You honestly believe they had military intelligence of an impending nuclear war five decades, maybe a century before it happened?'

Brady lifted his legs up to the water surface, comparing toes between his real foot and the prosthetic. 'That's—' He paused as he noticed the prosthetic toes were much faster and finely controlled than those on his real foot. 'Uh, that's kind of my point.'

'Okay, tell me this.' Benito pulled himself across the poolside, closer to Brady. 'You just came from outside the city walls, right?'

'Uh, yeah.'

'How's that radiation exposure treating you?' He watched Brady's face as the penny dropped. 'You know, the one that will kill us all if we weren't protected by the city perimeter super collider producing all that quark-gluon plasma blocking out the radiation? You see anything like that out there?'

'Oh my god.' Brady had become so engulfed in the conversation, he had forgotten the tension between the two and the bass in his voice had been lost to the upwards inflections of curiosity. 'Wait, what about the land?'

'What about it?'

'I saw it. It's a wreck out there.'

'Convenient, it all happened so close to the boundary, isn't it?'

'What about all the craft?'

'You honestly think if they could make it that close to the city, the city would still be here?'

'Obviously, the defences worked.'

Benito laughed. 'Obviously the duplicity worked!'

'Alright, so you are telling me, beyond all that carnage, there is fertile land?'

Benito lifted himself out of the pool. 'Guarantee it.'

'Seen it?'

'Don't need to. Wouldn't get far if I tried.' He picked up his towel and headed for the showers.

'What?' Brady stood to follow him. 'Just walk out.'

Benito hung his towel on the rack by the shower. 'You don't think anyone has tried?' The clear glass turned opaque as he shut and locked the door behind him. Over the noise of the shower, he shouted, 'Two miles out, boom!' He thumped the wall of the shower to emphasise the point. As Brady neared the showers, he was startled by the noise.

'Answer me this then.' Brady sealed himself into the adjacent shower and set the high pressure jets to "cool massage." 'If there is no wasteland out there, why are we all eating synth garbage?'

'You got me there,' said Benito. 'Lots of theories, and could be any number of reasons.'

'Like what? It's gotta be cheaper to grow stuff than synthesise it.'

'Not for everyone.'

'Well no, not if you've got a hydroponic farm underground, but if they've got nature on their side—'

'Maybe the whole thing is just part of their ruse,' he continued shouting after he shut down his shower, 'or maybe it's all part of a bigger plan.' Benito exited the shower, grabbed his towel and wrapped it around his waist.

Through the opaque privacy panel of his shower, Brady could see Benito's silhouette, along with two more people. He stood on tiptoes to clear the opaque panel and could just see the top of Mya's head. Just behind her, a man he hadn't met before. *Must be this Layne guy,* he thought.

'Benny,' Layne greeted him, eyeing him up, down, then winked. 'You've got a guest with a story?'

Having not noticed Brady peering over the top, Benito gestured to the other shower. 'In there.' He leaned his head into Brady's shower door to shout through. 'Meet me in the games room, two doors down on the left when you're done.' With that, he slapped the door twice with the palm of his hand and ushered Mya and Layne out. Just before he left, he shouted back, 'Take whatever clothes you want in the changing rooms.'

CHAPTER FIFTEEN

In neatly pressed trousers and shirt, Brady walked into Benito's games room. Immediately, he felt the musty aroma of old wood, rope and leather. It hung heavily in his nostrils, almost suffocating him. It was unlike anything he had experienced before, so he took in a deep breath, held it, then let it go. His eyebrows furrowed, taking a few shorter, sharp sniffs of the imposing aroma.

Benito's games room was a page right out of old English pub history. In the centre, a freshly racked snooker table was illuminated by the huge hanging light. The balls were pristine, and they reflected the glow of the lamps. The bar was full of empty bottles in optics and brass beer pumps, all for show.

Before taking too much else in, Brady watched as Mya threw the last of three darts at the board, its flight wobbling in the air as it flew. Her eyes widened in anticipation of finally hitting the treble twenty. The tip of the final dart clattered against her previous two marker darts that had sat high of the treble twenty. Her final throw, agonisingly close, fell to the ground. She dropped her head. Mya opened her wrist panel as she drudged to collect the darts. She played with a couple of settings before taking position at the oche. Zero thought, zero aim, she launched them, one, two, three. She had thrown the third before the thud of the second dart had landed. The final dart brushed the flights of the previous two, nestled in tightly to a perfect one hundred and eighty.

Brady turned his attention to Benito and Layne, who were perched by the bar. Benito was savouring a glass of red wine he had made himself whilst Layne tinkered with the rifle Mya had recovered from the attacker.

Almost everything was foreign to Brady, from the darts board to the snooker table and all the old paintings and twentieth century posters. He grabbed Mya's attention, nodding towards Layne.

'Layne, I guess?'

Layne scrunched his face up but didn't lose focus on the weapon. 'I can see the first thing he needs upgrading is his charm.'

Benito swirled the wine in his glass, pinching his mouth at the bitter taste before setting the glass down. 'Brady, this is Layne. He's our...' Brady could see him struggle. 'What are we calling you these days?'

Layne pulled some wires through from the stock of the gun, ripping them out and discarding them. 'Gopher.'

'Pain in the ass,' Mya said before laughing, then taking aim with her next round of darts.

Brady sarcastically grinned, hopping up onto the edge of the snooker table. He sat, legs unable to touch the floor, and ran the palm of his hand on the soft felt surface of the table.

'Brady, I'll cut to the chase.' As Benito took another mouthful of his wine, he struggled to swallow and tipped the remains of the glass down the bar drain. 'I've spoken to Doc and Mya.' He began approaching Brady. 'Putting it all together, I can see we are in a bit of a predicament.'

'We?' Brady grabbed the nearest ball, the yellow, and bounced it off the cushion back into his hand repeatedly. 'Or me?'

Benito leaned on the table edge. 'One way or another, it affects us all.'

Brady launched the yellow ball down the table, narrowly missing the pack of reds. 'Isn't up to me who this affects?' He watched the ball returning, trying not to move his hand, hoping it would return perfectly.

Benito stopped the ball before it reached Brady's hand. 'I'd say it was more down to fate.' He took aim for the pack and rolled the yellow into them with force; the balls smacked and scattered around the table.

Mya retrieved the darts from the board again and walked over to the table. 'Where else are you going to go, hun?'

He looked at her, then at the scattered balls, staring at the way they reflected what had happened to his life. 'Honestly, I don't know.'

Benito took a cue from the rack on the wall and chalked it. 'You and I both know you are worth a lot.' He leaned over the table and lined up the cue ball with a red in the opposite corner. 'So you know the fact you are still here means we aren't interested in cashing in.' He struck the ball as he finished speaking, sending a perfect shot and sinking the red, holding the cue ball firm to line up with a shot on the black.

'You've got a home here, Brady.' Mya spun around sharply and launched all three darts across the room from the tight angle. Two hit the bullseye, one fractionally outside.

Brady watched on, amazed at her accuracy from that distance and angle. 'Nice throw.' He looked around the room, drew a deep breath and said, 'I can't stay here though.'

Benito lined up the black, rolling the cue ball gently. 'Why not?' The black dropped over the edge of the pocket just as it was about to run out of steam. Benito had already walked around to retrieve the ball by the time it went in. 'I can't promise you a manor like this, but we have a fine range of tents.' He polished the black before setting it back down in place.

Layne clicked the last piece of the reassembled rifle back together. 'All at a discount price, too.' He cocked the high velocity barrel, and pulled the trigger to a satisfying click. 'There we go.' He hopped down from the stool and headed to join the others at the table. 'One assault rifle, complete without traceable software.' He handed the gun to Brady.

'What's this for?'

'Figure you might need it.'

Brady took the rifle in hand, trying to find a comfortable way to hold it. 'Uh, thanks, I guess.' He studied the switches and touch panel, noticing the I/O port next to it. 'Didn't get anywhere close to killing me, but my being here got others killed.' He lay the gun down on the snooker table cloth. 'That's why I can't stay here.'

Mya nudged the gun back towards him. 'That's why you have to stay.'

'Benito and his mansion aside,' said Brady, winking at Benito, 'everyone here is suffering enough.'

'Isn't that speaking volumes?' said Layne. 'We've been suffering perfectly fine on our own. What makes you think you're going to make us any better at it?'

Benito towered over the cue ball, aiming downwards at it as he looked up at Brady. 'You resent my home?' he asked, before striking at the ball, curving it around the muzzle of the rifle to a red beyond, dropping it in the pocket. 'You know, I built this all myself, with materials I reclaimed, myself.' He chalked the cue and lined up his next shot on the black. 'See, everything that's been put together here is temporary, even this house. Anyone comes down here looking for us...' he said as he stroked the black into the pocket next to Mya, who picked out the ball and placed it back for him, 'we pack it up and move.

'You just—' Brady said, before pausing to think 'Move this house?'

'Nope, we pack up everything else.' He took his next shot, easily sinking a red and lining up on the pink back to the pocket by Mya. 'This house is rigged to blow.' The pink went in and Mya replaced it on the table. As he moved to his next shot, he chalked the cue again. 'See, I'm willing to sacrifice everything for what we have.'

'So why not me?'

'That's the interesting thing, Mr Drummond.' He knelt down

and closed one eye, working out the next shot. 'If someone had asked me just a few days ago, whether I would sell a human commodity up the river for the good of us all,' he said as he found his angle and leaned over the table, stretching and lifting one leg up on the cushion, 'I'd have said, without hesitation.'

Brady waited for the shot. 'What's changed?' As the cue ball was about to strike the target ball, Brady lifted the red out of the way, causing Benito's shot to bounce off the cushion to nowhere.

As Brady placed the red back where it was, Benito chuckled softly. 'Now I know what I'm dealing with,' he said as set down the cue on the cloth. Brady had seen to it that his break was over. 'It's clear we could use you here.'

Brady stood up sharply, angered by the sentiment of yet another group of people wanting to use him. 'I'm not a tool!' His instinct was to grab snooker balls and launch them in anger, but as he reached, he saw Mya. Awkwardly, he stopped himself, then let out a build-up of frustration in a primal roar.

Brady noticed his scream had put the three at odds. 'Hey, calm down,' Benito said, gesturing and angering Brady further.

'Don't tell me to calm down!' He stormed around the table towards Benito, who backed away in the opposite direction, using the table as a barrier. 'I swear, if one more person tells me they've got plans for me, I'm putting a gun to my head and blasting this damn thing out myself!'

As Benito and Brady played cat and mouse around the table, Mya stepped in Brady's path. 'Nobody here wants to tell you how to live your life.'

Brady's touch paper had been lit. 'What do you know?' he screamed in her face, backing her up. 'Try talking to me when you find out you're just a glorified carry case.' He pushed his finger towards her face. 'Then come back and tell me nobody is trying to make me live my life like they want!'

Stunned by his turn, Mya looked scared and he could see it. He knew she was stronger and faster than him. He had seen that much himself. He could feel her attitude towards him shifting. In truth, he projected his fear through her. Regardless, he needed to reel himself back in.

'I'm sorry.' He began backing away, hands creating a barrier between them to show he meant no threat. 'I'm still processing everything.' Letting out a deep breath, he calmed. 'I've not even come to terms with the fact that what I thought was my career is gone...' He paused and leaned on the table. 'Let alone piecing together everything else.'

'I know, it's a lot.' Benito spoke softer than usual. 'Maybe I misspoke. When I say we can use you down here, I mean, you'd be good to have around. In whatever way that goes.' Layne looked at Benito, confused as to what he was saying.

Brady stood up straight. 'You mean you don't have grand plans for me?'

'We live as free as we can here.' Mya walked up to Brady and put her hand on his shoulder. 'You don't have to be anything you don't want to be.'

Layne snapped his head around to Mya. 'What are you two saying?' His face had scrunched up with the question. 'He's a super weapon, not a sous chef.'

Benito stared down Layne. 'Layne!' He grabbed his attention and Brady could see him mouth to Layne to stop. 'We don't dictate who anyone wants to be here.'

Layne relaxed himself. 'Sorry. I'm just emotional, is all. I saw Joshua in action. I know you've got him in you, but Benny is right, ain't my place.'

'You're one of us if you want to be, Brady.' Benito walked around the table to him. 'Whatever that means to you, we'll have your back.'

Brady took a moment, breathing deeply to steady his nerves. 'Look, it's not that I don't want to help, I can see you need it.' He put his hand on top of Mya's, still on his shoulder. 'I just don't know how to be that help.' The emotions he had been holding down had risen beyond the surface, and he began crying.

'It's okay hun.' Mya took him in her arms, pulling his head into her chest. 'You don't have to be anything you aren't comfortable with.'

Through teary eyes, Brady saw Layne point towards Brady and look at Benito. He saw Benito shake his head, telling him not to say whatever he was thinking, but it was too late. 'This is our big hope?' said Layne.

Brady looked up from Mya's chest at Layne, his eyes red and teary. He wanted to respond but choked up before any words could come out. Mya snarled at Layne. 'That's not helpful!'

Benito intensified his look to Layne, who acknowledged and backed down. 'Ignore Layne, he's just frustrated.' He patted Brady on his back. 'There's no pressure.'

'Let me handle this.' Mya nodded to Benito, demanding he give her the chance. 'Give us the room, guys.'

Benito nodded back then turned to Layne. 'Let's go.' He grabbed his arm and dragged him outside, leaving Brady and Mya alone.

With her arm firmly around his shoulder, Mya led Brady to the sofa booth in the corner of the room, sat him down, and slid in next to him. Brady tried to rub away his tears. Elena had brought him up to hide his emotions. She had always told him a man must be strong above all else. It had never made sense to him. He never understood why a man couldn't be vulnerable. Yet, she had repeated her mantra enough that it had stuck, and in that moment, nearly two decades of pent up emotion welled up through him and out his eyes.

He sucked in a few breaths, just enough to get in a few words, 'I'm sorry, it's pathetic.'

Mya gently took hold of his chin and turned his face towards her. 'Hey, it's not pathetic. You've been through hell. Lesser people would've broken down long before this.'

He found comfort in both her words, and her eyes, 'I just...' He couldn't control the sobbing any longer. 'I don't know who I am anymore.' Brady took a few deep breaths to try to control the tears, blowing out the anxiety on each exhale before drying his eyes on his sleeves.

'Let me tell you something most people don't ever figure out.' She spoke softly and quietly, scooting closer into him until she was all but whispering. 'Nobody really ever knows who they are, they just know how they feel in a moment.'

'How do you mean?'

'Human consciousness. It's only ever a sliver of a second. We all are malleable to the surrounding stimuli.' She placed her hand on his thigh. 'We are all just reactions in a moment, and once it has gone, so is that person who you were when you reacted.' Mya pulled Brady's head into her shoulder, gently kissing the top of his head.

'I don't think I follow.' Brady nestled in happily, feeling the warmth of her kiss on his scalp.

'Everyone thinks they are the sum of their past, but that's all just muscle memory. It's not real. You ever feel like you're a different person depending on who you are with, what you are doing?'

'I guess.'

'So it's like that. That's all the self ever is, how you react to the moment. Everything that has happened to you may run in your head telling you to be a certain way, but it's only the present moment of consciousness that lets the thoughts change them.'

Brady struggled with the concept, but liked hearing her speak softly, close to him. 'Yeah, I see what you mean.' His brows furrowed out of sight of Mya.

'Everything that has happened to you, has still happened, and none of it exists, so you can choose to let it shape who you are in the moment, or move on understanding you're only ever a product of the moment.'

Brady paused for thought. He couldn't tell if what she was saying was starting to make sense, or if he just wanted her to keep close. 'I guess I just don't know who I want to be, then.'

'Just trust your instinct in each moment and be who your heart tells you to be.' She lifted up his head and looked deep into his eyes. 'You don't need to let anything define you other than your heart.' Mya placed her hand on his chest.

Brady felt a thousand weights lift away as he looked at her. 'My heart is only saying one thing right now.'

Mya leaned in. 'So listen to it.'

The two grew closer until they felt the other's lips against their own. For a split second, Brady wished he didn't have tear stains down his cheeks and puffy eyes, but the thought passed quickly, returning to the moment. As the kiss began to turn from gentle to passionate, the chemistry between the two upped in intensity. They had begun to lose themselves in the moment when Mya remembered Benito and Layne were not going to give them very long and she pulled back.

Brady worried he had done something wrong, but her smile placated any feelings of rejection he had. She wiped away the tear stains on his cheeks with her thumbs, brought his head down to her mouth and kissed him on the forehead.

'That's a good start.' She smiled coyly. 'But you still need to figure out what you want going forward.'

'What choice do I have, really?'

'There's always a choice hun, you just have to work out which ones are worth consideration.'

'I'm not stupid, I mean, I've seen enough to know things need to change, but—' He hesitated, 'I don't know. AntiFa are trying to tell me I can help them take down the machine, and that's all well and good, but if it didn't make a difference with Joshua, why would I be different?'

She squeezed his hand tightly. 'Don't compare yourself to anyone.'

'No, I know. I guess I mean, they are so focused on long term that they are blind to right now.'

Mya slid away, creating room, before tapping her hand on her lap. Brady recognised the opportunity and pivoted around, laying on the sofa with his head on her thighs, staring up intently at her face.

'The future doesn't exist, there's only now.' She began stroking his head. His eyes grew heavy.

'Exactly. I come down here and see just how bad you guys have it. Well, not you guys, but you know what I mean.'

As her fingers caressed the contours of his face, Brady closed his eyes, though his eyeballs continued tracking the movement of her fingers through feel alone.

'I know, hun.'

'For as long as I'm alive, with this thing in my head, I'm on borrowed time. I may not know much about what's real and what I've been taught, but I know that much.' He opened one eye just enough to make out Mya. He could see her gazing into the distance with a forlorn look on her face. 'Wherever I go, whatever I do, I'll put people in danger. Maybe it's just easier to disappear completely and put an end to all of this.' As he said that, he closed his eye again and he felt the rise and fall of Mya's lap as she took a deep breath.

'That's an option,' she said. 'You can run. Take it to your grave.' As she spoke, he felt tears dripping onto his face.

Brady opened his eyes and sat upright. Mya's tears had been coming thick and fast. He pulled her around, lifting her legs up onto the sofa and pulling her in close. He took her legs and made them straddle him, before bringing her in even further. They were face to face. Tear to tear.

'On the other hand, they already know you are here, right? Already know I've been here.'

Mya croaked as she spoke. 'We have to assume that.'

'So really, I've already put you in jeopardy?'

'I don't see it that way, but okay.'

'So really, what is the outcome? I stay, they come, we fight, people die, eventually they will win. But, maybe there's another way.'

'And that is?'

'Back at AntiFa... okay, bear with me.' He motioned to get up, but Mya was blocking his path.

'Where are you going?'

Nowhere, just standing up.' His reassurance was enough for her to move her leg that prevented him standing. Brady walked to the snooker table and picked up two balls, the pink and one red. 'Back at AntiFa, I found out I'm not totally alone.' He headed back towards Mya, tapping the two balls against each other. 'This Joshua guy, right? They have a construct of his personality back at their base.'

Mya swung her legs around to the ground and leaned forwards. Her tears began to abate. 'And?'

'And it communicates with me. Or—' He paused. 'It recognises his thought patterns in the chip. Or something. Either way, I can talk with his memories.'

Mya looked puzzled. 'Where are you going with this?'

Brady began circling the balls around each other. 'It said it needs a specific brain pattern in a new host. So, I'm thinking.'

Mya stood. 'Thinking what, exactly? You want to make this someone else's problem?'

Brady stopped spinning the balls and looked at her. 'Yeah. Well, no, not someone. Something, though.'

Mya shook her head, blank-faced. 'I don't understand.'

Brady handed her the red ball. 'So that ball, that's one of the husks. There's gotta be one out there that matches the profile. And this ball,' he said and held his up hand, 'is me. We take the implant outta my head—' He tapped his ball against hers. 'And put it in the husk. You know, once we find one.' She hadn't noticed, but Brady had swapped the two balls around. He held the red and Mya, the pink.

'Then what?'

'Look at the husk again.' He motioned to her hand.

'What? So now I have you? I don't get it.'

Brady walked back to the snooker table. 'Exactly. I stay with you. And the chip...' He swept his arm across the loose red balls remaining on the table, made a little hole and placed the red he was holding in the middle. 'Well... The chip gets lost in the pack.' He scattered the balls violently around the table.

Mya placed the pink ball down on the side table. 'I still don't understand how that helps anything.'

Brady gathered the coloured balls remaining on the table, along with the cue ball. 'Look, they don't want me, just that technology, right? If we leave it here,' he said as he gestured to the scattered reds, 'we can move out of sight.' He began putting the coloured balls down the pockets. 'They will be too busy sifting through the pack to come after us.' He finally dropped the cue ball down the pocket. 'By the time they find which one is which, we can be long gone.'

Mya slumped onto the armrest of the sofa. 'Okay, I understand in theory, but what good is it when Doc has already said he doesn't know how to do anything with the implant? We don't have the knowledge to pull this off. Besides, that won't change the fact that MediTech will think you have it still.'

Brady made his way back to the sofa and stood in front of Mya, taking her hands. 'We don't, but AntiFa do. They've done it before, and I bet that knowledge is on this personality construct.

Or hell, maybe in the memories stored in the damn chip. As for MediTech, that's simple.' He knelt down to her height. 'We make a holo recording, implanting it in one of them. Then show them being released into that hoard out there.'

Mya shook her head. 'But we still don't have the knowledge.'

Brady stood back up. 'Look, this Joshua couldn't handle MediTech even with AntiFa's backing. So what chance do I have, even with your limited resources? None. But, maybe, just maybe I can become enough to hold my own against AntiFa and get the construct out of their base.'

Mya reeled back. 'Oh, so MediTech on our doorstep isn't enough, you want to pick a fight with them too?'

'I don't want to pick a fight with them. Ideally, I want to get in and out with it. I have the advantage. I know where they are, they have no idea where I am.' He sat next to her and pulled her down onto his lap.

'I don't know about this,' she said.

'The way I see it, I've got two choices. I run for as long as I can, and hope it's not too late for everyone else.' He took a deep breath. 'Or I take a chance on losing it and coming with you. Then just maybe I can make some lives better.'

Mya looked deep into his eyes. 'Does that mean—'

'I think so.' Brady pulled her in for a kiss. His lips gently brushed hers before he pulled away again. 'The only way I can stay with you is if they aren't looking for me. The only way to do that, is this. Trust me.'

Mya continued to stare at him. He could feel her fighting with her thoughts, before she eventually whispered in his ear. 'Don't let them push you too far.'

CHAPTER SIXTEEN

Brady and Mya sat in uncomfortable silence inside Doc's surgery tent. He could see Benito and Layne quietly discussing outside, their mumbled whispers audible but indecipherable.

Brady stared at Mya's restless leg, his shallow breaths no more stable.

Mya broke the silence. 'Okay, I understand why you want to do this, I even commend it in many ways.' She rubbed her eyes, pinching the bridge of her nose. 'But do you really need to do so much, so soon?'

Brady took in a deep breath through his nostrils, the air whistling as it forced through his deviated septum. 'I appreciate you're looking out for me, but this has to work or I can never be free of it.' Brady puffed his cheeks and let go a whoosh of air. 'We have to press the advantage I have.'

Mya pushed down on her leg to stop the jitters. 'But the overhaul you spoke of, this is like preparing for war.'

'Prepare for the worst, hope for the best.'

'I don't think you've really thought through the worst. If it doesn't go to plan, innocent people might die.'

Brady let out an exasperated sigh. 'What makes you think they are innocent? What, because they want to fight MediTech? What about the fact they are willing to sacrifice me for their cause? To hijack my entire life, for what? To continue some endless fight they can't win?'

Mya sat up straight. 'Why are you sighing at me?'

He turned back to her. 'I'm not sighing at you, I'm just—'

'You just sighed at me.'

'I sighed because I'm frustrated. I didn't sigh at you.'

'And why are you frustrated?' Mya stood abruptly. 'Because I'm concerned about you?'

Brady was getting flustered. 'No, I meant—' He groaned.

'Don't groan at me either!'

Brady threw his head upwards, eyes shut. 'I am not groaning at you.'

Mya's hands went to her hips. 'Stop getting shirty. I can't help caring.'

'I know.' He brought his head back down to meet her eyes. 'I know you care, about everyone, me, it's one of the things I love about you, but honestly—' He froze.

Mya grinned. 'One of the things you what?'

Brady fought a nervous laugh, knowing it was too soon to be saying, let alone thinking anything along those lines, but equally pleased that it appeared to have thrown Mya off her train of thought. He was considering his response when, to his delight, the Doc joined them, cold crate in hand.

Mya winked at Brady. 'Doc's always saving people.'

Doc looked at them both. Brady could tell he was confused by Mya's wink, though he soon lost interest. He set the crate down on the floor as Mya tried to force eye contact with Brady, who, in turn, tried to stop a smile from breaking his poker face.

'When you two are done doing whatever it is you're doing,' Doc said and snapped his fingers, getting their attention, 'you might want to pay attention.'

Mya turned to him. 'What you got, Doc?'

He kicked the cold crate gently. 'Best I could do. It's not a lot, but it's a start.'

The reality of the situation kicked in for Brady much harder than Doc had kicked the crate. He sat back down on the operating table, feeling like Doc was about to deliver terminal, news when Benito and Layne joined them.

Brady saw a look of concern on Benito's face as he ushered

Layne to deliver the verdict of their private conversation.

'Look, in theory the plan is solid, but there's no way you go it alone,' said Layne.

Mya stepped back. Brady could see she was eager to say something, but bit her tongue. Brady smiled and winked at her, subtly so the others didn't see, then turned to address Layne.

'The whole point of this is to not put others in danger, so if I drag anyone else in with me, doesn't that negate the entire purpose?'

Layne scoffed. 'Trust me, they won't let you just walk out with their treasure. They'll kill you if it means protecting their work. These people are sycophants, I know it, I've seen it up close and personal, you know?'

Brady could see Benito's look of confusion before he even spoke. 'Sycophants? You mean zealots, Layne.'

Layne shrugged. 'Whatever it is. They'll die for their cause.'

Mya shook her head. 'Martyrs.'

'Fine,' said Layne. 'Martyrs. It doesn't matter, you need backup, mate.'

Brady looked at the crate the Doc had wheeled in again, contemplating how all the parts in there would fit into his body. 'And I'm telling you, one person sneaking in is the way to go. I got myself out, even before all this.' He pointed to the crate. 'Better, stronger, faster, right? With it, I'll be in and out before they know what hit them.'

Benito stepped forward. 'Layne is right, you can't go it alone. If this is going to work, we have to give it everything.'

Brady looked to Mya, then subtly nodded in Benito's direction, mouthing what do I do. She nodded a *yes*. Brady nodded in agreement, turning back to Benito. 'Okay, I guess you're not going to let it go.'

'You better be right about getting in there. You sure you know the way?' said Benito.

Brady thought for a moment. 'I mean, I have an idea. I think I can retrace my steps.'

Layne picked up one of the surgical tools and began examining it curiously. 'Still won't be enough.'

Mya leaned forwards. 'There's a problem?'

Layne continued with the tool, fixated on its sharp point. 'Not if we want to avoid casualties. I might not agree with these people, but they aren't bad people.' Doc looked to Brady, then purposefully to the tool, then the table. 'If we can avoid conflict, we should.'

'Like I say, that's why I figure one body is better than a bunch.' Gently, Brady took the instrument from Layne and set it back down. Doc smiled at him in gratitude. 'But what else do you suggest?'

Aghast that Brady had removed his fixation, Layne began reading information on the monitors. 'We need to get them away.'

Benito, having taken a seat on the edge of a table, stood back up. 'And how do you propose this?'

Layne was still fixated on the monitor. 'MediTech is after our boy, right?' Brady looked over at Mya, and mouthed the words *our boy* to her. She met it with a subtle look to let it go as Layne tore himself away from the monitor and faced Brady. 'So let's let them think they've got a lead. You say they sprang to your aid before, right?' Brady nodded in affirmation. 'Cool, so they'll do it again.'

Mya powered up to Layne. 'And how on earth are we going to achieve something like that?'

'Hang on,' said Benito. He looked around, clearly putting pieces of a puzzle together. 'This guy. This friend of yours who sold you down the river.' His face contorted slowly into a grin. 'He is now.'

Brady looked to Benito, teeth clenched, pupils dilated. 'Do it.'

Mya interjected, pushing Brady away to create some space

between the two men. She leaned into his ear and whispered, 'Keep quiet on that. Let me dig.' She turned the pushback into a hug and dropped the whispered tone. 'I have to go now.' She softly kissed his cheek.

'Stay?'

'Couldn't even if I wanted to, got a shift up top in an hour.' Mya left, dragging her hand across his arm to his hand as she left. He watched her every step until she was out of sight, then stared blankly at the exit of the tent. Then he heard her shout. 'I'll be back tomorrow.'

Doc coughed for Brady's attention. 'We doing this?' Brady heard the words, but they aimlessly meandered around his mind like white noise. 'Drummond!'

Finally the time delay caught up, and Brady jolted, as if his gearbox had slipped from neutral to drive. 'What did you say?' He already knew, but the instinct to duck and weave was as strong as it would be in a fight.

Doc patted the bed. A cold, clinical gesture for a cold, clinical setup. Brady took the invitation regardless. For every second that Mya had been gone, his anxiety worsened, almost as though it was inversely proportional to her proximity. Worriedly, he looked around, taking time to pause on each face. First Layne, then Benito, then the masked, barely visible face of Doc. His life was in their hands now, these men he had just met.

Benito placed an arm around his shoulder, shepherding him towards the table. 'What did she say?' Brady felt the force he was applying, pushing him forwards. The gesture may have appeared caring, yet it felt anything but.

Putting up just enough resistance to let Benito feel the pushback, Brady shifted, uncomfortable in his grasp. 'That's between us.'

Benito's stride paused. 'I really don't like it when people keep things from me.' Brady felt a tightening of Benito's grip on his shoulder. 'You have to trust me if we want this to work, right?'

Brady side-eyed him. 'Goes two ways, doesn't it?'

Benito slapped Brady's back. 'I've only just met you. That will come in time.'

Brady pressed his tongue on his top teeth and drew in a sharp breath, hissing and squeaking. 'You just met Mya, too?'

Layne lurched forward, removing Benito's arm from Brady and squeezing between the two. 'Guys, chill.' He gently elbowed Benito in the side. 'Benny, if it's their business, that's cool.'

As they reached the surgical bed, Benito broke away. 'Brady, I'm sorry. Layne is right, your business is your business.' He picked up the crate of everything that was about to make its way into Brady's body and placed it on the table next to the bed. 'I just have a duty of care here. Any second now, we could be wiped out like a wasp nest.'

Brady took the Doc's lead and climbed onto the bed. He sat at its edge for a moment, eyeing up Benito. 'Then let's spend less time doubting each other and get it going.' He swung his legs up and around. He looked at Doc and nodded. 'Let's go.'

Doc fiddled with the computer system and powered up a holo of Brady's anatomy. Fully interactive and explosible, from the dermal layers, right down to his skeletal core. Brady watched as he flipped through the layers, zooming in and out on various areas.

'That supposed to be me?' said Brady.

'Table's scanning you as we speak. It's literally you. Cough.'

Brady narrowed his eyes, questioning Doc's instruction. Doc nodded in affirmation. Taking the cue, Brady coughed and watched a deep red pulse emanate from his chest on the holo. He did it again, just as a test.

'What's the point of that?'

'It shows trauma sites. Means during surgery, I get alerts of anything going wrong.'

'That's good to know.' Brady realised after he spoke that it may not have been a positive thing. 'Wait, do you expect things to go wrong?'

'Expecting is preparing.'

Far from being filled with confidence, Brady gazed at the crate. 'So what's in there?'

'First thing's first.' Doc double tapped the holo on Brady's eyes, expanding the view to his eyeball. 'Retinal overlay. Nice and simple, we put a membrane on your pupil, which expands around your eye.' The holo rendered a video of the process. Brady watched the small patch placed on the pupil quickly expand, engulfing the eye. 'You won't feel this one, but it will eventually have to be replaced, and that bit isn't as pleasant.'

'Okay.' Brady was hesitant, yet intrigued at the same time. 'So what does it do?'

'Basic stuff really, heads up display with bio-monitoring, interacts with other systems we install for a complete visual overhaul. Maps, targeting, reprogrammable reticules, heat and threat detection, that sort of stuff.'

'Like a comms lens?'

'I suppose, aside from all the other things I just mentioned,' said Doc just as Brady caught the tail-end of him rolling his eyes.

'Okay, well, what else?'

Doc zoomed back out on the holo, then into Brady's right hand. 'I've got one epidermal hand graft. Reprogrammable finger prints, scanning system, climbing barbs, not that it's much use to you as I only have the one.'

'Why give it to me if it's no use?'

'It's useful as a single, can get you through ID print security as well as unlocking most print-locked weapons, and the scanning is good. It's just the climbing barb tech is useless unless you have both hands.'

'How come you've only got one, then?'

Doc looked at him, contemplating whether he really was as stupid as he sounded. 'Because the body I got it from only had one arm.' He gestured to highlight the obviousness of the answer.

'Okay, so I'll buy a second at some point, or what?'

'Given that they are highly illegal and rarer than most tech, you'd be lucky', he said and zoomed back out. 'Only person I've ever met with them is Mya, so you'll have to ask for her hand.'

Brady chuckled to himself. 'Maybe I will one day.'

Brady could tell his joke had not landed, seeing Doc still ultra-focused on the displays.

'Well, good luck with that.' He expanded on the forearm. 'Here's where things get a little more invasive.'

Brady baulked. 'Nice.'

'Full forearm bone replacements, pneumatic actuators for high-impact striking, electro-charged muscle fibres increasing strength and speed and, my favourite part.' He selected the demonstration on the model, showing a quill of needles rising up through the skin, before firing out like a porcupine. 'Hypodermic quill.'

Brady looked confused. 'Seems kind of unnecessary if I have a gun.'

Doc smiled wryly. 'Guns don't have the capability of lacing their bullets with coatings, nor can they hit targets unnoticed.'

'What kind of coatings?'

'All sorts. Fast or slow acting poisons and venoms, sedatives, trackers.' Deep in thought, he counted off on his fingers. 'Hallucinogens, viruses, both organic and electronic. Those are just the ones off the top of my head.'

'Useful, then,' said Brady.

'Oh, and the quills are so strong and finely tipped, they'll pretty much penetrate anything they strike.'

'Great, Doc, but the plan is to avoid conflict. This all seems pretty aggressive.'

Doc zoomed the image in on Brady's chest, slid away the

dermal layers and took away the rib cage. 'In case you didn't notice, we don't exactly have access to much. I'm just working with what I have.'

Brady stared at his organs in three dimensions, floating in front of him before pushing Doc's hand away. 'I don't want to see any of it, just tell me.'

He could tell Doc was disappointed. 'Fine.' He tore himself away from the medical schematics. 'Only other tech I could get at the moment that wasn't a write-off, heart mesh and valve replacements, controllable heart rates for any given scenarios, comms and positioning implant, basically most of the systems that can pair up with the eye mesh.'

'So you're turning me into a walking computer?'

'As much as I can,' said Doc.

'Anything else?'

'Cranial armour and EMP shielding, and got you a second prosthetic leg, slightly newer model, but I'll tweak the settings and dampen the response time so you don't walk around in circles, plus I can swap out the tendons on the old one to match so you'll be able to get a pneumatic push off the calves.'

Brady looked down at his prosthesis. 'What does that mean?'

Doc looked to Benito. Brady could see his exasperation. 'You can jump better, run faster, kick harder.'

Brady nodded in approval. 'Okay, so is that it?'

Doc thought for a second, adding, 'Well, there's one more thing, but it's more of a temporary solution and honestly, it's going to hurt like hell.'

Brady's arms folded in front of his chest, defending himself from the idea of something that painful. 'What is it?'

Doc placed a hand on Brady's shoulder sympathetically. 'Normally I'd refrain from doing this, but let's face facts, if you have to go up there, you'll be a hunted man.' He pointed skyward with his other hand. 'We don't have any epidermal armour and frankly, we are low on exoskeletal armour too, so—' He closed his eyes. 'We are looking at subcutaneous render.'

'That doesn't sound that bad... is it?'

Doc drew in a deep breath. 'The subcutaneous layer is pretty much all fat and connective tissue. I'm going to have to inject you with a super-heated gel which, when it has mixed with the fat and cools, renders into a tough ballistic dampener.'

Brady's eyes shut tight, trying not to think about what Doc had told him. 'So, uh, this is for bullet-proofing?'

Let's call it—' Doc hesitated. 'Bullet slowing.'

Brady's eyes opened wide as he shifted uncomfortably in the bed. 'So, you're going to inject me with hot tar and it just, slows bullets? It doesn't actually stop them?'

Doc just nodded. 'Best I can do.'

The two men remained in silence for long moments, Brady trying to comprehend the idea of being filled with super-hot gel, Doc at a loss for words.

Brady began laughing as an outlet for his nerves. It grew throughout his body until he had to shout it out. The despondent cry of anguish, combined with the frantic rubbing of his face, just about calmed him. 'Do it.'

'Are you sure?' Doc looked over to Layne. Brady took one look at Layne's face and knew this was going to hurt.

'Just do it.' His cheeks puffed. 'Do whatever you need to, just stop talking about it and do it.' Brady became agitated and his natural leg began shaking. He closed his eyes again, psyching himself up for the ordeal that lay ahead.

***

Up in the city, Mya had almost made it through the busiest shift. Tired and worried about Brady, the last thing she needed was her head pounding as a result of the repetitive drone of industrial dance music from the club nearby.

The entertainment district was teeming with life. It was an evening like any other, except for Mya, everything had changed. The bustle of life seemed more pointless; the smiles around her, just that bit more deluded.

She was finishing up serving an older couple when she noticed Nerea passing by. Her usually perfect make-up had been smeared by tears, and her eyes were tired. Mya knew Dan was the cause. For a moment, she contemplated letting the girl walk by, but decided she may be able to gain some information to give her a head start on getting to the root cause of Dan's betrayal.

'Hey!' she shouted, and waved to Nerea, who did not notice, seemingly so wrapped up in her emotions she would have carried on past a neon flashing sign with her name on it. Mya jumped over the bar and sped after her, grabbing her arm and causing her to jump out of her skin and scream.

'Get off me! What do you want?' As she calmed down, she recognised Mya and breathed a sigh of relief. 'Oh it's you, sorry!'

'No, I'm sorry for startling you.' Mya let her go. 'Are you okay? You look like you could use a drink.' She waved over to the bar in invitation.

'I could use more than one.' Nerea smiled as she answered. It looked at odds with the mess on her face.

Nerea took a stool at the bar as Mya returned behind it, nodding an apology to her counterpart. Mya pulled two glasses of blended synth scotch and slid one to Nerea. 'On me.' She immediately drank her own in a single mouthful and hissed at the raw flavour.

Grabbing the glass and pulling it close, Nerea span it around on the bar for a few moments, looking down into the mini vortex she had created in the glass. 'Gracias.' She downed the scotch without registering how bad it was, tapped the glass on the bar and tipped her head up at Mya, who dutifully took the vessel.

'Looks like I was right.' Mya laughed, grabbing the tumbler and pressing it to the optic to pour another. 'You want to talk about it?' Mya drew a second measure into the glass and pretended it took longer than it did, keeping an eye on Nerea in the mirror.

'It's a long story. Might take a whole bottle.' Mya could see the questioning face as she dawdled. 'Something wrong?'

'Oh, no.' Mya turned back with the drink. 'Was just thinking about making it a triple for you.' The fact Nerea had noticed spooked her. She knew people, she served hundreds every week and knew the difference between people watching, and movement studying. *This girl's into something,* she thought. Mya knelt behind the bar and emerged with a half full bottle of the really nasty synth grain, placing it in front of Nerea.

'What's this?'

'Something between booze and disinfectant.' She uncorked the bottle and wafted it in front of Nerea's nose, who was taken aback by the almost caustic aroma. Mya knew the only people who didn't react to the pungent smell had been trained by MediTech. *Not with them,* she thought. Their grunts grew up on the stuff during basic training and had developed an immunity. 'It's free, though.'

Nerea took her glass, drank the double Mya had poured in two purposeful sips, then poured in some of the bottle. She looked at it dubiously before having a taster sip. It hit the back of her throat like a fire and she let out a puff of air as though she were releasing a mouthful of smoke, coughing and gagging.

Mya laughed. 'We usually cut that with something.' She knew the local crime syndicate pretty well and knew they had a favourite club drink; any grain alcohol mixed with taurine liquor, and synthesised orange juice. She produced a bottle of each and placed them in front of Nerea, waiting for any kind of reaction. There was none. *Either she is good, or that ain't it.*

Nerea eyed the taurine, but went for the orange, mixing in a good amount to dilute. She took another sip. Her eyes winced, the sharpness of the synth orange juice causing it. 'That's better.'

'So tell me...' Mya said and leaned over the bar to her, 'what's going on? I'm guessing, either something really bad has happened, or Dan has happened.' She poured herself the same to join in, adding in the taurine. *Can't be involved, must just be upset.*

Nerea took another, longer sip, steadying her nerves. 'Bingo.'

'Dan?'

Nerea nodded as she looked deep into her drink. 'It's over.'

Mya reached forward, giving her the lightest of touches. 'I'm sorry to hear that.'

'Don't be. I don't even know why I'm upset.' She finished her drink and began making another. 'We didn't love each other. We both knew it.'

'Still, you shared time together, you'll always have a bond.' Mya noticed another customer waiting and moved down the bar to serve them.

'Maybe. I just wish it had ended differently.'

Mya asked her customers, 'Same again?' They nodded, and she began pouring two glasses of clear, nondescript liquor before shouting back over to Nerea. 'He wasn't cheating, was he?'

She shook her head, nursing her next drink. 'No. Well, not that I know of. Worse.'

Mya slid the payment scanner over the bar, and after a swift fingerprint credit transaction, Mya moved back to Nerea. 'He didn't hit you, did he?'

Nerea scoffed. 'Would've been the last thing he did.' She slid the drink away, clearly beginning to feel the potent affect.

Mya packed away the bottles, tipped the last of her drink away, and said, 'So what was it, if you don't mind my asking?'

'Drugs.'

Mya looked surprised. She knew she shouldn't have been. The signs were all there, and she suddenly pieced them together. 'I can't believe I didn't see it. Like what stuff?'

'He wouldn't tell me, but I found some high grade DoSe amphetamine.' She smacked the bar top and stood in anger. 'So not only was he on some serious stuff, he obviously had a contact in the high ups.'

'Real DoSe?'

'Premium grade.'

'Sorry hun, one sec.' Mya ducked down behind the bar and out of sight. She thought back to the attacker. Recalled that he couldn't have been MediTech themselves. The puzzle was growing and the pieces weren't quite fitting together.

'Thing is,' Nerea said, 'I don't know what I'm angrier about. The drugs, or the fact he's clearly involved in something bigger to get a hold of it.'

Mya took a deep breath before resurfacing. 'Wow yeah, that's definitely a strange one.'

'It is. The other thing, is now I don't know if Brady is somehow involved.'

Mya, aghast by the mention of Brady, did her best to feign surprise. 'Brady?'

'Yeah, you can't tell me it doesn't seem a little suspicious he's gone off the radar since that fight.' Mya could tell Nerea was looking for a tell, but she remained steadfast. 'Now this with Dan. I don't know. Seems a bit suspect, no?'

Mya made a point of looking down and left, a slight head tilt to sell the ruse of trying to recall anything she may have been able to remember. 'Could be. I just assumed he was laying low and healing up.' She could tell Nerea was suspicious, just from the micro-expressions on her face, but she continued to play it as cool as she could.

'Hmm, yes. I suppose that could be it.' The shift in Nerea's tone confirmed her thoughts, though she could tell Nerea was not about to question it.

'Another one?' asked Mya. She knew Nerea was done, but was baiting for a reaction that never came.

'No, thank you, Mya. I think I'm going to try and get some sleep. My head is swimming.' Nerea stood, a little wobbly from the alcohol, but steadied herself on the bar.

Mya smiled. 'Take care of yourself, hun.' Nerea didn't respond. Mya watched her carefully as she left the bar. Unwittingly, Nerea had given her what she needed to press Dan. But he would have to wait a little. She still had a bar to manage for another hour.

CHAPTER SEVENTEEN

Tears streamed down Mya's face. Brady's screams of pain echoed throughout the undercity complex.

She sat with Layne in the mess tent on the centre table as the eyes of the other citizens eating there were on her. A disgusted look on his face, Layne tore a chunk out of the roasted mushroom and algae stuffed rat skewer he held in one hand, whilst his other clamped onto a tankard of weakly distilled vodka. The sinew of the rat stuck in his teeth as he chewed and chewed at the dry, pungent mass.

'Quit crying,' Layne mumbled through his full mouth. 'He'll be fine.' He took a big gulp of the vodka to wash the food down. 'I was.'

Mya wiped away tears, but couldn't damn the flood. She sniffled. 'He doesn't have fried neurals, you sadist.'

Layne dismissed her with a shrug as she watched Samantha approach. Bathed in sweat and blood from assisting the operations on Brady, she was clearly too exhausted to have scrubbed down. Mya studied Samantha's facial expressions to try to ascertain how it had gone, but it was hard to tell beyond her half down mask and the blood and sweat.

'How is he?' Layne set aside his drink and food. Mya wanted to ask, but she couldn't quite bring herself to face the answer.

Samantha pulled her mask off completely. 'There were—' She hesitated, enough that Mya feared the worse. 'Complications, but he's going to be okay.'

Mya exhaled deeply in relief, releasing the fear she had held onto since Brady had agreed to the augmentations.

'What complications?' said Layne. The coldness in his voice

seemed out of sorts with Mya.

'He's lucky.' Samantha took a seat opposite, grabbed Layne's vodka and took a long drink. 'We found a blood clot in his brain, evidence of blunt force trauma.'

Mya leaned across the table. 'Is he okay?'

'He is now. That was a ticking time bomb.'

Layne snatched his tankard back. 'What about the procedures? Is he good to go?'

'Is that all you care about?' Mya slapped him on the arm with the back of her hand.

'All due respect Mya,' he said and turned to her, barely acknowledging the slap, 'I'm looking for the bigger picture here.'

She shook her head in disbelief. 'He's a human being.'

Layne slurped at the vodka, swilling it around his mouth and gargling before swallowing it down. 'Yeah, but until we get this done, we are all human beings with a dwindling clock.'

Mya's eyes began welling up once more, so she took some deep breaths to try preventing the next wave of tears coming through. She tightened her eyes, feeling the pressure build.

'Did the upgrades take?' Layne tore another chunk of rat from the skewer and chewed aggressively.

'Whatever this implant is in him, it's assimilating anything instantly.' Samantha peeled the bloodstained gloves off her arms, looking around for somewhere to discard them. The handful of other people in the mess tent watched, many sliding away the food that was hard enough to swallow without such a sight.

Layne swallowed his mouthful and shuddered at the taste. 'We are right to push his limits, then?'

Giving up on finding anywhere appropriate to get rid of her surgical gloves, Samantha headed to the mess tent entrance and tossed them carelessly outside. 'In all honesty, I don't know if he has any.'

'We are good to go, then?' Layne stood and tossed down the

last morsels he couldn't manage to swallow.

Walking back to the table from the entrance, Samantha gestured apologies to the other diners. 'He'll need some time, but it's certainly better than expected.'

Mya stood abruptly. 'I'm going to see him.' She hurried towards the entrance.

Samantha stuck out her arm to stop her. 'He lost consciousness.'

Mya ignored her, forcing herself through the arm barrier and quickly leaving.

***

Mya entered the surgical tent to find Brady laying in the bed. His eyes were open, but he was devoid of energy. Her eyes widened as she saw him. Her heart sunk. He tried to greet her, but his voice crackled in nothing but a throaty noise.

'It's okay,' she said. 'Don't push yourself.'

Doc had been scrubbing down since the operation was over and still had blood and pneumatic fluids staining his arms. Mya glanced between him and the bucket of discarded flesh from Brady's body. Her stomach churned as her face drained of colour. She had seen gruesome sights countless times and never reacted, but this wasn't just gruesome, it was Brady.

Doc shook his hands to get the water off. 'I'll administer an adrenaline shot in a moment, but everything looks good.'

Mya reached a hand out to steady herself on the monitor cart next to Brady's bed. 'What about the clot?'

'Almost certainly a result of a pneumatic punch.'

The wheels of the cart moved and Mya with it, so she took the pressure off it and barely managed to stabilize herself. 'Well he fought in the natural leagues, could that be it?'

'Nothing natural about what caused that. His cranium was

fractured so badly I'm surprised he didn't die instantly.'

Mya looked over at Brady, helplessly lying on the bed. She was thankful he had made it this far and her concerns over how much he had been through with the surgery began melting away when weighed up with the fact it had saved his life.

Doc prepared the adrenaline and whipped away the cover from Brady's torso. Mya baulked at the amount of surgery sites and tissue bruising all over his body, then noticed the red raw appearance of his skin. Doc tried to fire the adrenaline shot through Brady's chest, but his hardened subcutaneous tissue broke the needle.

'Interesting,' said Doc.

'Something wrong?' Mya said, clocking the broken needle.

'It shouldn't have rendered this hard this fast. But this is what we are seeing with him, there's no resistance to anything we have installed. It's like his body soaks up procedures like a sponge.' He took out another application head and replaced it with the broken one on the injector before opening Brady's mouth and administering the shot into his tongue.

'Is that safe?' Mya asked.

'Just about the only place I can get the needle through now.'

Brady jolted upright as the adrenaline surged through his heart. Mya began to panic as she watched Brady's frantic reaction, but her panic abated as he calmed. She looked him deep in the eyes, doing her best to present him with a calming face.

'How are you doing?' She immediately thought the question was stupid, given the circumstances.

Brady gritted his teeth. 'I'm okay.' The nature of his answer did little reassure her, but she remained calm for his sake.

'The pain will last a couple of hours, so take this.' Doc handed him a tablet. 'It'll take the edge off.'

Brady took the tablet and swallowed. 'What is it?'

'Signal inhibitor. It'll reprogram your nervous system's signals to block out pain processing. Works for about an hour before it loses charge, but you'll be over the worst of it by then.'

'How did everything else go? Am I indestructible now?' Mya could tell he was putting on a brave face for her and yet, she still found comfort in it.

Mya smiled. 'You're less destructible.'

'I'll take what I can get.'

She bent over him and put her hand on his face gently. 'You nearly died.'

'Sure felt like it.'

'Not in the operation.' She moved her hand to the crown of his head where she could see the shaved patch and big scar.

Brady looked confused. 'When?'

'They saved your life. You had a blood clot in your brain.' Mya gently ran the tip of her finger across the scar line.

Brady's eyes perked up. 'Seriously?'

Doc spun the monitor cart around and fiddled with the controls. 'And a broken skull.'

'And now?' Brady tried to sit upright a little, but Mya could tell the pain was still too insufferable as he resigned to laying back down.

'Now you just have a thick head.' Mya laughed, trying to mask her worry. 'Doc thinks it was a pneumatic punch.'

Mya watched Brady's face, seeing him clearly trying to piece together the puzzle. She took her hand from the scar and gently held his face, then forced a smile, but could feel how fake it must've appeared before she dropped it.

'The fight?' said Brady.

As Doc finished up with the monitor systems and turned his attention to Brady, Mya moved aside so he could shine a torch into Brady's eye. 'I said it can't be fighting, though. No way a clean puncher would do that much damage.' As Doc switched through the spectrum of light on his torch, Mya watched as

Brady's ocular membranes reacted, glistening in different colours.

'Clean?' Brady jerked away from the light in his eyes. 'If that was a clean fight, then this is MediTech headquarters.' Brady tried to manoeuvre himself to get out of the bed. Mya readied herself to help, but as he took weight on his arm, he collapsed back down.

'Sam replaced the broken skull sections with graphene plating, so if you're going to fall, fall on that part.' Doc left the bed and manipulated the holo display with Brady's vitals. Mya tried to decipher what was on show, but it meant nothing to her.

As Brady tried to move again, Mya placed a hand on his chest, stopping his attempt. 'So when am I ready to cause a fuss?' he said.

Mya watched the displays as Doc paid close attention to Brady's heart rate and blood pressure. 'Day or two, everything needs to settle in.' It was higher than he would like but not in the danger zone.

Brady looked at Mya, and saw his eyes zip in and out of focus. 'How do I get rid of this display? It's all I can see.' Instinctively, he reached out to try to operate the display as if it were touch operational. Mya heard the sharp thwack of Brady's razor grips as they released. She jumped back, fearful of how close she was. She wasn't sure who it surprised more, Brady or herself.

Mya laughed, nervously. The adrenaline rush abated and she calmed when she saw Brady's face soften and smile at her reaction.

'It's ocular,' said Doc. 'Works with psychic feedback. You just look at the options and think about what you want to do.'

'Yeah, but how do I make it go away?' Mya recognised Brady's erratic eye movement. She'd gone through the same when she first had ocular overlays. The first time she tried to navigate them, she ended up with motion sickness from the constant, fine movements. By the looks of it, Brady was feeling that too.

Doc turned away from the holo display to watch Brady

struggling. 'Just think it.'

'It doesn't appear to be that simple, Doc. I can't focus on any one option, it's like the whole thing is juddering in front of me.'

'Children have these and figure it out in minutes. It's not hard.'

Mya gently patted Brady on the shoulder. 'I hate them, can't use them.' She opened her wrist monitor to show him. 'That's why I'm old-fashioned.'

'Can I get one of those?'

'Doc looked over to see what he was referring to, and said, 'Suppose you want a thirty PSI exo-skeletal crust replacement and a mark one SimTech respiratory mesh too?' Doc scoffed as if he were in the company of fellow medical practitioners who would find his quip funny.

Mya guided Brady's face back towards herself. 'Forget that. You'll figure it out. It will just take time.' She took his hand. 'But we need to work out the whole Dan business before anything else.'

Mya had lit a fuse in Brady and she could tell. His teeth gritted, and his eyes pinched closed. Even through his anger, she noticed him calm. His breathing became more steady. She recognised this, too. The inhibitors had clearly started to beat his pain levels. She watched for a moment, before his eyes snapped back open.

'I'm going to kill him.'

Brady began to stand, but Mya held him down. Not because he couldn't handle it this time; he was ready, she could see that much. 'Calm down, I've got something.'

Mya felt him try to bolt upright. As he tried to lift, she forced him down again with relative ease. She knew after his strengthening upgrades, he wouldn't always be so weak, but she took advantage of the fact his body was still tired from the procedures.

'Let me go.' He struggled but got nowhere.

'Just listen to me. I ran in to his ex.' She overtly looked in Doc's direction, making it clear to Brady they needed the room.

He sighed. 'Doc. Leave us a minute, will you?'

Doc obliged, and Mya watched closely as he began stripping out of his surgical overalls and headed out to shower down. She could see he was exhausted and probably glad of the break anyway.

Brady slid Mya's hand off him. She didn't resist. 'Ex? What do you mean, his ex?'

'Nerea ended it.'

'When? Why?'

'Two nights ago.' Mya knelt in front of Brady to get closer to his level. 'He's on DoSe, the good stuff.'

Mya backed off and Brady stood out of bed without resistance. 'I knew there was something like that.' He wobbled briefly, and Mya thought about catching him but by the time she processed it, he had balanced himself. 'Wait, DoSe? Real DoSe?'

Mya stood, ignoring the stomach-churning gore around. 'Yep.'

'So, MediTech?'

Mya shook her head. 'Not them. Like I said before, they would've sent down a carpet bombing.'

She tracked his movements as Brady wandered the tent slowly as he assimilated to the new body setup. 'So if it wasn't them,' he said and peered into the medical waste bucket. Mya saw his reaction to what lay in there; he was as disgusted as she had been. 'Who was it?'

'That's what we need to find out.'

'And how do we do that?'

'We have an advantage.' She cleared space on a table and leaned into it. 'He doesn't know you know it was him.' Mya could see Brady was deep in thought as he studied the readouts on Doc's holo display. She gave him a moment to gather himself.

'What can I do, though? Can't go up and see him, can't call him in case whoever he is working for can trace me here.'

'Who says you can't go up there?' Mya placed her arms around Brady from behind, holding him softly, speaking into his ear.

He looked over his shoulder at her. 'Benito, you. Everyone.'

'We said you can't live up there.'

'Yes, but if I go up there, all hell breaks loose, right?'

'Only if they know.' She paused, taking the opportunity to smell his head. For as much as he had now become a machine, she still recognised his aroma. 'One of the perks of your ocular system, there's a little interference setting, scrambles signals from things like facial recognition.' She gently kissed the nape of his neck. 'You go up there as a ghost, just can't go through any official channels.'

'Like what?'

'Anything requiring registration? You can't transit. It will flag unlicensed and the area gets locked down.' She stretched her arms forward and began counting off her points on her fingers. 'Nothing medical, no access to apartments, businesses, industrial sector.' She was about to mention point five on her little finger when Brady interrupted.

'Basically anything, then. Can I eat?'

'You can spend creds once you're in somewhere. Can't just walk into any old place now, though. Got to know they aren't identity verifying.'

'So how can I get to Dan if I can't get past anything?'

'I'm not saying you can't get into any of those places. I'm saying *you* can't get into any of those places.'

'What?' He turned around, still in her arms. The dopey, confused look on his face was endearing to her.

'You can't, but your body can. You just need to scan someone's biometrics who has authority but isn't located anywhere else and you can go where you like.'

'Isn't located anywhere else? How is that possible?'

Mya received a message from Benito on her wrist comms and she broke their embrace. 'Well, they need to be in public spaces and you need to know they aren't going to attempt any scans while you are using their biometrics.'

Mya watched as Brady, having discovered the mechanism of making a fist to reveal his forearm dart launcher, played with how quickly he could make it appear and disappear. Each time they engaged, the combat reticule on his ocular replacements popped up, switching the colour of his eyes to red. He was like a boy with a toy, deep in his new discovery, so Mya coughed to grab his attention.

'Were you listening?'

'Sorry, yeah, got to be in public.' He suddenly stopped fiddling about. 'Hang on, how do I make sure they don't scan in anywhere while I'm using their identity?'

Mya gave him a stern look. 'Generally,' she said, sighing, 'we have to neutralise them.'

'You kill people just to get around?'

'No, no, no.' She pumped the brakes heavily. 'Usually sedation and isolating them from where they could be found.'

Brady let out a puff. 'I was seriously worried then. What happens when they wake up? Surely they'll ask questions?'

'That's where someone like me comes in. We hang around and tell them they passed out, so we carried them out the way.'

'Okay, put it another way.' His eyes switched away from red, then to blue, then green. Mya could tell he was circling through new options and not really paying full attention. It annoyed her. 'What happens if they wake up, don't buy your story and go off to get scanned somewhere, say a security post?'

Mya shrugged. 'That's only happened twice before. The last time—' She looked around to the side of the tent as if she had X-ray vision. 'It was Samantha.'

Brady's eyes widened. 'You kidnap them?' He staggered

slightly. 'Woah, when I open my eyes more, the image gets bigger.' As Brady played with the feature, opening and closing his eyes, she grew ever more frustrated, sharply turning away to hide her aggravation.

'Well, yes.' Mya turned back to face him. 'But we just show them our world, explain why we did what we did and then offer to let them return.' She checked her comms again. One more message from Benito. She knew he was getting agitated himself. 'So far, they've both stayed.'

'Who was the other?' He was still playing with his systems. She shook her head as he released the palm hooks and watched, her foot tapping the ground rapidly as he engaged the climbing membrane on his hand and began testing its grip on the ground.

Suddenly, Mya's aggravation subsided, replaced with a wave of sadness crashing over her. Everything since the raid on the silicone processing plant had gone wrong had happened in such quick succession that she had yet to process the deaths of those involved. None more so than Olly's.

As Mya began to cry, Brady looked up from his experimentation. 'I'm sorry.'

She spoke through shortened breath. 'It's okay.'

'You don't have to talk about it. Let's just focus on Dan.'

Mya sucked up her tears and shook it off. She would still need to grieve, but now was not the time. She nodded to Brady as her comms pinged once more.

Layne waited outside the tent as Mya emerged with Brady. She recognised Olly's .58 calibre pistol as he held it. The tears she had just managed to control welled back up immediately. Olly had recovered it from a skirmish he'd had with Joshua at his side and he had kept it well over the years, and had fired it just the once. The recoil from the shot had left a scar above his eye, such was the pure force. Joshua had had it specially made with a massive increase in PSI over the standard model, and it took Joshua's bionic strength to be able to handle such a punch.

Layne waved Brady over. 'Come here.' He held out the pistol, waiting for Brady to reach him.

'What's this?' As Brady eyed the gun, Mya could tell he was intimidated by the imposing size of such an unwieldy killing machine.

'Just take it. It belongs to you now.' Layne thrust it towards him.

Brady backed off. 'You already gave me a gun.'

'This one's different. Speak to that memory of yours, it was his.' Layne jabbed the butt into Brady's solar plexus. Despite his rendered flesh, Mya saw it still left an impression. 'It's got a kick you ain't ready for, but once you can wield that piece, you'll be what you need to be.' As Brady took the gun, the sheer weight was evident. His arm dropped and as he lilted to one side, Mya saw the little smirk on Layne's face.

Seeing Brady holding that cannon, remembering Olly, it was all too much for Mya. Like the passing of the torch of death, she couldn't bear to look.

CHAPTER EIGHTEEN

Dan sat in his apartment, sweat beads racing each other down his face as he shivered uncontrollably. His foot tapped frantically on the floor as he tried to figure out how he could convince Xiao to hook him up with some more DoSe. Failing that, where he could get some semi passable synthetic knock-off just to keep him hanging on. His thoughts were disturbed when the doorbell rang. He looked at the identification. *Don't know that name, can't matter.*

His brief respite from the gloomy thought that he could be standing on the precipice of death was over. He had no time for strangers when he was grieving for himself, but as soon as he lulled back into the notion of his own mortality, the bell rang once more. Same identification.

Every time Dan began to relax again, the bell rang. *Whoever they are, they're persistent. I'll give them that.* Then it dawned on him, if Xiao was going to send someone around to drop off some DoSe, he wouldn't know their identity. With that thought, he dragged himself up and over to the door panel. Every fibre of his being hurt from moving. He could hear the muted woosh of blood through restricted arteries in his neck. He felt his heart stop, he froze, counting the seconds. Eighteen was his record, but this pause had made it to eleven already as he began to feel the early stages of unconsciousness washing down him like cold water. His vision was becoming dark when the sudden, uncomfortable flutter of a restarted heart tickled in his chest.

As the blood surged back into his brain, he recalled why he was up in the first place. As much as he would kill to just collapse, salvation was probably just in reach. His hopefulness withered when he answered and saw Brady on the screen. So disappointed he was to see his friend, he almost forgot about the identification mix-up.

Dan could tell he looked different. It wasn't the Brady he had known. 'Brady, uh, hey. How's it going?'

'Yeah.' Brady beamed a smile. Dan knew it was Brady's smile of recognition for something that amused him, but he couldn't fathom what was so funny. 'Yeah, I'm really good, mate.'

Dan leaned his weight on the wall, the disappointment from seeing Brady and his physical exhaustion compounded. 'Glad to hear.'

'Are you going to let me in or we having a conversation like this?' said Brady.

Dan unlocked the door and opened it a crack before sauntering back to his pit of despair. He heard the door open behind him, hurrying as best he could to get to a seat before Brady could notice his laboured movement. He bounced between supporting objects and the mess on the floor before finally making it to the sofa, collapsing into it just as his body gave up.

Brady followed, clearly hit by the smell in the apartment that Dan no longer noticed. It was musty, as though it had not been disturbed in years, but also had the thickness of fresh sweat and decay. Dan's body was slowly beginning to decompose. That was the smell that lingered. He knew it. He had grown accustomed to it, but he could see just how much it turned Brady's stomach.

Dan watched his friend taking in the squalor he lived in, cautiously stepping over everything in his way. The look of pity he was expecting wasn't there. Beyond the revolt, there was an air of expectancy, as though none of it had surprised him. Brady hadn't been to Dan's in months, and the degradation since then was exorbitant, yet he wasn't reacting.

'Come on Dan,' he said, holding his nose, 'I knew it would be bad, but this is something else.'

Dan had slumped back into the small nook he had crafted for himself amid the refuse on the sofa. 'What? What do you mean, expected?'

Brady grinned, immediately amping up Dan's unease. 'Certain things have come to light.' He carefully perched himself on the arm of the sofa.

Dan shuffled uncomfortably. 'What sort of things?' Then another through struck him like a hammer. 'Wait. Where the hell have you been these last few days? Nobody has seen a single sign from you.'

'Oh I've been about,' said Brady, chuckling lightly to himself.

'Nah you haven't. One minute we know where you are, the next—' Dan caught his mistake, pumping the brakes and hoping Brady hadn't.

'Wait. We?' Brady stood up, looming over Dan.

Dan wished his brain wasn't so foggy. The small lapse of concentration had pulled a thread and he knew it. He floundered. 'We. Yeah, we.'

'We who?' said Brady.

'We. You know.' He was panicking, but then he noticed Brady's eyes. The unmistakeable hue of retinal overlays. 'Your eyes. What have you done?'

Brady scoffed, shaking his head. 'Nice try mate. Who is we?'

Dan looked Brady up and down, taking him in with a finer detail than he had for years. Looking for any signs of further alterations. Nothing else was apparent, but he had an air of confidence that Dan had never seen before.

Brady looked behind to the coffee table. Without care, he swept aside the junk to make a space for himself. He sat, perched at the edge, leaning forwards. 'Well? You going to answer me or what?'

Dan could almost feel a spotlight beaming onto him. But he

had bought just enough time for his laboured brain to come up with something. 'We, your friends.'

'Friends?' Brady's pause was enough to make Dan squirm. 'What friends?'

Dan was glad his nervous system was so severely hampered, otherwise his panic would've manifested physically. Internally twisting, his numb body remained still. 'You know, me, Nerea. Even Mya doesn't know where you've been.'

Brady remained cool. 'Mya? What makes you think that?'

Brady's intense gaze was starting to burn into Dan. He avoided eye contact. 'She was speaking to Nerea.'

Brady stretched out his leg, placing his foot on the edge of the sofa, uncomfortably close to Dan. 'And what did she say?'

'I don't know mate, just that she hadn't seen you for a while.' Dan shifted away from Brady's foot.

'I should really catch up with her.' Brady stood up and wandered to Dan's kitchen corner. He opened the fridge, looking inside. Dan knew there was little in there, but kept an eye on him.

'So are you going to tell me what has happened to you or do I have to guess?' said Dan. He scanned the room to look for anything conspicuous whilst Brady was engrossed in the empty fridge.

'I'm not really here to talk about myself to be honest, mate!' Brady peeled himself away from the fridge.

'So what do you want?'

'What do I want?' Brady said, clearly scouring the room. 'Can't I come and see how my best friend is doing?'

Dan could tell from his tone that there was definitely more to this than met the eye. 'Look mate, I know you, I can see something is up, so just tell me.'

Brady abandoned his search, looked directly at Dan and grinned. 'As if you don't know.'

Dan's heart leapt from his chest. 'What do you mean?'

'How's the DoSe going?' Brady, brushed the old, rehydrated food containers from the couch and sat next to Dan. 'You're on the good stuff, right?'

Dan felt a weight lift from him. *Just the gear, I can handle that.* He briefly let a smile slip before realising it could lead to suspicion and quickly straightened up again. 'Damn, okay, so you know. What now?'

'What do you mean, what now?' Brady feigned his best concerned face, but Dan saw right through it. 'Talk to me, mate. Why didn't you ever say anything? I could've helped you.'

Dan studied him for a moment. 'How could you help?' There was a certain sincerity to Brady's demeanour, but it was tinged with an ulterior motive; he had studied Brady for years, and knew him down to the smallest sign. 'You've had enough going on yourself.'

'Dan, this has obviously been going on longer than a few weeks.' He waved around the room, showing Dan the mess as if he were unaware. 'Look at the state of it, mate!'

'So you came to gloat, is that it?'

'Come on, you know me better than that.' Brady slapped Dan's leg. 'Of course I have.'

The two men laughed. Dan's was not authentic and he knew immediately nor was Brady's. The hope he had that Brady knew nothing beyond his addiction had fallen away like old rendering. His chest tightened, heart rate increased. Brady's laugh made way for a sinister look, twisting the knife into Dan's chest.

Dan broke. 'Seriously, why are you here?'

'I'm telling you.' Brady tilted his head, the patronisation too much to bear. 'I came to see how you're doing.'

Dan stared directly into his eyes, devoid of expression. 'So that's it. Just checking in as a friend?'

'Yeah, of course, mate.' Brady, noticing Dan's stash of room temperature beers, grabbed two bottles and cracked them both open. 'I'm worried about you.' He handed one to Dan and began drinking the other.

Dan played with the etching on the bottle, running his fingers over the contours, unsure whether a beer and dulling his senses was the best thing at that juncture. His illness did enough of that for him and the peak of the last dose of drugs was beginning to wear off. Equally, he knew that by not drinking it would almost certainly raise Brady's suspicions.

Against his better judgment, Dan took a swig. 'So what now? Going to lecture me on the perils of drug abuse?'

'Why you gotta be like that?' Brady took a gulp of the beer; his face afterwards said it all.

'Oh come on Brady, as if you haven't loved playing the high and mighty, Mr clean living, holier than thou card since, well, forever.' Dan set the beer aside. As if his body wasn't crying in enough pain, the chemicals and alcohol only served to worsen it.

Brady took a long drink from the bottle, swallowing down two gulps. 'Why can't you just let me be your friend?'

'Alright, you want to get into this? Really?' Dan leaned forward, rustling the refuse. 'You've never known how to be my friend. It's always been about you. What you needed, how you were going to get your training in. Never me, and you never cared.' He slumped back down. 'Some best friend you are.'

Brady began laughing. Dan's body tensed. 'Are you seriously going to lecture me on the merits of friendship?'

'What is that supposed to mean?' Dan, in his anger, battled through the pain to stand. 'You're going to tell me I'm wrong?'

'I'm going to tell you one thing.' Brady downed the last of the beer and tossed the bottle casually into the mess. 'I know what you did.'

As soon as he heard those words, Dan's stomach tightened into knots. He had been swimming against the tide since he saw Brady on the holo. Now the water had turned to a quagmire. The moment was as surreal to him as the kick of an overdose, and hoped that if he said nothing and stayed still for long enough, it would go away.

Brady snapped his fingers repeatedly. 'Anyone in there got anything to say?'

Dan shut his eyes. Somewhere in his head, there must've been a reasonable explanation that could placate Brady long enough to get him out of the apartment. If he could manage that feat, he could disappear into a hole and rot in peace. All thoughts of how to survive his disease had been kicked to the curb by the guilt of what he had done to Brady. Under the spotlight, he no longer felt a reason to preserve himself.

He heard movement, then felt a solid flick and the sting of Brady's fingernail, right in the middle of his forehead. Dan flinched, but his eyes remained shut tight. Then he felt a powerful grip on his cheeks and jaw, squeezing tightly, squashing his lips. He could feel the nerves where his teeth met his jaw. The pain was oddly satisfying, which made a difference from the numbness, at least.

Dan opened his eyes and was met by an intense stare from Brady that he had never seen before. He had always known Brady was tough, he had to be, but this man in front of him was someone he hadn't met before. He was scared. 'I don't know what to say to you.' He forced his words through his tightened mouth. 'I'm so sorry, I didn't have a choice.'

'There's always a choice. Yours was to give me up to killers.' Dan felt the pressure release as Brady stepped away.

Dan cursed his neural regulators. He was genuinely shocked, but knew all too well that from the outside looking in, it would appear like this was old news. 'Killers?'

'Yeah, killers, what did you think?' Brady's scrutiny of his lack of physical reaction was all too apparent.

'I swear, he said he just wanted to get to you before MediTech.'

Dan did his best to emphasise his remorse, but even he could hear that his own tone was forced. 'He promised me you'd be safe.'

Dan watched Brady ruminate, burying the impulse to add more details. As the silence continued, he grew more and more awkward. The words were vying to blurt out, like pressure building up in a jet. As Brady spoke, he breathed a sigh of relief.

'He? Who is he?' Brady pushed back into Dan's space. He had nowhere to go, as the sofa behind him blocked him in.

Dan had seen Brady put many fighters on the back foot, and had always cheered for him, but suddenly, he knew how they felt and he didn't like it. But he knew that whilst they all cowered against the ropes, they had all lost. Not once had they tried to come out swinging.

'He. Doesn't matter.' Dan left a gap in his defence, waiting for Brady to take the bait. As he saw him attempt to speak, he swung again. 'Actually, you know what? He's my dealer.'

'What do you mean, dealer?' Brady's lack of surprise belied his question.

'Yeah, you already know I'm into it, huh?' Dan moved forwards and Brady took a step back, creating space. 'You just don't care, right?' Dan seized the gap, escaping the vice that Brady had created between him and the sofa and headed for the bathroom, slamming the door shut behind him.

Dan leant over the basin, caked in residue. He looked at himself in the mirror, noting how pale his face had become. He sniffed as the stagnant water in the base of the shower permeated into his nostrils. *How long has the drain been clogged? A week? Two maybe.* He ran the cold tap and watched as the water rose in the sink. A chunk or two of old vomit came up and floated, swirling in the displacement as the fresh water ran.

'How're you going to make this about you, man?' Brady shouted through the door.

Dan cupped a handful of water and splashed it on his face. 'Oh it's not about me, it never is.'

He heard Brady laughing. 'Are you really going there again?'

The water in the sink was rising rapidly. He shut the tap off and perched on the edge of the sink, leaning down to the toilet and lightly putting pressure on the flush button, ensuring a slow trickle of water into the pan. 'Going where?'

'You already tried this earlier. That DoSe getting to your memory?'

'DoSe? I never said it was DoSe, so how do you know that?'

'Yeah mate, stop changing the subject. Who is your dealer?'

Dan stamped the ground with his foot. 'I don't know, just some guy.'

'Just some guy? You seriously expect me to believe that just some guy came hunting me down? Are you stupid or what?'

Dan slumped. 'Look, I don't know who he is, it's all pretty anonymous.'

'Can't be that anonymous if he got to me through you.'

Dan was digging his hole deeper and deeper and he knew it. He begged his muted brain to come up with the right sequence of words to put a stop to it all, but the brain fog was too thick. He sat in silence. Maybe if he closed his eyes and remained quiet for long enough, Brady would eventually disappear. His wish was shot down by the loud pounding on the door.

'Are you going to say something? Or ever come out? You can't hide in there all day.' Brady's combined laugh and groan of exasperation was loud enough to be heard, muffled by the closed door, but enough to turn the screw.

'I'm peeing, give me a minute. Can't you hear?'

'Nobody pees for that long. You think I'm stupid or what?'

Dan sighed, increasing the pressure on the flush mechanism to instigate a full flush. 'I'm done man, I can't help it, it's the DoSe.'

'Just hurry up and get out here.'

Dan stared himself down in the mirror. His eyes pinched, head dropped. With tightened jaw, he let out a cry of anguish, so dampened it could not be heard by Brady, but it was enough to at least begin unknotting his stomach.

Dan opened the bathroom door, met by anger on Brady's face. He attempted to breeze past him, but Brady blocked his way. He didn't have the strength to move him, reluctantly stepping back, and met his eyes.

The moment he saw the hurt behind the anger of his friend, Dan lost all fight. the withdrawals grew worse by the minute and the guilt only compounded his down-slide.

'I can't anymore, Brades. Just... I don't know, tell me what you want to know.' Just as he spoke, Dan felt a wave of darkness crashing in on him. Brady, the room and everything in it began to fade away and he felt a chill through his veins. What was left of his vision, a dark, blurry mess, seemed to zoom in and out in front of his face. Then he felt the cold wall against his shoulder, then face. All went black.

As Dan opened his eyes, he recognised the ceiling. Every stain, every crack in the rendering. He was in his bed. Still woozy, he gingerly sat up to find Brady perched at the foot of his bed. Brady remained motionless, staring at the wall opposite.

'What happened?' Dan already knew the answer, but he didn't want to dive straight back into the interrogation.

'You passed out.' Brady's voice was downbeat. Dan had expected a continuation of the anger and this surprised him.

'I'm surprised you didn't leave me there.' He attempted to laugh, but it soon turned to a cough.

'Thought about it.'

'What changed your mind?'

Brady finally turned to face him. 'Look at the state of you, Dan. Trust me, I want to be angry at you, but.' He shook his head. 'I don't know man, it's like you aren't even you.'

Dan smiled, sadly. 'So what now?'

'You've still got some explaining to do, no matter what else.' Brady shuffled around. 'Start with this guy trying to kill me.'

Feeling a heavy weight on his chest, Dan realised Brady had put him under the covers. He pushed the duvet off himself, but it brought no relief. He rubbed his face with both hands, and took a deep breath, letting it out before he began. 'Okay. But first thing's first. Are you sure he was trying to kill you? I swear this guy did not want you dead.'

Brady muttered something under his breath but Dan couldn't hear. He was about to chase up when Brady spoke. 'You expect me to believe that?'

'I swear man, I would never have agreed if I thought he would kill you.'

Brady shook his head. 'Okay, let me try again. Did you really believe that?'

'Answer my question. Did he actually try to kill you?'

He could see Brady pause for thought. 'He came in all guns blazing. So yeah. I reckon so.'

'Came in where?'

'You should know.'

'Honestly I don't. Look, I just put a tracker on Mya, I could tell she knew where you were. That's as much as I knew.'

Brady stood up and paced back and forth. Dan waited, giving him time to ruminate. Eventually Brady stopped in his tracks. 'Okay, so maybe he wasn't. I don't know. He had to fight through others.'

Dan, rejuvenated by the breakthrough, sat further upright. 'Well there you go.'

'Okay, let's say for argument's sake, he wasn't. I still need to know who this person who sent him is.'

'I really don't know who he is.' He immediately noticed the look Brady gave him. He wasn't buying it and it was clear. 'Okay fine. You want to know? It's the truth I don't know who he is. But

I know he's working against MediTech from the inside.'

'You what?' Brady marched up to the side of the bed, looming over Dan. 'He's MediTech and you gave me up?'

Dan attempted to get up, but Brady pinned him down. The force on his chest was unlike anything he had felt before. Dan struggled, but could not move. 'Listen to what I said, he is working against them. I'm pretty sure he's part of the Russian-Asian alliance.'

Brady backed off, swivelled to the wall, and punched. The impact shook the room and cracked the solid duracrete. He shook his fist loose and grimaced, before turning back to Dan. 'What the hell are you thinking? It's not bad enough I've got—' He stopped abruptly.

'Got what?' Dan already knew the answer, but he wanted to hear him say it.

'Don't avoid the question. You're giving me up to some foreign agent now?'

'I don't know, I'm just guessing he is. I never met him. He called me up one day, said he could hook me up with real DoSe but I had to let him know your movements.'

'How long ago?'

'Three, four months maybe.'

Brady looked clearly confused. 'Wait, so why now?'

'I seriously don't know, man. Something to do with the fight maybe.'

Brady grabbed Dan's hand, twisting it back. 'Do you really not know?'

Dan cried in pain. 'Okay, okay.' Brady let his hand go. His face had once again become angry. 'Yeah I know. Okay, you happy now?'

Brady thumped down into the bed. 'And how do you know that?'

Dan sighed. 'I'm with AntiFa, man.' He saw the shock on

Brady's face. 'I've been keeping an eye on you since we were kids.'

Brady flew into a rage in front of Dan's eyes, smashing anything he could see and sweeping broken remnants around. 'Are you kidding me? My whole life you've just been some spy?'

'No man, it's not like that, I didn't choose it, I just did it. Our friendship is real to me.'

Brady grabbed the edge of the desk and ripped it from the ground, tearing chunks of floor from where it had been anchored with it. Even with his nervous system dulled, Dan felt the unmistakeable pangs of fear and apprehension, seeing just how strong Brady had become.

Brady held the desk aloft, wielding it like a weapon. Dan mustered up all his energy and rolled out of bed to the opposite side. Panicked, he looked for something to act as a defence, but there was nothing aside from dirty clothes and empty beer cans.

Brady primed the desk for a strike. 'Give me one good reason I don't take you out right now!'

Dan backed into the corner. 'You know what? Do it, I'm dead anyway.'

'You're dead to me.'

Dan saw Brady relax his stance a little. He knew he wasn't going to do anything; still, he had to play cautious. 'You know what? I don't blame you. But, mate, this isn't you. You aren't a killer.'

Brady screamed in frustration, turned away from Dan and launched the desk at the wall. The noise of the impact was almost deafening. Dan heard the muffled shouts of his neighbour through the wall as he reeled back, banging against the corner of the room. The desk had broken into two pieces and cracked the wall, a spiderweb vein running from the damage point, straight to the point Brady had punched earlier. Dan's apartment was breaking apart. It mirrored his own demise.

Brady leaned into the wall and slid down to the floor. 'How can you be working with them and still give me up?'

Dan walked around the bed towards him. 'I don't have a choice, man. Look at me. I'm dying.'

Brady looked up at him, solemnly. 'So just screw everyone so long as you can numb the pain, huh?'

Dan knelt down in front of Brady. 'It's not just that.'

'So what else?'

Dan sighed. 'This tech you've got, the guy told me if he gets hold of it, his plan is to replicate it and make it available to everyone. It could save my life. Not just mine. Everyone's.' He reached out to Brady, but was brushed away. 'I'm not afraid of death, but you know what scares me most? That I don't die, I just become a zombie.'

Brady looked up at Dan, and could tell by the look on his face that something had resonated with him. Like he had seen exactly what Dan had meant. And in that moment, Dan pieced together exactly where Brady had been.

'You've seen it for yourself, haven't you?'

Brady nodded. Said nothing.

'You get it then, right? I am really, genuinely sorry, but mate, I can't give that chance up.'

Brady stood abruptly. 'I don't want to hear any more of it. You need to do something for me or I swear, either I take you out, or give you up.'

Brady began leaving the bedroom and Dan followed through to the living room. 'Like what?'

'I need Joshua.' Brady continued towards the front door. 'And I need you to clear my way.'

Dan stopped dead. 'What? No chance.'

Brady turned back to him. 'Look, it's happening, but with your help, nobody gets hurt.' He paused. 'Without it. Well.'

Dan didn't know how to react. He was caught between a rock

and a hard place. He slumped into the sofa, staring beyond Brady as though he weren't there, saying nothing.

Brady opened the front door and stepped half out. 'I'll ping you the details. You know what to do.'

Dan watched as he left, shell-shocked and torn.

CHAPTER NINETEEN

Brady wore the holo-projected face of a middle-aged man. Hood up and hat pulled down to obscure the view as much as possible, he moved quickly through the streets outside the primary school in Dan's block. He had timed it perfectly with the end of the school day. Hordes of children jovially celebrated their freedom for the day, meeting their transports on the roads. Hundreds of shuttle buses lined up in military fashion, each in their respective zones to ferry the passengers to their living blocks.

Beyond the noise and business, he could see the exit to the industrial transit lounge. As long as his disguise and identification got him through there, he was clear to access the maintenance tunnel that would take him back down below.

He weaved his way through the exodus of children with speed and agility. The looks he received made him uneasy, but he soon realised that, given his disguise, he looked a lot like someone these children had probably been warned to steer clear of. He quickened his pace, not wanting to appear as though he was lingering.

Soon enough, he was at the terminal to the transit lounge. He held his breath as he approached. The identification had worked to get him up there, but the words of warning about how long false ID worked for echoed in his mind.

Cautiously, he placed his hand on the access terminal and waited. The display in front cycled quickly through biometrics, randomly selecting which secondary form of identification it required. Brady called up his HUD, quickly navigating to his hack options. He guided the reticule over the access terminal and waited for the options to display.

It was a race against time now. He wasn't au fait enough with his systems yet to be as slick as he would like, he just needed his system to offer up the backdoor option to force facial recognition.

One by one, his options turned red. There was nothing left. He had missed the window of opportunity and all he could do was hope. He closed his HUD and looked at the terminal monitor. DNA match selected. Nothing he could do. The timer had begun. Five second countdown before alarm bells rang. What were his choices? Run through the crowd, hope to jump on a shuttle unseen? No chance. Brute force the transit door? Even less.

His thoughts were interrupted by the all too familiar ringing of the alarm. Then the hiss of the door to the lounge as it began to open. He already knew what would be meeting him. He backed off quickly, aiming his arm at the ground before the door. He switched his ocular implants to heat detection, then fired a smoke missile from his wrist rocket to the ground.

The billowing thick smoke obscured everything, but Brady could see the two heat signatures of the bodies of MediTech security at the doorway. His hand had been forced.

Without a thought, he launched himself at one, powerfully landing a knee blow to their chest. He heard the crack of ribs and the exhalation of breath. One down.

He had to move quickly or lose his advantage. No time to draw weapons, no time for anything slick or clever. He jumped on the back of the second guard, and using one hand, he ripped away their helmet. The other hand smothered their face. Brady selected claw grip deployment from his system. The wrenching sound of metal tearing flesh was gruesome. It turned his stomach. He retracted his grips and the body of the guard dropped like a ragdoll in front of him.

The two heat signatures lay motionless on the floor. Warmth radiated from the head of the second guard. He knew it was their blood. Dead.

He had to run.

***

Brady had the underground complex in sight. He recalled the first time he ran the gauntlet of husks alone, and all that fear over these creatures he now felt nothing but pity for. As much as he didn't believe Dan's revelation that his contact could lead to the prevention of any more of these poor souls, he wanted it to be true.

The gate groaned opened before he even reached it. Mya waited for him as he ran towards it. As he grew closer, he noticed her expression change from glee to concern. He already knew why; he could feel his own aura. The heavy guilt of taking a life shrouded him like a cloak of darkness.

As Brady reached her, they said nothing. He was immediately greeted by her warm embrace. He felt her grip tighten, pulling him into a sanctuary that he had not felt since Elena's hugs during his childhood. But the memory of those had been tarnished, and this new home felt more needed than ever.

'They're dead,' he said. A whisper, reverberating with dread. 'I never—'

'It's okay.' Mya stopped his words. 'I know.'

Brady buried his face further into her neck. Her skin was warm and soft. His safe place. 'How?'

'It's obvious, hun.' Her words, muffled by the grinding as the gates closed behind them, still sounded sweet to him.

He pulled back to look at her. Tears welling in his eyes, his tightened lips began to quiver. 'I hate this feeling.'

She took the back of his head and pulled it back into her chest. 'I know you do, he was your friend after all.' She kissed the top of his head lightly.

Brady pulled away again. Sharper this time. 'What? Not Dan, no.' His voice cracked. 'I could've. For a minute I wanted to.'

Mya looked puzzled. 'Then who?'

Brady wiped the tears from his face and cleared his throat. 'MediTech. Guards. Two of them.'

As Brady began to pull away, Mya released her grip on his arms.. 'So he was working with them?'

'What?' said Brady.

She looked confused. 'Wait, not at his place? Then where?'

Brady rubbed his face, and could feel a burning sensation in his eyes, knowing the tears and his ocular overlays didn't mix well. 'No. Transit entrance. ID hack failed, set off alarm and then, well.'

Mya breathed a clear sigh of relief. 'That's different hun. You know they would've killed you on sight.'

Brady felt the words cut like a knife. 'Different? I still killed them. Doesn't matter how or where, does it? I'm a murderer. What the hell?' He felt anger building inside.

Mya's face scrunched up, as though he had just told her the most ridiculous story. 'That doesn't make you a murderer, as they are the enemy of us all; it makes you a soldier. You did what you had to.'

'They were still people, and I took their lives. That's murder, and just because you dress it up as something else, doesn't mean that beneath it all, it isn't the same damn thing.' He turned to walk away. 'I don't know how you can be so flippant. I expected it from them, not you.' Brady stormed away, deeper into the complex.

'Hun, I'm sorry, I didn't mean it like that!' Brady remained unfazed by her words and continued his march. 'Brady!'

He quickened his pace, shaking his head in disbelief. 'I don't want to hear it right now!'

Brady stormed towards Benito's home, ignoring the continued shouts from Mya. He turned back to see her remaining where she was, hanging her head, looking dejected. He fought the urge to turn back, knowing all too well that the emotions running through him would only serve to escalate things with her. It was better to leave it be.

Benito's door opened before Brady even reached it. Of course Benito knew he was coming. *Doesn't miss a trick.*

'So, we on?' Benito's directness was jarring. For a man everyone in the undercity seemed to revere, Brady could not understand why. His moments of pleasantness were too few and far between to be the real Benito. Brady wondered, was it his outsider perspective that allowed him to see what others could not?

'Nice to be back, glad I made it.' Brady avoided eye contact as he brushed past Benito. He felt his hand on his shoulder, trying to stop him, but he was having none of it.

'There's really no need for the attitude, and if my curtness is grating, it is only because of the importance of this situation.' Benito held his hands up in a gesture of apology.

Brady was sure Benito's attitude was masking the truth, but he played along. 'Okay, fine. Let's just leave it there.'

'I take it you do have some sort of update?' said Benito.

Brady gestured with his head for Benito to follow him into the living room. 'Pretty big one.'

Brady immediately took a seat in Benito's armchair. He spread his legs, making a pointed display and watched as Benito weighed up whether to take the bait. Benito looked straight into Brady's eyes and smiled before taking a seat on his sofa and calling up on his comms. 'Layne. Living room. Bring everyone.'

'Not Mya,' said Brady. Benito met him with a questioning glance and Brady shook his head with purpose. Benito nodded in agreement.

'Leave Mya out of it, Layne.' His eye returned to normal as comms ended. 'What's that about?'

'Not the time. Let's just keep this about the plan.'

'Maybe it's not my business anyway, but just answer this, is there something that can compromise what we need to do?'

Brady closed his eyes and drew in a composing breath. 'No. Nothing like that.'

'Then it isn't my business unless it becomes my business,' said Benito.

Brady chuckled quietly. 'Yes, I get it.'

The two shared an awkward silence. Brady felt as if it was going to last forever, until the door opened and Layne entered, followed by Doc and Samantha. Their faces were more welcome than normal to Brady for the break of the silence they provided.

Benito stood to greet them. 'All here. Let's get down to business. Brady, what have you got for us?'

Layne winked at Brady as he walked past to perch on the edge of Benito's coffee table. 'No messing about, huh?' Doc and Samantha took seats on the sofa as Benito sat back down.

'Alright then, I'll cut to the chase.' Brady sat forward. 'So this friend of mine... Turns out I've been a project for him since we were kids.'

Benito and Layne shared a look before Benito addressed Brady. 'What does that mean?'

'Means we've got a way in with AntiFa. Don't need to create a stir any more. He will clear them out for us.'

Layne stood abruptly. 'AntiFa? No way that guy was AntiFa.'

'You're right there. My friend, okay, let's call him my contact now, we aren't friends.' Brady cracked his knuckles, but there was no release and no noise. He looked down at his hands; *one more thing to get used to.* 'I'll just say he's in deep with someone. MediTech maybe, maybe a foreign agent working them within.'

Samantha immediately became uneasy, shifting uncomfortably on the sofa. 'Foreign agent? This is getting out of hand.' Brady noticed her mannerisms change. She must have been scared. Then it occurred to him. *Why aren't I?* Everything had been happening so quickly, he'd never taken a moment to truly contemplate the severity of the situation. Dealing with his fate was one thing, getting embroiled in a global political matter, until that very moment, hadn't seemed quite as monumental as it was.

Brady's deepened thought process was interrupted by Benito. 'Are you kidding me?'

'Nope.' Brady looked back at Samantha. She was definitely more alert than he had seen her before. 'Well I don't know for sure, nor does he. But could be.'

Layne had been relaxed until this point, but his hackles were raised now. 'Assuming he is both, why come after you?'

'Same reason as everyone else. He knows what I've got.'

'Layne is right,' said Benito. 'If he's some kind of double agent, going after you is just going to get him caught.'

'Well, you know whoever came down for me wasn't MediTech, so what other option does that leave?'

'You're taking this all on your friend's word? The same friend who you just said has been deceiving you all your life?' Benito raised an eyebrow at Brady, patronising, yet he had a point.

'I trust him as far as I can throw him.'

'Could have thrown him,' said Layne, grinning to himself.

Brady looked at Layne, wondering why brevity in this situation was called for. 'I don't trust him, but it makes sense, right? MediTech want this thing, AntiFa want this thing. Why wouldn't other nations? He said this man can replicate it, use it to save lives. Even said he would save my—' He caught himself before he said it. 'Contact.'

Doc laughed. 'So besides untrustworthy, he is also naïve?'

'Doc is right.' Samantha stood. 'If he is what your friend says he is, you won't ever be coming back here. Nor will he.'

'Still.' Benito got up and headed to his liquor cabinet. 'For sake of argument, let's say he is. Wouldn't it be interesting if he found himself between jobs?' He perused his collection, settling on an unlabelled bottle of brown liquor. He uncorked the bottle and took a long, meaningful sniff. 'Could be pretty beneficial to have someone with that kind of knowledge.'

Brady watched on as Layne joined Benito at the cabinet, grabbing a glass for himself and setting it down, expectantly. 'Before you explain that, pour me one.'

Benito looked in Brady's direction and pointed the bottle in his direction. 'You, too?'

Brady shook his head to decline. 'You think this guy would just join you if you asked nicely?'

Benito turned back to the bar and grabbed a glass, pouring one for himself, then setting the bottle down. 'Someone in that unique position comes with some pretty clear strings attached to them, don't you think?' He took a sip, and Brady saw the reaction to the burning liquor on his face even from across the room. He was glad he'd declined the offer. 'Be pretty easy to pull them and make him dance.'

Doc tilted his neck to the side, adding pressure with his hands. The crack of his spinal fluids was loud. 'With what he might know, I'd tend to agree.' He bent his neck the other way, cracking once more. 'But theory and practice are two very different concepts.'

Brady was watching a stand-off between Layne and Benito over who would pour Layne's drink. Eventually Layne caved. He poured a long glass, keeping his stare on Benito the entire time until it nearly spilled over. Layne stopped just in time and bent down to slurp the excess. 'I know what you are thinking,' said Layne, words muffled by the act of swallowing. 'What if he's wrong. We just set ourselves up to be annihilated.'

Benito grabbed the bottle back and corked it. 'Brady.' He turned his attention. 'If you had to bet Mya's life, which way would you go?'

'On the guy being a mole?' He saw Benito nod. 'I don't know. More I think about, the more confident I am.'

Samantha sighed. 'Now is hardly a time for gambling. We're in survival mode. Any minute now his presence could bring an army down. Maybe we should hit pause on anything grander until we have worked this mess out.'

Brady looked around at everyone else. They were quiet, and each seemed to be ruminating with their own thoughts. Benito, in particular, looked deep in a quandary. He swilled his drink, looking inside as though he was reading his fortune in tea leaves.

The silence was beginning to make Brady uncomfortable, so he stood. 'I don't agree. Look, even if we pull this off and get this thing hidden, it's only a matter of time before they find it. We need to replicate it before that happens, then who cares? We can hand it to them and end all this.'

Doc laughed. 'You think they will just let you walk then?'

'It doesn't matter about me. I'm dead either way, but one scenario means it's all for nothing. The other, well maybe my life will mean something if it's the means to you saving thousands.'

Layne put his glass down. 'Mya won't like to hear that.'

'Good thing she isn't here, then, isn't it?' said Brady.

Benito sauntered over to Brady and put his hand on his shoulder. He was more gentle than usual. 'Are you sure you want to risk this?'

Brady looked at Benito, his eyes remaining steely and determined. Not the look of wariness he usually had with him. 'You and I both know it was always going to be the outcome. At least we can be honest about it now.'

Benito nodded. 'You concentrate on getting what we need. I'll find this guy.'

'How? We have no idea who he is,' said Brady.

Benito gently patted him. 'When you tell your friend to clear out the obstacles and set up a meeting with him. We can take care of the rest.'

Brady walked away from Benito around the back of the armchair and leaned over it. 'Then what? He doesn't know who he is, either.'

Benito grinned. 'But he knows how to get in touch with him. That's the first step we need.'

'You are biting off more than you can chew,' said Samantha.

Doc stood, joining Samantha. He put one arm around her. 'They are right though. Time isn't something we have. How they haven't already brought the hammer down is beyond me.'

Layne made his way to them, forcing himself between the two and placing his arms around them both. 'What are we waiting for then? Let's get a wriggle on, eh Benny?'

Benito took a long, hard look at Brady. 'You sure you are ready for this?'

Brady looked down between the chair and his body, to his feet. 'What other choice is there?' He looked up, doing his best to appear confident, through his nerves were churning.

Benito turned to the other three. 'Doc, Sam, anything else you can do this end for him?'

Samantha broke away from Layne's arm. 'Nothing. Final check on his systems to make sure there aren't any glitches, that's about it.'

Benito walked to the living room door, opened it and ushered Doc, Samantha and Layne out. 'Give us a moment.' The three diligently obliged, leaving Brady and Benito alone.

Brady watched on as Benito shut the door and turned back to him. 'I know you don't trust me. Truth be told, I don't trust you yet either.' He walked to his chair and took a seat, waving Brady to come around and sit on the sofa. 'Thing is, that's probably why we will eventually be good together.' Brady made his way to the sofa, labouring as he did. 'Too many people just give out their trust and you know why?'

Brady sat, crossing his legs in an over-exaggerated movement. 'No, why is that then?'

'Because they aren't worthy of it themselves. They don't value it as a commodity, so when someone like you comes along and questions my intentions.'

Brady began to speak but was immediately cut off.

'Come on, I know. And I respect it,' said Benito. 'It means I know you are on edge. And if you are on edge, it means you and I are on the same page.'

Brady uncrossed his legs and sat forward, imposing his frame. 'So why don't you trust me?'

Benito sank deeper into his armchair. 'It's not that I don't trust you, more I don't know if I can trust your judgement.'

'If you've got something to say, just say it.'

'This friend, or whatever. How sure are you the whole thing isn't a setup?' Benito raised one eyebrow. 'I assume you scrutinise others as much as you do me?'

Brady chuckled. 'I'm not even going to answer that.'

Benito stood. 'You better be right. I don't think you'll like the outcome if you aren't.' He began heading towards the door.

'Is that a threat?'

Benito paused, didn't look back. 'Not a threat. Call it a warning.' He slowly pushed the door handle down. 'If there're any doubts, now is the time to tell me.' With that, he left the room.

Brady remained seated, listening to his footsteps when he heard him talking. 'He's all yours.' Brady sat forward, perched on the edge of the sofa. His hand slid down to his wait, ready by the butt of his handgun. He tensed up, watching the door handle dip. As it slowly opened, his hand twitched. When he saw Samantha's face in the gap, he relaxed, exhaling a sigh of relief.

'I'm just going to do a quick scan.' She pulled out her portable system monitor from her jacket pocket. 'Won't take long.' She placed two probes on his temples and began the checks.

Brady sat patiently as she went through the motions. 'What are you looking for?'

Engrossed in the monitor, she almost missed the question. 'Just integration, making sure everything is working as intended.'

'And?'

As she finished the process, she removed the probes. 'All checks out. You're good to go, even if you are biting off more than you can chew.'

Brady grinned. 'Turns out my capacity to chew things is a lot greater than I realised.'

Samantha slipped her monitoring device away and held her hands aloft. She mumbled something inaudible as she walked back out, leaving Brady alone again. He called up his comms overlay and wrote out a message to Dan. EVACUATE – 7AM TOMORROW – MEET ME AT THE OLD PLAYHOUSE – THIRD FLOOR AT 6:45.

Brady sat, contemplating what was to come. Thoughts of what could happen if Dan didn't play ball and evacuate AntiFa's compound terrified him. He looked at the palm of his hand, extracting and retracting the grapple claws over and over. It was one thing taking the life of a MediTech guard, and whilst he had no love for what AntiFa had done to him, the thought of having to take their lives just didn't sit right with him.

He wished he could hit pause. A stay of execution, to figure this all out. He was caught in a snowball effect, always moving, constantly gathering momentum. Merely hours were left before he would meet Layne to carry it out, hours before Benito's mysterious plan to get to Dan's contact. And those words he left him with. That he would be the one to suffer greatest if Dan betrayed him again.

He needed some sleep, but he already knew it would elude him.

CHAPTER TWENTY

A cold vortex of air blew down through the gaping hole in the mezzanine above the undercity, whipping up a dust devil around Brady and Layne's feet as they stared up though the chasm. The relentless shuffle of husks grew ever nearer to them from all direction, like walls closing in. With a sharp click, Layne loaded a grappling hook to his handgun and took aim through the hole.

'You sure this is the way?' Layne clipped the carabinier to his belt.

'Hundred percent.' Brady called up his HUD and scanned for structures within his newly increased jumping distance. The reticule whizzed around, looking for a suitable anchor point, eventually flickering green as it settled on the contorted remnants of a support beam that hung below the hole.

Layne's tactical armour suit was clearly a better fit than Brady's. Custom built, rather than the ill-fitted dregs that Brady had scrambled together from the enclave's lost and found. It was clear enough to him that the lost part referred to the lives of whoever had been wearing the pieces prior. He felt as though he was wearing a patchwork quilt of lives gone by.

'I'll see you up there.' Layne's gun crackled. The hook fizzed through the air, and the spool of single, thin-thread biridium unfurled, whipping the air as it snaked its way up. The thud of his hook striking a target was subdued, too far away to hear the true impact. Before Brady knew it, Layne had activated the winch and shot up and out of sight like a rag-doll pulled behind a jet engine.

Brady was left standing as the trudging pincer movement of the husks was getting ever closer. His heart raced, it wasn't them he was worried about, rather, the impending leap. His systems made it look like child's play, breaking down a superhuman feat into mere algorithms.

In a perfect world, he would've had more time to bolster his confidence enough to make the leap, but it was either fight or flight now. Any further hesitance and he would have no choice but to kill that which he wished to save. He primed himself, coiled like a spring, ready for launch. Looking at his trajectory, the proximity to what remained of a solid wall was nerve-wracking. *Not enough space there, surely.*

With no choice but to trust the calculations, he launched. With a force he had never experienced before, he rocketed through the air. His target hurtled ever closer. And that wall. *Gonna hit it.* His body tensed, ready for impact and he cried out in fear. Ever closer, he panicked. *Hooks!* He had forgotten to deploy them. Too late. *Try and grab it anyway.*

He stretched out his hands, instinctually guarding himself from the inevitable crash. The wall narrowly missed his left shoulder and with a loud, crunching sound, he swung from the beam. His left hand had made impact. *System's must've pre-selected hooks.* The momentum swung him like a pendulum. He heard the rapid retraction of the hooks and once more he was airborne. This time, like a loose wrecking ball, his flight arched him through the chasm.

His knees hit the ground first. Didn't hurt like he expected. Tumbling like a lifeless body cast aside, he rolled, slid and finally came to a halt just inches from the partially destroyed gate, with Layne's grappling hook jammed through the bars.

'Fun, right?' Layne chuckled, looming over him.

Brady, white as a ghost, panted frantically as he fixated his gaze on a sharp end of railing that pointed directly between his eyes. The sight of it sent shivers from his eyeballs down to his stomach.

His gaze was broken when he saw Layne thrust his hand in front of him. Brady took hold and Layne lifted him up. 'Something like that.'

Layne let him go and tussled with the grappling hook, thrusting it further through the bar to release it. 'Man it's cold up here.'

'You should feel it when you're dragging yourself through with a shattered leg.' Brady looked back down through the hole at the husks below, recalling how he had felt the last time he stood on the precipice.

'Well, you made it, that's the main thing. Different this time.' Layne slapped him on the back, it made him jump. He stumbled slightly towards the fall, but caught himself in time.

Brady took one last look, then turned away. 'We gotta get moving, it's a long way.'

Layne nodded in agreement, falling in line behind Brady as he led them through the corridors. They traced his footsteps in reverse, winding through the corridors, into the gun room and out, down the ladder to the ground below.

Layne looked back up the walls to where they had descended from. 'Man, I don't know how you managed to climb that in the state you were in.'

Brady was busy scanning the wreckages ahead for heat signatures. 'Honestly I don't remember much of it. Adrenaline I guess. Will to survive maybe.'

Layne spun around, surveying the horizon. 'Never occurred to you to go that way?' He pointed out into the distance. On the horizon, the darkness was broken by the beginnings of sunrise.

Brady turned off heat scanning to look at where he was pointing. 'Uh, no.' His voice was weakened by amazement at the sight.

Brady glanced over at Layne, who was transfixed. 'I've never seen something so powerful, yet beautiful at the same time.'

Layne wiped the tears that had begun to well in his eyes.

Brady looked back to the horizon, amazed by how much it had come up since he had looked away. 'You never saw it during the war?'

Layne remained quiet for a moment, taking it all in. 'Sure, I saw it. But without ever seeing it. Not really.'

'How can you see something without seeing it?' asked Brady.

Layne tore himself away from the rising sun. 'Why were you so engrossed looking down through the mezzanine? You saw it before.'

Brady thought about it for a moment. It was true that he didn't realise the scope of the husks the first time around, as he'd been too focused on fear and survival. 'Alright, I get it.' He took another long look at the ever-growing ball of red. The light emanating had begun to intensify, painting a picture of hued streaks on the canvas of clouds. 'We've got to move though. The window is closing.' With that, he hurried towards the wreckages.

Brady looked back to Layne, gesturing to follow. As Layne caught up, he could see him studying the carcasses of the vehicles closely. 'What's up?'

Layne stopped at the exterior of the Russian Air Assault body. He pressed his hand against the panel, formed a fist and tapped, with a hollow clunk. 'What the hell?'

Brady stepped over debris to enter the shell, then looked around to Layne. 'What's up?'

'This is fake,' said Layne as he wrenched a panel away. Between the exterior and interior skin, the hull was hollow. 'They never made these with aluminium, they were titan alloy.' He pushed his head inside the gap he had created. 'And there's nothing in here. Where are the cables?'

Brady took a look at the panels himself, not really sure what he was looking for. 'So what are you saying?'

Layne emerged. 'False flag attacks. Make the population fear the outside world and they won't be curious about it.'

'Are you serious?' said Brady, his brows furrowed in confusion.

Layne joined him inside the fuselage. 'Worked, didn't it? Everyone in that city suckles the teat with gratitude.'

Brady bent down at the hatch. 'I guess. Benito said something similar.'

'Always surprised the lengths they go to.' Layne knelt down beside him. 'Anyway, doesn't matter. This the way in?'

'Yup. Pretty damn heavy. Give me a hand with it.' Brady grabbed the handle on top, making room for Layne to get a hold on it as well.

'Heavy for you before, now give it a try,' said Layne, backing off to make room.

Brady looked at Layne, who just smiled. He took a more solid grip and braced to lift. It was easier. Much easier. With little effort, Brady had lifted the hatch clean open, swinging it over the hinges and dropping it to the ground.

Layne peered inside the tunnel network below. 'Quick in, quick out, right?

Brady took in a deep breath, bolstering his nerves. Even if Dan had cleared the way for him, something about going back into the Lion's den was terrifying. Gingerly, he began to lower himself.

The tunnels were narrower than he remembered. Claustrophobic, even. He carefully took the last step down, moving to make room for Layne, and crouching. He looked up at the hatch, watching Layne descend. On his HUD, he selected the private comms channel with Layne and sent him a message, using his thought feedback to type: QUIETLY.

He saw Layne looking down over his shoulder at him before he received a response: EASIER TO BE QUIET WHEN I DON'T HAVE TO READ YOUR MESSAGES.

As Layne stepped off the ladder, Brady gestured for him to

crouch with him. He sent the next communication: JUST FOLLOW ME. Layne nodded in agreement and Brady set off down the dark, quiet tunnels of the maze.

The heat radiated off the pipes just as he remembered. Sweat dripped from both of their brows, their breathing, short and tight. Brady didn't remember the amount of cobwebs he now felt suffocated by with each one that grasped his face.

He could feel Layne behind him, almost breathing down his neck. Too close for comfort. *Wish he'd back off.* Brady forgot his thought to text was on and the message sent through to Layne. Brady snapped his head back around, and the look on Layne's face told him the message had gone through.

Layne gave him some breathing room and Brady continued to lead them through the maze of the maintenance tunnels, trying desperately to recall which twist he needed to take. Everything looked the same. *Have I gone full circle?* Only time would tell. Couldn't let on that he was lost, and had to seem confident. *Carry on for long enough and get lucky.* The complex was somewhere close, it had to be. Then it dawned on him, if anyone had discovered the panel he'd twisted to escape to these tunnels, chances are they would have repaired it. He began to panic, as the cramped tunnels began to close in yet more.

Brady looked back to Layne, and could sense him losing faith in his leadership. Then, Layne's message appeared on Brady's HUD: SWITCH TO IR, OVERLAY HEAT SENSOR. TRACE THE INSFRASTRUCTURE.

He switched both overlays on and swept around the tunnels. He could see Layne, burning brightly in his view, and turned away to the darkness, taking a moment to readjust his vision. And then he saw the faintest hope. In the distance, a thin wisp of marginal heat. He had no idea what it was, but it had to be a sign of life.

As they crawled ever closer, the source became more apparent.

Electrical cables and wires carrying current around AntiFa's complex, had to be. The goal was in sight, and for every inch he grew closer, the greater his nervous anticipation. Still, no sign of body heat, so maybe Dan had made good on his word.

After what had felt like an eternity of guesswork and hope, Brady had led them to the breach. The panel he had escaped through remained twisted open. He was surprised it had not been found and sealed, but it certainly made it easier. He looked over his shoulder to Layne, motioning that they needed to squeeze through.

It was eerily quiet in AntiFa's compound. Brady recalled the hum of machinery the last time he was there. It was missing. The doors he could see were ajar, and there were empty crates all down the corridors. Something didn't feel right at all.

'What are you waiting for?' Layne's whisper was enough to startle Brady.

'I don't like this.' Brady did another full sweep; zero heat signatures.

'What's the problem? This is what we wanted.' Layne stood tall and relaxed himself.

Brady followed suit, and as uneasy as he felt, he knew there was no imminent danger. 'I don't know, it feels more abandoned.'

Layne brazenly powered down the corridor, sticking his head into rooms as he made his way down. He stopped briefly to shout back at Brady. 'You sure this is the right place?'

Brady began to catch up with him. 'This is definitely the place.' He peered inside a crate; nothing. 'Something has happened.'

'Let's just get the databank and bug out.' Layne entered one of the rooms, disappearing from Brady's sight.

As Brady joined Layne, the sight of a desolate room with nothing but abandoned cables laying around caused panic. He turned tail and began running, out through the corridor and down to the server room. The door into it was open, just like the others.

He paused and took a deep breath before entering.

'Where did you go?' Layne's voice was distant.

'Down here!' Brady stood in the room he had woken up in. Just as he feared, it was gone. The signs were clear; they had made a hasty retreat. He stood alone with the echoes of everything said the last time he was there when Layne's hasty arrival broke his concentration.

'What are you doing?'

Brady looked at him, solemn and dejected. 'It's gone.'

Layne looked around at the empty room. 'This was it?'

Brady remained silent as he surveyed the room, looking to find anything they may have left behind in their haste, but the exodus had clearly been thorough, if rushed.

Layne inspected the cables protruding from the wall. 'I'm just saying, whatever's going on in your head, couldn't you have imagined it?'

Brady recognised the trunking of cables Layne was inspecting as the same that would have been directly ported into the server with Joshua's data. He noticed the rendering of the wall had cracked, seeing the flakes of plaster on the ground by it. 'They moved quick. Look at that, ripping things out like they needed to be gone in a flash.'

Layne craned his neck around to Brady. 'What are you saying?'

Brady became flustered, and switched back on the heat sensors and frantically scanned around. 'We need to go.'

Layne stood. 'Go? We need to find this thing, man.'

Brady grabbed him, pulling him towards the door. 'Run!'

Out of breath, drenched in sweat, Brady and Layne made it back to the end of the tunnels. Brady stared up at the ladder to the hatch, still open. *Probably should've closed it to cover tracks. Too late.* He held on to Layne's shoulder, chest tightening. Hyperventilating. Lack of oxygen, panic, exhaustion; the imperfect cocktail.

He felt Layne's hands on his head, grasping and positioning to meet his eyes. He mouthed the word breathe. *How can he be so calm? He's sweating like me.* Layne moved one hand to Brady's diaphragm, palm placed across, putting pressure on, then releasing. At first, awkward, suffocating, it soon became reassuring. He was learning to breathe again, like it was a skill he'd never had. With each breath came a calmer moment.

'You good?' said Layne.

Brady just nodded. It was easing, but he couldn't muster a response. Layne pointed at his own chest, then up at the hatch. Brady knew what it meant, and shuffled aside to make room and watched as Layne began to scale.

Brady took a grip on the rungs and lifted himself up a couple. It was hard going. He watched as Layne got higher and higher, and the gap between them got bigger. *Concentrate on your breathing.* He took two deep breaths for every rung. Before he knew it, Layne had disappeared up and out. But he was calming. It was becoming easier.

The sun was fully in the sky when he poked his head up through the hatch. Too bright, in fact. It was burning his retinas. He hauled himself up with one arm shielding his wet eyes. As he adjusted, he could see the figure of Layne ahead. Kneeling. Arms up and behind his head. *Why?*

As his eyes began to adjust to the overwhelming power of the sunlight, the picture became clearer. MediTech security force, five strong. One gun aimed at the back of Layne's head. The others' guns on Brady.

Incoming message notification flashed on his display, so he opened his HUD. Layne's message read: TAKE THIS ONE OUT AND RUN – WILL DEAL WITH REST.

'Get the hands up!' The instruction from the guard was clear.

Brady complied. He needed time to allow the combat interface to calculate the best strategy. Quickly, he marked Layne as friendly and set all other people to threat.

'On your knees, Mr Drummond!' The guard stepped towards him.

If it weren't already apparent, hearing his name told Brady that this was no coincidence. Someone had set them up. Slowly, he motioned as though he were complying, down as far as one knee. The combat implant had finalised the plan of attack, marking the guard behind Layne as priority one and ordering the others sequentially by threat to life.

The reticule chose the first move. A leap to the top of the hull. The trajectory overlay showed him the exact point during the jump he needed to draw and fire shots at the executioner. Adrenaline surged, and he could hear his heart beating. Time appeared to slowed down. The release of dopamine from his neural enhancement let him perceive it in a broader scope.

'I said knees!' The guard's words were elongated and deepened. They almost echoed themselves through Brady's heightened perception of time. He had to make the move.

Brady leapt, twisting his body into the position required to take the shot. His hand whipped his pistol out from its clip. He heard the bustle of motion from the response to his movement. He saw Layne, in slow motion, begin to drop his hands from his head. The executioner tore his attention from Layne to Brady.

Bang. One shot from Brady's hand gun and the executioner was done. The mist of red danced from his head, painting an evolving picture in the air as the guard's body slowly fell to the ground.

He heard the echoed pops and saw concentrated muzzle flashes from Layne's guns as Layne broke forwards for cover.

Before he knew it, Brady landed on the top of the hull, with a clear run down the exterior. His neurals began to level and time reverted to normal, the cacophony of gunshots beginning to catch up. Fighting the strong instinct to turn back and help Layne,

Brady slid down the exterior of the ship.

Brady's feet hit the ground running. The gunshots were becoming less frequent. The fact they were still going meant Layne was alive. Brady was at full speed in a split second, barrelling towards the city's walls. He looked on his HUD's feedback data; thirty-eight miles per hour sprint speed.

He slowed it down, hesitating over his decision. Looking back, he wondered how he could leave Layne so easily. Sure, it was his instruction, but still, he couldn't shake the feeling he should have stayed behind to help.

Ominously, the gunshots abated. One way or another, the fight was over. He could stick around to see, risking the fallout in the case that Layne would not emerge victorious, or scale the walls and retreat to the undercity. Brady looked back and forth between the ladder up and the aircraft graveyard in the distance.

He stepped up, pausing from moving up whilst he battled with his decision. Nothing moved from the ship wreckages. Up it was. Frantically he began climbing, making light work of the ladder that had caused him so much trouble the first time.

Each rung he climbed, his conscience grew heavier. Looking back, there was still no movement from the wreckages. If Layne had been victorious, why wasn't he catching up? If MediTech had taken Layne down, why weren't they? He had to go back.

Gun out, sweeping the crash site ahead, Brady switched to heat signature. Four motionless bodies beginning to cool down within the shell. He burst from cover to cover, each time pausing to perform another tactical sweep. Still just the three bodies. No other movement.

Cautiously he entered the vessel, his gun leading the way. He turned off heat signature and assessed the scene. All four bodies were MediTech. No sign of Layne or the fourth guard. Brady inspected the bodies of Layne's kills one by one. A simple chest shot on the first. The second, raked by multiple shots all over their body. The third had no visible signs of ballistics, but on closer inspection, Brady noticed the head at an angle telling him Layne must have snapped the neck. Then he saw blood on the ground. Three distinct patterns, all trailing outside.

Brady followed the trail of blood for a long stretch, heading away from the city into the barren wasteland. As it began to fade, he switched back to heat signature. In the distance, he could make out a signal. Gun drawn and pointed towards it, he ran.

As he got closer, he could tell that the signature was a mix of two bodies on top of each other. He switched back to normal vision. The MediTech guard lay motionless on the ground, Layne's legs wrapped around their neck in a triangle choke hold.

'Layne!' Brady lowered his gun and hurried over, but there was no response.

He assessed the scene. The guard had taken two shots, shoulder and midriff. Layne had been bleeding profusely from his thigh around the guard's face. His eyes were closed, unlike the open, lifeless eyes of the guard. Brady knelt down beside him, released the leg lock and felt for a pulse. It was faint, but there.

'Layne!' Brady shook him. Nothing.

Quickly, he fumbled through the guard's uniform, looking in the pockets and pouches. Finally, he found the med kit, tore it apart and found an adrenal shot. He ripped open Layne's jacket, tore his t-shirt and bit the needle's cap off. With a quick flick of the vial and a short squirt, he pierced his chest. As Brady plunged the liquid into Layne, his body convulsed. Coughing and wheezing, Layne came to.

'Are you okay?' Brady retracted the needle.

Layne, in the midst of hyperventilating, tried to speak but it was inaudible.

'Come on, I'm gonna get you back.' Brady began to slide Layne away from the guard.

'I told you to run,' said Layne, weakened by the ordeal. He

coughed and spluttered.

'Good thing I didn't.' Brady released the leg under the guard and crouched over Layne, ready to lift him.

'Too late. I'm bleeding out.' He coughed again. 'Just go.'

Brady looked at the wound to his leg. It was worse than appeared. Still haemorrhaging blood, probably worsened by movement. 'Hang on.'

'Go!' Layne was weakening more.

Brady searched the med kit again for anything to help, but he came up short. He began to panic, his eyes darting around everywhere as he tried to think of something, anything, to stem the bleed. Then he noticed the guard's assault rifle.

He took hold and aimed out towards the wasteland, squeezing the trigger. Nothing. He recalled Mya and Benito mentioning DNA lock on them. Brady manipulated the guard's body, placing their hand on the rifle, then slipped their finger over the trigger and over the top of it with his own, and squeezed. The incessant burst of fire rang out. Brady fought hard against the recoil, allowing the gun to continue until the ammunition had depleted.

He looked at the muzzle. Red hot from sustained fire. *Perfect.* He tore Layne's trousers around the wound and laid the muzzle across it. The searing fizzle of melting flesh was drowned out by the groans from Layne. But they weren't of pain; Brady knew he didn't feel any. They must have been in frustration.

The smell of burning flesh was turning Brady's stomach, and holding the muzzle in place, he looked away and gagged.

'More could come. Just go.' Layne's instruction was louder, more anger in the voice.

Brady looked him in the eyes. 'I'm not leaving you here!'

'I'm not important anyway!'

Brady looked back at the wound, satisfied the red hot muzzle had cauterised it as much as possible. He tossed the gun aside and grabbed the med bag. He produced from it another syringe. This one was a heavy dose sedative. He looked at Layne, whose shaking head movements tried to protest, but Brady persevered. He slipped the needle into Layne's neck and watched as his eyes grew heavy, before finally closing.

Brady hoisted Layne over his shoulder and hurried, as quickly as he could with the extra weight, back towards the city walls.

CHAPTER TWENTY-ONE

Exhausted, on the brink of collapse, Brady dropped Layne's body on the ground in front of the undercity compound's gates. Short of breath, he stumbled forwards, hitting the ramshackle panels with a dull thud.

He slumped in a heap on the ground, elbowing the gate to get attention with one arm, the other hand primed on his holstered gun as he watched the husks close in on them. He knew if it came down to it, he would have to protect Layne.

No movement on the gate, so he banged harder, more frequently.

'Open up, Layne needs help!' Brady's voice reverberated around the undercity as his hand began to twitch, hovering by his gun.

Still with no movement on the gate, Brady hauled himself to his feet. He looked up at the scale of the gate in front, then back over his shoulder to the husks and their slow, yet relentless shuffle towards Layne's unconscious body. He banged his fist over and over against the gate, screaming at the top of his lungs.

There was no response yet again. He switched to heat signature; no sign of anyone inside. *What the hell is happening?* He looked back up and let out a guttural scream, extracted his grip hooks, and began the climb. One eye at the peak, one behind for Layne's safety, he gave all he had left to give to reach the top.

As Brady straddled the top of the gate, barbed wire tearing his combat suit, unable to penetrate his hardened dermal layer, he took a final gauge of the husks' proximity. They were close. Too close. He looked down inside the complex, nothing there to break his fall and no time to care. He leapt.

The crash of his landing was loud. Real loud. His cry in pain, louder. He dragged himself up to his feet and hobbled to the gate release controls. He had no idea of the code to open up, so his system would have to backdoor the security. Physically shaking, both from the pain and the impatience, he instructed his hacks to get going.

'Come on come on come on!' He looked at the gate, wondering if it would be quicker to brute force them open, but he realised how foolish that notion was.

'Hang on Layne!' The algorithms were running through countless code sequences, each one failing to trigger the release.

Outside the gate, Brady could swear he heard the shuffle of husk feet as well as their monotonous groans. He groaned himself in frustration, when finally, the hack reticule pinged green. The panel lit up with the release button, and he immediately jabbed at it and heard the mechanism of the gate begin to whir and grind.

He limped to the gate, jittering as he waited for it to open enough for him to squeeze through. The wait was painful as the gate slowly drew open. Brady reached into the small gap and tried to create extra leverage.

As the gap widened just enough to see out, the husks were looming over Layne. Two directly by him, heads snap-tilting one way, then the other, as though processing. Their movement was jerky, like small flinches as each piece of information overloaded their senses. Countless more continued their instinctual trudge towards their prey.

Brady chomped at the bit to get out and help Layne; the gap was widening, and he could almost fit through. He slid in sideways, feeling the crushing pressure on his chest and back, but it slowly abated until he was free enough to shimmy through. Brady heard the rip of his jacket as it caught the gate.

Finally free, he limped towards Layne, watching as the husks surveyed their spoils. Still only two in touching distance of

Layne's body, so if he could beat the rest, he stood a chance without resorting to firepower, but his laboured pace was almost a match for theirs.

As Brady neared, one of the husks bent down beside Layne, beginning to handle him, like it was reading Braille on his skin. Brady reached Brady ahead of the horde by the narrowest of margins. He grabbed the husk who was exploring Dan's body by the shoulders and yanked back.

The groan of the husk as it was off balanced was like nothing Brady had ever heard. Somewhere between the creaking of wood and the low whine of his car engine at top speed. As the vacant mind tried to come to terms with the fact it was laying on its back, the other husk looking over Layne turned its attention to Brady. The soulless eyes met him head on, yet, it was as if he wasn't there.

It lurched forward, and Brady jumped back out of reach. He set his legs the best he could and swung. He was off balance, but his accuracy was good enough. His fist caught the husk on the jaw. A little off centre, but enough force to knock it down.

He grabbed Layne by his uninjured leg and began to drag him back to the complex. The husk he'd thrown to the ground was slowly figuring out how to pick itself up. The one he punched was temporarily immobilised. But the horde continued to close.

Watching as the husks gained ground, Brady continued to drag Layne's body, inching closer and closer to the wide open gate. The husks were moving quicker than him and the gap was dwindling. He panicked and strained to pull the weight, but he was close. One more effort and Layne would be clear of the gate and inside.

Brady dropped Layne's leg to the ground and threw himself at the control panel. Luckily, still activated by his hack, he pounded the close button and stood at the gateway, ready. It whirred and clunked into action, slowly beginning to close. Brady stared out at the incoming husks as the gate swept across in front of him. The clank of the locking mechanism as it shut fully was a relief. He dropped to his knees, breathing deeply, and took his weight with his palm pressed on the gate in gratitude.

His respite was short-lived as the thought of what the husks may have done to Layne before he intervened hit him. He hobbled over to Layne and looked over. No obvious signs of anything. Brady licked the back of his hand and hovered it by Layne's mouth and nose. He felt the brush of breath on the back of it. *Thank hell.*

There was nothing he could do for him. He knew he needed to find Doc or Samantha. That's when the eerie quiet on the compound made itself apparent to him. *Where is everyone?* He looked around for any sign of disturbance. Nothing. He looked back at Layne; *could I just leave him there? What other choice do I have?*

Brady limped through the complex, scouring for anything that might give him a clue as to what had happened. It all looked normal; empty, but normal. The mess tent, empty. Medical tents, no sign of life, patients gone. He headed to Benito's villa. Still silent ahead, it was eerie, like a haunted house.

The front door was ajar. Brady unsheathed his gun and cautiously entered. The barrel of his gun scanned in front of him, down corridors, through open doors to the living room, games room, kitchen. All utterly abandoned. He was running out of ideas.

'Anyone here?' He aimed his gun up the stairs in case of movement. The silence was response enough. *What else?*

Brady scoured the swimming pool. Still, no sign of life. Returning to the hallway, he decided to head back outside. He relaxed his gun; clearly there was no threat and he made his way around to the bunker entrance.

The hatch was open. Slowly, Brady hobbled down the stairs. In the vestibule, he could see little else other than the closed security door to the bunker itself.

Brady approached the door curiously. Shut tight. Locked down. He knocked on the door with the butt of his gun, the tinny clank reverberating in the vestibule ringing in his ears.

'Who's there?' came a muffled male voice from inside. Too distorted to be recognisable. 'We are locked in here!'

The response startled Brady. He hesitated. *Trapped, or a trap*?

Brady pressed his face against the door. 'Who is in there?'

'Who's out there?'

Brady pulled his face back. 'You first!'

Even with his aural enhancements, Brady couldn't make out any of the chattering behind the door. Whatever they were saying to each other, they were taking their time about it.

'Answer this, is Doc in there?' Brady had momentarily forgotten the need to get Layne help.

'Brady? Is that you?' He relaxed the moment he heard his name. Whoever it was, they knew him.

Brady released the door, and as the two panels peeled apart he saw Doc standing ahead of twenty, maybe twenty-five guns aimed at him. One by one, the barrels dropped.

'What happened here?' Brady holstered his own gun. Everyone had been crammed into the bunker, patients and all.

Doc stepped outside. 'After Benito left, we got a message about MediTech vehicles scouring the area. We moved everyone down here, and next thing we know, the door's locked from outside.'

Brady stepped aside to make room for the exodus of people. 'Yeah, we ran into them.'

'We?' Doc looked concerned. 'Where is Layne? Tell me he made it.'

'Barely. He's taken pretty bad damage; you need to help him.' He scoured the people leaving, scrutinising each one as they passed him. 'Where're Mya and Samantha?'

'We haven't seen Samantha at all. Benito took Mya with him. Let's deal with Layne first, we can figure the rest out afterwards.'

Brady motioned Doc to follow him as he led him up and out of the bunker vestibule.

***

Brady perched at the end of Layne's bed post-surgery. Doc was busy analysing Layne's vitals on the monitors.

'Here's the thing, Doc.' Brady got up from the bed. 'They knew exactly where to be and when. Benito runs off and all of a sudden, I'm ambushed. No way they weren't tipped off.'

Layne tried to speak, but the gastric suction tube down his throat made it impossible. Brady gestured for him to relax. 'I never trusted that guy, he said something about me regretting it and now he's gone and taken Mya with him. I don't like this at all.'

Doc fiddled with the adrenal and hormonal support levels on the screen to get the balance required before tearing himself away. 'Granted, it doesn't look great.' He began to remove the suction pipe from Layne's oesophagus. 'You can't seriously believe he would throw away everything he has helped to build here.'

A creeping, crawling sensation flustered Brady at the sight of the tube being extracted. 'He never had any leverage before, right? All of a sudden I turn up here with this thing he could use to bargain his way to who knows what.'

Layne gurgled as the last of the tube was extracted. He spluttered, leaned over to the side and spat out a mouthful of blood and fluids. 'It has merit. He went to see your friend, so you need to figure out what happened.' He rolled back over, swallowing hard, clearly feeling discomfort from the intrusion.

Brady turned away and walked to the tent entrance, staring outside for a while. 'If anything has happened to Mya, you know

I'll kill him.'

Layne sat upright. 'Seems more likely your friend is behind this if you ask me.'

Brady turned back to Layne. 'Only one way to find out.' With that, Brady left the tent.

***

Brady had made his way up to one of the compound watchtowers. The view out over the undercity stretched as far as the eye could see. He set up a high-end encryption holo-call to Dan on his HUD.

As Dan answered, his holo projection fired to life in front of Brady. 'Who is this?'

Brady knew at the other end his image was scrambled as the ID had been masked. Dan would have no idea who was on the call. 'What happened?'

Dan's holo leaned forward towards Brady, evidently scrutinising the image he was seeing to discern who it may be. 'Tell me who this is.' His holo image looked different to the last time Brady saw him. Less like a man on the brink of death. Perkier, more alert.

'Keep clean, keep lean,' said Brady. It was a phrase Elena had used so often during his childhood that Dan was as aware of it as he was.

Dan's holo-projection reeled backwards. 'Brady? Where the hell are you?'

'Cut the crap, Dan. Tell me exactly what happened, right now.'

'You tell me.' Dan's arms raised upwards. Brady tried to discern whether his physical reaction to the question meant he genuinely didn't know, or if it was a hard sell. The holo-projection hid too much to get a good read.

'Don't play dumb, Dan.'

'Who's playing dumb? I went to meet you like you asked, but you never showed up.'

It gave Brady pause for thought. Sounded genuine. Maybe Dan really was as in the dark as himself. 'Nobody came?'

'I waited there for an hour mate, nobody showed up. Who should I have been expecting if it wasn't you?'

'You haven't seen Mya?'

'Mya? I haven't seen her for days. You sent her to meet me?'

'Something of that order.'

'Brady, I promise you I never saw her. Ask her yourself.'

'I can't ask her myself, I have no idea where she is.'

Dan's holo-projection began to pace back and forth, evidently deep in thought. 'Seriously mate, I don't know a damn thing.'

Brady studied him, again not getting enough to ascertain genuineness. 'Shelve that a second. What happened with AntiFa?'

Dan snapped his attention back to Brady. 'Okay, that I don't know totally. I did what you asked. Ella screamed about compromising them, but cut me off immediately.'

'The whole place was deserted. They took everything man, Joshua and all.'

'I figured as much, but she's severed her link with me. I can't get through to any of them. Trust me mate, I've been trying.'

Brady sighed. 'Meet me.'

'Meet you? Are you going to show up this time?'

'An hour. Where we used to shoot hoops.' Brady severed the call and hurried down from the watchtower.

CHAPTER TWENTY-TWO

Three levels above the mezzanine, on the outer perimeter of his old home tower, Brady skulked in the shadows of the abandoned buildings by the old anti-gravity basketball court he had played on as a child. He wore the face of an elderly man, adorned in a long duster jacket and with a baseball cap obscuring himself. He reminisced over the times he had spent on that court, floating ten feet high to slamdunk the ball as an eight year old.

He grew sad, seeing the state of disrepair and abandonment all around, like a life that had decayed into a horror story. He didn't feel safe, either. Even with his bio-tech enhancements, these areas were almost lawless. Drug abuse, murder, any form of depravity; if they took place anywhere, it was places just like this.

Suddenly, Brady noticed movement across the court. It could've been Dan, whoever it was was about the right height and shape. But it was early yet, and if he knew anything about who his friend really was, it was that punctuality was not his strong suit. He remained lurking, waiting to get a clear view. The figure of a man was joined by someone else. Brady ducked down behind the building's generator block, peering cautiously over to see what was going on.

The two figures met in the centre of the court, exchanged a brief nod of acknowledgement, then the man that Brady momentarily thought could've been Dan produced something from inside his coat. The other withdrew something themselves, and there was a quick exchange.

It all seemed done and dusted, but as the second person turned to leave, the first quickly rifled in their pocket, flung their hands over the head of the person leaving and pulled back tightly. He couldn't see it, but from the movement, it was clear to Brady he was being garrotted.

The man flailed wildly as he suffocated, and Brady watched on in abject horror as their limb movements became smaller and smaller. He thought about helping, but he just couldn't give himself away like that. Who knew who this person was, and who knew if anyone else was watching. He had no option but to hide and watch the murder.

What made him feel much, much more uncomfortable, was seeing the murderer carry away his victim, knowing that with a cause of death like that, the body would be butchered and on the black market in the morning, consumed by those either too naïve to believe it, or too uncaring to mind.

Brady remained in his hiding place, shocked and appalled. Another ten minutes went by before he finally saw Dan approach. This time it was definitely him; he recognised the obnoxious swagger he had in his gait that he'd developed when they were teenagers in an effort to look cool.

A quick scan on heat signature told Brady that aside from the retreating murderer, getting further and further away, they were alone. He emerged from the shadows and went to meet Dan.

Dan was startled by Brady's appearance. 'Is that you?'

'You're not going to believe what I just saw.' Brady continued to approach, knowing that despite his appearance, the voice would be a dead giveaway.

'Down here mate. I probably will.' Dan extended his hand to shake.

Brady looked at his hand and purposefully left him hanging. 'Meat market murder.' Brady could see Dan was offended by his rejection of the handshake, but did not care.

Dan shrugged. 'Yep. Happens all the time.' He looked around the court. 'You remember all the times we played here? Crazy to see it like this.'

Brady laughed. 'Don't come all familiar, Daniel. All that? The whole life we shared, yeah, that's gone as far as I'm concerned.'

Dan groaned. 'Don't say that mate, it still means something. It has to.'

Brady stared daggers at Dan. 'Drop it. I'm here for one thing and one thing only. Answers. Mya. The meeting. What do you know?'

Dan widened his eyes, not breaking contact with Brady. 'Look mate, I swear to you, I know as much as you do.'

'Yeah?' Brady looked him up and down. 'Because the way I see it, is all those shakes, that whole walking dead vibe you had? Gone.'

Dan's face turned steely. 'When you came to my place, I was waiting for my hookup for, well, I'm not going down that road. They came after you left. I'm still riding that wave, but I swear, I haven't done anything that your brain is concocting.'

Brady squared up to Dan. 'Don't get glib with me, I'm really not far from losing it.'

Dan reached out an arm to create separation. 'Okay okay, just calm down mate. I give you my word, and I know that might not mean much anymore, but I went to the meeting place, nobody, and I mean nobody showed. I didn't say anything to anyone about it. As much as you don't want to believe this right now, I'm on your side.'

Dan's words lit Brady's touchpaper. 'My side? You know the only person who I feel like they are on my side right now is Mya, and I have no idea where she is. What's worse, the last time I spoke to her, I lost it with her. I can't bear the thought that the last thing I said to her was in anger.'

'You know her, she was always running off, and I bet she'll turn up sooner rather than later,' said Dan.

Brady hung his head. 'Nah, now I know where she was always

going and she ain't there. Something is up.'

Dan held his hands up to Brady. 'Mate, if I knew anything, I'd tell you.'

Brady narrowed his eyes, scrutinising Dan. 'And why would I believe you? You sold me out before, why would I think you wouldn't try it again? Just this time the wrong people got mixed up in it.'

'People?' said Dan.

'Person, then, stop splitting hairs.' Brady puffed through his cheeks to release the building anger.

'Well, whatever. I swear to you, I didn't have anything to do with whatever you think is going on.' Dan looked quizzically at Brady. 'Hang on, if you weren't meeting me, why Mya? And what was it all about, anyway?'

Brady contemplated whether it would make any difference if Dan knew the plan or not at this stage. He wandered around in circles, mulling it over before feigning a shot towards the hoop as if he had a ball in hand.

'Alright, if you aren't going to answer that, tell me why you wanted Joshua,' said Dan.

Brady, fresh from the jump shot, turned back to Dan. 'You want to know? I need him to get this damn thing out of my head. That's why I went there. You wanna know why I set up the meeting with you? Maybe this guy of yours is legit. Maybe he can help replicate the tech to save lives. We wanted to use you to get to him.'

'We? Who is we? You and Mya?'

Brady slowly walked back to Dan. 'That doesn't matter.'

'Okay, but tell me this, why do you think Joshua's construct can help you?' Dan looked genuinely confused. 'And even if he could, you can't just take it out. It needs a host to remain viable. You can't just throw that potential away, Brady.'

Brady tapped on his head. 'I know this. I needed Joshua,

because he must know about transferring it. Put it back into hiding. They'll get me.' He paused. 'That's a matter of time. As long as they don't get that, there's still hope to end the suffering of thousands. Millions, maybe.'

Dan looked shocked. 'You want to what? Just burden someone else with it?'

'Worked for you guys, right?' Brady grinned sinisterly.

'You can't just do that.' He tried to continue, but Brady interrupted.

'Why the hell not? Who are you to tell me what I can do with this gift?'

Dan shook his head. 'You know it can only be implanted in utero, so what? You're just gonna lump some poor kid with it until you can figure something out?'

Brady laughed haughtily. 'How is that any different to what you did?'

'Me?!' Dan shoved Brady in the chest. 'I had nothing to do with that! It should've—' He stopped.

Brady had clenched his fist ready to retaliate, but the way Dan cut himself off caught him off guard. 'Should've what?'

Dan became more solemn and turned away from Brady. 'It should've been me. Or could've. I don't know.'

Brady span him back around. 'What the hell does that mean?'

Dan stared at him. Looking deep into his eyes, Brady stared back at him. A dawning realisation began to come over him, something he had perhaps always known, but dismissed. He needed to hear it though.

'I'm your brother. We're twins. Fraternal. Fifty-fifty who would end up carrying that thing.' Dan's eyes began to well up.

Even though he knew it was coming, the truth hit Brady in the gut like a missile strike. He didn't know what to say, what to do, how to react.

'A part of you had to have known,' said Dan.

'But, I knew your parents, Dan.'

'They weren't my parents. Not my real ones.'

Brady's head span with the revelation. Anger, confusion, denial, all mixed into a storm. He snapped. 'So you tried to sell your own brother out?!'

Dan perked up. 'You know what? Yeah, yeah. Maybe I did.' He bent over, screaming a deep, primal urge. 'If I had that thing I wouldn't be dying, and you took that from me!'

Brady looked up to the ceiling, then back down. 'You're dying because you got greedy with the tech, so don't give me that pity play.'

Dan stood back up straight, widening his shoulders. 'So what? I wanted to live. You have no idea—' He was cut short. Brady saw his eye light up as a call came in.

'Who is it?' said Brady, panicking.

'Him.' Dan's head snapped around, left, right, looking for any signs of anyone around.

Brady began to move. 'Answer it. Don't let him know I'm here.' He scurried away behind the pole holding up the hoop. A poor hiding place, but maybe enough. 'Put him on holo!'

'X.' Dan transferred the call to holo. Xiao's image was scrambled as always. 'Why are you calling me?'

'Cut the chatter. Explain why the same girl who killed my last operative came to meet you in his place.'

Dan's face dropped. 'What?'

Brady had to fight the urge to burst forth on hearing this.

'Do not play dumb with me Mr Price.'

'What conversation?' Dan was clearly panicked.

'I told you not to play dumb with me. My patience is wearing thin, boy.'

'Where is she?' said Dan, face white as a sheet.

'My operative has her. He is trying to get the information out of her but she seems to be a rather stubborn one. We will see how long that lasts.'

'Don't hurt her!'

'It's too late for that. I know you are meeting the target now. Bring him to the coordinates I am sending through or she dies.' Xiao's holo disappeared.

Brady bounded over to Dan. 'What the hell? I swear, if anything happens to her I will kill him, you, dammit, everyone.'

Dan ran his hand down his face. 'I don't know what's going on, Brady, you have to trust me.'

Brady grabbed his arm and began to pull him towards the exit of the court. 'Let's go.'

Dan put the brakes on. 'You can't go there, he is clearly dangerous.'

Brady pulled even harder. 'I can't leave her there, either.'

'What do you think, you can just walk in and he will let her go?'

'I'll think of something, but let's just go before it's too late. I swear, if she is...' Brady doubled their speed. Dan struggled to keep up with him. 'I can't even think about it, but if it comes down to me, or you, or her, you know what I'll do.'

***

The coordinates had led them to the central plaza on level thirteen. It was teeming with life, from young families, to groups of friends, all enjoying the day. Patches of artificial grass, holographic fauna, benches and artwork all circled a huge clock tower. The holographic clock face had the time and date at 11:23am, 19th February.

Brady and Dan stood in the midst of the activity, bemused as to why the location was there. Brady scoured the area for any signs out of the ordinary, but all he could see was regular people, living their regular lives.

Brady grabbed Dan's arm. 'You sure this is the right place?'

Dan seemed to check his system. 'Coordinates match. Has to be.'

'Why would he send us here? This makes no sense.'

Dan gestured to his head. 'Hang on, incoming message.'

'What does it say?'

'Hard to see. Back of clock tower.' Dan looked at Brady and gestured to see what he wanted to do.

Brady thought for a moment, looking around to the clock tower. 'Okay. Let's do it. You set on the play?'

Dan nodded in agreement and they made their way around the back of the tower. Brady had been inside once before, as a child. Years ago, citizens had access to climb the tower for the views, but he recalled it shutting down for safety concerns almost ten years ago.

He looked to Dan, then held his hand up to tell him to hang on as he switched to heat signature and scanned through the door. The entrance was clear, so he looked upwards at the tower and could make out two bodies in the belfry. He put two fingers up to Dan, then pointed upwards to show him where they were. Slowly, he tried the door. It was unlocked, but moved with a stiff swing.

Inside, the old reception room was lifeless. The counter that used to be manned was covered in dust. The seating, shrouded in sheets. Little light made it inside, but it was enough to get a general idea.

Brady closed the door a little behind them, leaving a crack for light, and pulled Dan in close. 'Okay. Play back my holo. I'll scale up outside, you keep him talking, just don't say anything stupid.'

Dan closed his eyes tightly. 'And Mya?'

A wave of anxiety tickled Brady. 'Just make sure she's okay. If —' He swallowed hard. 'If she isn't, abort and run.'

Dan motioned his arms around. 'Where?'

Brady let out a puff of air. 'I don't know, alright, we will just cross that bridge when we come to it. You good?'

Dan nodded in agreement, but Brady saw he was nervous. He called up the holo recording of Brady they had made and projected it a few feet away from himself. Brady studied it for a moment before activating his prism field disrupter, shrouding himself in a blur. He squeezed through the door back outside.

Brady looked at his arms; he could only see the effects of the disrupter. It was like looking through himself, but the background was distorted and fractured. He deployed his climbing grips and began to slowly scale up the exterior of the tower.

Looking down from halfway up, he began to feel giddy. It was disorientating, not being able to see his lower body properly. He felt disconnected from himself, as though his legs weren't really attached to him anymore. He had to push through the sensation and carry on. Tracking Dan through heat signature, he could see he was one flight of stairs above.

Fighting his subconscious will to look back down, Brady continued to climb. Dan's signature was getting further and further away, but Brady knew he couldn't quicken his pace. He had to remain quiet and move slowly, else the prism field shrouding him would become too obvious to anyone with eyes on the tower.

Dan was getting perilously close to the other signatures. Looked like two, maybe three more flights of stairs. Brady's heart was beginning to race from the combination of physical excursion and anticipation, thumping in his chest like a metronome gathering pace

Brady maintained his pace as Dan's signature made it to the top level. Brady was close enough to make out the other two signatures with more clarity. Someone standing, the other was sitting, but motionless. He feared the worst, but if that was Mya as he presumed, she was still warm, at least.

He could hear the murmur of chatter, but not well enough to

make any of it out. He just had to hope that Dan could stay cool enough to sell the bluff that the holo projection was actually Brady. The standing signature appeared to approach Dan, arms raised in his direction. Had to have been a gun pointed at him. Dan's arms raised above his head. *Just hang on.*

It was getting perilously close to Dan. Much closer and the façade of the holo would be clear. Brady could see Dan backing off from the other heat source, creating space. *Clever.*

The voices were becoming clear as Brady continued to climb. He could just about recognise Dan's voice; the other was thickly accented. *Russian?*

A few more feet up and Brady could finally discern what was being said.

'She's not moving, how do I know she is okay?' said Dan.

'I don't care. You leave him. We deliver her.' The voice was deep, definitely a Russian accent, speaking in short, sharp sentences.

'I need to see she is alive, at least,' said Dan.

Brady was edging ever closer as the man responded. 'You make no demand. Trust or you die also.'

'Also?' Dan's voice got louder. Brady's eyes widened. 'So she is dead?'

'No her, him, him.' The heat signature seemed to point to an empty space. Brady knew immediately it was his holo. 'Wait.' It began to move forwards. 'This holo!' It snapped back towards Dan. Brady had no choice but to rush. He clambered the rest of the way frantically.

'It's okay, it's okay, he is downstairs. We just wanted to make sure she was alive.' Dan's signature dropped to its knees. 'I swear, I will call him up now, just please, please don't shoot!'

'You not move! Make him come now!'

Brady had no choice but to spring to action. He hauled himself up onto the roof and ran across the tiled spire to position himself above the heat sources.

'What is that?' the Russian man said.

Brady heard a small explosive. Dan had deployed the smoke grenade that Brady had tasked him with if he needed cover. Directly above the Russian, Brady lifted his leg and brought it crashing down, heel-first into the roof. The tiles broke easily, weakening the area he was stood on so much that the entire section collapsed.

Inside the thick hue of smoke, Brady landed directly on the Russian. The man dropped his assault rifle and Brady immediately kicked it out of reach. Then he felt the hands of the man grasp at him, throwing him off to the side.

The two men sprang to their feet and immediately started trading blows. Brady took shots to the face and body. They were so hard, he felt every one despite his dermal hardening, clear indication that the man was highly enhanced. He landed many himself, shots he thought would knock him down, but he stood toe to toe with him.

'Get her, get out!' Brady ducked and weaved as he shouted instruction to Dan.

The smoke was still thick and smothering. He couldn't see anything aside from the opponent in front. But he heard movement from behind.

A shin kick cracked across his face, sending him backwards, but he maintained enough balance to retaliate, launching a knee strike into the man's torso. He heard the breath escaping from the impact, but the man refused to go down. Blow after blow rained back and forth, the balance between the two, perfect. Neither could get the upper hand.

Brady reached for his handgun multiple times, but the attacks kept coming at a relentless pace. He had to guard and counter too often to have time to unsheathe his weapon. Suddenly, he felt the full force of a driving tackle into his midriff. The Russian took him to the ground, on top, in control.

'Got her!' said Dan. Brady still couldn't see beyond a few feet through the smoke, but the words were a relief.

Brady groaned under the weight of the Russian's knee pressing into his chest. 'Go!' He bellowed a rousing roar, tipping the Russian off-balance just enough to free himself.

Brady swung his legs into a hold on the Russian's neck, but he slithered out before he could exert any pressure. Brady felt the full force of an elbow, striking him in the temple. Amidst the ruckus, Brady could hear the movement of Dan, escaping the room. He rolled, twice over, to one side, spinning himself into a pivot on one foot as he whipped the other leg around with force, his heel catching the Russian's chin solidly.

The man spun to the ground, and it was the blow Brady needed to get the edge. No time to let up, he pounced, straddling the Russian as he lay on the ground. Relentlessly, Brady brought his fists into the man's face. Over, and over, until there was blood spraying with each strike. In his left hand, he raised the man's head, his right drawn back for a full-force hook.

The crunch was loud. Broken jaw. But Brady's anger and hatred did not subside. Another crunching fist strike to the nose. One to the eye. Bang. Bang. He continued, a man possessed, until the Russian's face was no longer recognisable.

He screamed at the top of his lungs and threw one final, all-in punch. That was it. He was dead. Brady stared at the annihilation he had caused. His face had flushed red with anger, but it was abating, tinged with a guilt over what he had done, though it was guilt mixed with fear. Fear of himself. What he was capable of if pushed.

Brady had to shake it off. He needed to catch-up with Dan, find out what was going on with Mya. He still was none the wiser; *is she even alive?*

Brady raced down the stairs after Dan, limping, and bleeding from his nose and mouth. He stumbled down seven flights before he caught site of Dan and Mya. She was clearly conscious, struggling to move, but Dan was guiding her down.

'Mya!' Brady slipped and bumped down a few steps as she turned around. Her face was in worse shape than his own, swollen eyes she clearly struggled to see out of, and blood and bruises all over.

'Brady!' Her voice was croaked and quiet, but even through the evident pain she was in, he saw the attempted smile.

'I thought I'd lost you!' He picked himself up and bounded down towards her.

'It's okay.' She was clearly struggling to even support herself. As she was about to collapse, Dan had to crouch down to take her weight.

'It's okay, don't talk, let's just get you out of here.' Brady gently took her other side and helped Dan walk her down the rest of the stairs.

Outside, the noise of commotion was evident. Brady stuck his head outside first, immediately seeing increased movement from the crowds. The people were clearly panicked, which meant only one thing. 'MediTech!' said Brady. 'We need to get out of here asap.'

Dan let Mya go into Brady's clutches. 'Take her. I'll draw them away.'

Brady stared at him. 'What're you going to do?'

Dan looked forlorn. 'Don't worry about it. Just, go mate.'

'Bro. I can help you.' Brady hadn't noticed until that moment, but Dan had picked up the Russian's assault rifle and had it slung over his shoulder. Dan took it off, primed the loading sequence and ran outside.

'Dan!' Brady followed up his pleas. He couldn't leave Mya to chase him down. Dan ignored his shout anyway.

He heard the sound of shots fired, then the screams of terror for the people around. Peeking out carefully, he saw the MediTech team running. He didn't have eyes on Dan any more. All he could do was hope he would make it.

He took Mya's face ever so gently, kissed her forehead and smiled. 'You know I love you, right?'

She nodded, just slightly, but enough to answer him.

'We got to move.' He led her out, slowly so as to not hurt her. Scanning around, he could see the crowd had tightened. If he could get her over to them, they had the best chance of blending in and making it out of there.

CHAPTER TWENTY-THREE

Brady sat by Mya's medical bed as she slept. He had been there for the last six hours; he hadn't slept in nearly two full days and his eyes burned and itched. He was beginning to nod off, when he heard Mya stirring.

He leaned in. 'Hey.' He gently kissed her cheek and ever so lightly pressed his cheek against hers. 'I thought I'd lost you. Don't do this to me again, I much prefer being the one all battered and broken.' He kissed her cheek again and pulled away.

Mya smiled at him the best she could. Brady made a conscious effort not to react as her swollen face tried to move. 'I do, too.' She chuckled, wincing at the pain in her torso as she did.

Grinning, Brady put his hand to her chin. 'It's okay, you don't have to talk if it hurts.'

Mya sucked air in through her teeth. 'I can talk, just don't make me laugh, idiot.'

Brady smiled and shook his head at her. 'Idiot now? What happened to hun?'

'That's for the punters.' Mya coughed, wincing again and holding her ribs. 'You get the reality now.'

Brady winked at her. 'Maybe I'll like the reality better.'

She shrugged. 'We will see.'

He grinned, scoffed. 'Yeah, we will.'

Mya shuffled up the bed, her pain levels clear to see as she did. 'Any word on Dan?'

Brady shook his head, staring vacantly.

'Maybe he'll be okay.' Mya reached out to hold his arm.

Brady sniffed loudly. 'You don't believe that, let's not pretend. I want to know what happened with you? And Benito.'

Mya looked at him for a while before responding. 'All I know, is one minute we are on our way to meet up with Dan, then boom, bag over my head, sedatives, I guess, as well, because I woke up in that chair.'

Brady's face flushed with the anger as he recalled the ordeal. 'But what about Benito?'

'I don't know. He was there, then he wasn't,' said Mya.

Brady looked around the room. 'Snake.'

Mya's brow furrowed; it wasn't that noticeable beyond the swelling, but Brady could tell. 'You don't really think—'

Brady interrupted her. 'Nah, I know. MediTech knew exactly where to be and when. Now this with you and what, he's conveniently just gone? Let's not be dumb about this.'

Mya swallowed a mouthful of saliva that had built up. 'They were there because you smashed down through the ceiling, so what did you think? They wouldn't get all that on their monitoring?'

Brady stood up. 'I'm not talking about that.'

'Then what?'

He paced at the foot of the bed. 'Layne and I were ambushed the second we got out of the AntiFa compound.'

Mya shuffled her legs over as Brady sat at the end of the bed. 'Is Layne okay?'

Brady began to softly massage Mya's exposed foot. 'Just about. One more life I saved.' He chuckled, then stopped himself.

Mya sighed. 'Probably makes you even now.'

'Seriously, though.' Brady looked back around to her. 'I'm telling you, Benito has sold us all out. I didn't even say, when I got back here with Layne, everyone had been locked inside his bunker.'

Mya pulled her foot away. 'What?'

Brady swung himself around the bed, then sat crossed-legged

looking at her. 'Yep. You believe me now?'

Mya seemed to stare off into space for a good thirty seconds. 'Okay, it doesn't look good. But tell me you got the data you needed out, tell me you can get rid of this thing.'

Brady looked at her solemnly. 'Nope. Compound was abandoned. Wouldn't have mattered anyway.'

Mya looked confused. 'Why not?'

Brady blew out his breath. 'Doesn't work the way we hoped. Gotta be transferred in the womb. Besides, removing it will almost certainly kill me anyway.'

'And how do you know this?' asked Mya.

'Dan.' Brady shuffled up towards her more. 'That's how it ended up in me. Could've been him.'

Mya shut her eyes. 'What does that mean? Him?'

Brady laid down, nestling in next to her. 'He's my brother. Twins.' He placed his arm around her gently.

Mya sunk into his embrace. 'I'd say I'm surprised, but, and I don't know why, I'm just not.'

Brady kissed the top of Mya's head. 'Yeah, me neither. I think I sort of always knew.'

Mya took in a deep breath, then let it out. 'So what now?'

Brady pressed his forehead against hers. 'First things first, we gotta get you better so we can get the hell out of here.'

'What do you mean?' she said.

He took hold of her hand. 'We can't stay here. Not anymore. Not any of us.'

She nestled her head into him. 'What about you?'

Brady sighed heavily. 'You know, I tried to run from this thing, I tried ignoring it. I wanted to get rid of it and just I don't know, survive. What's left but to embrace it? To take it on and hell, even if we can't do anything to replicate it, work to make our lives just a little easier?'

'How will that make it any easier for you?' said Mya.

Brady stroked her hair. 'I don't mean me. Maybe my fate is sealed.'

'Don't say that.' Her voice croaked.

'I know, but it's the truth. But I'll be damned if I don't take them down with me. Maybe AntiFa were right, maybe my destiny is to just be a thorn in their side. If they are so hell-bent on taking me out, the least I can do is get what I can out of them and spread it around. What's that ancient fable? Steal from the rich, give to the poor.'

She gripped his hand tighter. 'I don't know if I like that.'

Brady pulled her head up gently and kissed her, deeply, with a muted passion. 'I don't really either, but what's the alternative?' He leaned his forehead against hers. 'But that's for another time. Right now, just heal up. I can't lose you. I won't.'

Mya pulled her head away sharply. 'And what if I lose you?' She punched him in the arm.

Brady let out a yelp, exaggerated for effect. 'What's that for?'

Mya looked unimpressed. 'Don't be such a baby.'

Brady chuckled. 'You know, I think I liked you better when you treated me like your customers. You were actually nice to me then.'

Mya stuck her tongue out at him. 'Well I didn't know you were such a baby, then, did I?'

Brady's stomach fluttered; something about the way she was playfully insulting him was setting him off. Was he falling deeper, or just suffering the sensation of repressing his instinct to insult her back? He couldn't quite tell the feelings apart. He was amused, annoyed, yet drawn to her in equal measures.

'Don't avoid my question,' said Mya.

Brady looked away from her, rubbed his face and let out a quiet groan. 'Let's just not think about that right now. Why don't we just leave this whole place? Like, get out the city. Benito said there's land out there, like real land, not a wasteland.'

Mya tutted. 'Maybe there is, maybe there isn't, but you can't just go look for it. They'll have ways of finding you wherever you go.'

'Well, why even stay in this country? It's messed up. Let's go to the EU.'

Mya laughed. 'Oh yes, we can just get on a transport and go there. Don't be stupid, you know that can't happen.'

'There has to be some way. Isn't there an old tunnel under the water or something? I swear I remember hearing about it in school.'

My laughed even harder. 'Are you joking me, Brady? You think they didn't fill that in or destroy it the moment the segregated from the rest of the world? Come on, you aren't that dumb, arc you?'

Brady clenched his jaw and tightened his stomach. He needed to be rid of the agitation that was growing. 'Okay, fine. Then we build a raft and sail it across, or row it, or whatever.'

Mya looked dumbfounded. 'Oh my god, Brady, be real. There's no way in hell that can happen. MediTech will see it and hey, even if they didn't, you think you'd survive the crossing? And, even if you did that, you think the EU will just let you walk in?'

Brady groaned in exasperation. 'America, then.'

'Oh, just build a raft and row to America? Do you have any idea how far that is?'

'Not a raft—' He stopped himself shy of screaming profanity. 'Sneak onto a transport and then, I don't know, disappear over there. MediTech can't have eyes on all that amount of land. It's huge.'

Mya sighed, then took his hand and pulled it into her chest. 'Look, Brady, I really like that you have this wild optimistic side, but you have to let those ideas go and be realistic. We are trapped here, just like everyone else. And even if you, we, whatever, could somehow elude detection to get somewhere, what do you suggest? We just abandon everyone else. I thought you wanted to help.'

'Well you come up with something then.'

'There's a whole big undercity, so we don't have to stay right here. We can move this whole thing out of sight. It doesn't matter where we go, as long as we go together. But we can't solve this right now. Tomorrow is a new day; we can work it out then.'

Brady took a long, deep breath as Mya nestled into him again. 'You're right. And like I said, you need to rest. To be honest, I do, too.'

'So sleep here. We will figure this out.' She squeezed his hand tightly and closed her eyes, her head buried into him. He could feel the breath and the movement. It was comforting.

As he lay there, still and quiet, the constant noises in his head began to dampen for the first time in a long time. It was hypnotic, the silence of abandonment of thought. Eerie, sure, but he felt safer with her by his side. Not at peace, not yet. But peaceful. Contempt, at the least. He knew Mya was right, the journey would be long, but this moment was worth tucking the battles that lay ahead away for.

Slowly and systematically, he felt his muscles begin to relax. The in and out motion of Mya's chest as she breathed was soothing. He held his breath a beat, to match hers.

Printed in Great Britain
by Amazon